BETRAYED

REBECCA YORK

Published by Sourcebooks Casablanca, an imprint of Sourcebooks, Inc.
P.O. Box 4410, Naperville, Illinois 60567-4410
(630) 961-3900
Fax: (630) 961-2168
www.sourcebooks.com

Printed and bound in Canada.
MBP 10 9 8 7 6 5 4 3 2 1

Chapter 1

"I DON'T WANT TO KILL YOU."

Bueno, Elena Reyes thought as she flicked her gaze from the man's eyes to the automatic pistol he held in his hand and back again. *Dios*, if she'd only gone to the human resources department in the morning instead of after lunch, she wouldn't be in this fix.

She'd been in the front office talking to the receptionist, Lisa Walters, when they'd both heard loud voices in the back.

"That's Joe Duckworth," Lisa had murmured. "He was let go last week, and he came storming in to talk to Mr. Perkins."

As the volume of the altercation increased, the women had exchanged glances.

"Maybe I'd better come back later," Elena had said, taking a step toward the door.

Before she could leave, Mr. Perkins had stumbled into the reception area, with Duckworth behind him, holding a gun.

And now Elena and the human resources staff were gathered together in the reception area, listening to the man's rambling demands. Air-conditioning poured from the vents in the ceiling, making her feel as if someone had pushed her into an open grave. She wanted to rub her arms with her palms to warm herself, but she kept her hands at her sides.

Don't draw attention to yourself. Blend in. Those were rules she'd unconsciously followed since before her parents had brought her to the United States.

The gunman kept speaking in a high, whiny voice that grated on her ears and her nerve endings.

"But you don't understand the position I'm in. What other choice do I have?"

She wanted to answer, but she kept to her previous decision and let him do the talking.

Yes, that was safer. His eyes told her that he wasn't sure what he wanted, although he was prepared to do whatever was needed to get it.

"Everybody stay calm," he said.

Sure, when he could blow them away at any moment.

In the past twenty minutes, she and the other hostages had learned a lot about him. Joe Duckworth had been a loyal employee of S&D Systems for two years after moving to Maryland from North Carolina. His wife had hated living in a crummy apartment in the North so she'd gone back home to her family. Joe had been driving back and forth on weekends, trying to get her to change her mind. That had taken a toll on him, and it wasn't his fault that his work had suffered.

In the past few minutes, he'd switched from his life story to his demands. He wanted his job reinstated. He wanted back pay. He wanted the respect that was due a man of his considerable talents. He'd been on the phone to Lincoln Kinkead, president of S&D. So at least management knew what was going on up here. But the survival of the men and women trapped in the HR department, herself included, depended on a lot of factors.

Had Duckworth already gone too far to back down?

Had his wife come back for a visit? Was she lying dead on the kitchen floor? If so, he had nothing more to lose, and this rant was just his way of working himself up to the big moment when he killed himself and took a bunch of innocent S&D employees with him.

Madre de Dios. The Spanish phrase brought a flash of annoyance. She'd worked hard to think in English. And she always did, unless she was under stress.

She risked taking her gaze off Duckworth for a moment, checking out the six other hostages in the room. There were five women and one man. Mr. Perkins, the sixty-year-old head of personnel, and five much younger female employees who worked for him, including Lisa, the receptionist, a slender brunette wearing a white blouse and black slacks. She was the one who looked like she was going to do something stupid. Elena tried to catch her eye, but the woman was staring into space with a fixed expression on her face.

Relax. Just relax. Don't do anything foolish.

Elena repeated the words in her head, trying to project them toward Lisa, but the woman didn't seem to be getting the message.

She made a moaning sound, and as Elena watched in horror, she leaped out of her chair behind the reception desk and ran for the door. Before she reached it, Duckworth shot her in the back, and she went down, her face pressed against the gray vinyl tile floor.

The rest of the captives watched in frozen horror, but Elena couldn't simply leave her lying there.

"I have to help her," she said in a voice she struggled to hold steady. Forcing herself to walk slowly, she crossed the room and knelt by Lisa. The woman's breathing was labored, and blood stained the back of her white blouse.

"We need something to stop the bleeding," Elena said. "She left a jacket on the back of her chair. Someone bring it to me."

One of the other captives brought Elena the jacket, and she folded it up and pressed it to Lisa's back, wishing she could do more for the woman.

"Just take it easy. You're going to be okay," she whispered.

Lisa moaned and turned her head, giving Elena a pleading look.

"Let me find something to cover you." She turned to the woman who had brought the jacket. "Can you apply pressure?"

She gave a small nod.

Straightening, Elena looked around at the anxious faces watching her, then searched for something to use as a blanket.

As she surveyed the room, she flashed back to another time when her life had been in danger. Then she'd been a little girl, with no idea how to save herself. Now she was older and, she hoped, wiser.

It had been back in San Marcos, where her family had lived before they'd come to the U.S. as political refugees eighteen years ago.

It had happened on one of the local shopping days, which was nothing like shopping in North America.

She and her mother and brother, Alesandro, who was two years older than Elena, had gone to the open-air market in the town square near their home to buy food and look at the used clothing that got shipped south from the United States. Momma had bought tomatoes and squash, and they were heading for the fish stalls when a squad of soldiers came running through the crowd, shouting orders and pushing people aside. They were looking for rebels who had dashed between the stalls, trying to escape from the troops.

The soldiers found the rebels, and the two groups started shooting.

Momma rushed Elena and Alesandro toward the edge of the market, but at the first sound of gunfire, she pushed Alesandro to the cracked pavement and covered him with her body. Elena huddled next to them, shielding her head with her arms and shivering as bullets flew around them. When the shooting stopped, a lot of rebels lay bleeding on the pavement, along with a few soldiers and some unlucky civilians who had gotten caught in the crossfire.

As soon as the government troops let the shoppers go, Momma whisked Alesandro and Elena home. But Elena would never forget that day. Not just the terror of the gunfight but the knowledge that her mother had been focused on saving her son—not her daughter.

Until then, Elena had sensed only that her brother was more important to Momma and Papa than she was. The gun battle at the market left her with a sharp pain in her stomach.

After that, her parents began making plans to get out of San Marcos. When she listened to them talking in low voices at night about their arrangements, she couldn't shake the secret fear that they would leave her behind.

But to her vast relief, they'd brought her to the United States with them, where she prospered, always trying to prove to them that they should love her as much as they loved her brother.

Well, that had been early motivation. Later the drive to succeed had been for herself alone. She'd worked hard to learn English, gone to Montgomery College on scholarships, gotten a degree in computer science, and been hired by S&D in the information technology department. She'd already gotten promoted, and outside of work, she'd been doing equally well. She had her own apartment. She was completely self-sufficient. And she'd been able to buy herself nice furniture, nice clothing, and a nice car.

Now the life she'd made for herself might be snuffed out because she'd come up to the HR department to check on a malfunctioning communications link.

Unfortunately, Duckworth had already been in the back, making demands and babbling about why he thought S&D had screwed him.

He was watching her as she crossed to the coatrack, but he was still talking to the room in general. She longed to tune him out, but she forced herself to pay attention to the flow of words, listening for clues to his state of mind. As she returned to Lisa with a raincoat, he started to pace back and forth, making her think that his mental state was deteriorating.

He moved the gun from his right hand to his left, shook out his wrist, and clasped the weapon in his right hand again.

All eyes were focused on that shift. But as Elena kept her gaze on the gunman, she saw something that made her heart stop, then start up again in double time. Duckworth was standing with his back to the window, and there was a flicker of movement behind him where there should be nothing to see—unless it was a bird or a plane—since they were on the eighth floor of the S&D building.

As she stood with her breath shallow in her lungs, a face emerged behind Duckworth, a man with medium-length dark hair, wearing a running suit and protective goggles that partly obscured his face. She was sure that only one man at S&D would do something so daring—and crazy.

Shane Gallagher, the new head of security.

He'd been at the company for a few months, and he'd come around to interview a lot of people in the workforce. He'd said he wanted to get familiar with the employees, but she had the feeling he had some hidden agenda that he wasn't sharing. Which was one of the reasons she'd been cautious around him. The other was that she was attracted to him, which was dangerous, as far as she was concerned. He was a tough, no-nonsense guy who reminded her too much of the military officers back home. She should stay away from him. Without being obvious about it, of course, because that would make him wonder what she had to hide.

But now he was here—poised to do something about the hostage situation.

He was hanging on to a rope. With one hand, he pushed the goggles onto his forehead and looked into the room. She saw him focus on Duckworth, then flick his attention to her. Across fifteen feet of charged space, their eyes met. He held her gaze, and she was fairly sure she knew what he wanted her to do—keep Duckworth's attention away from the window. While Gallagher did what?

As he pulled the goggles back over his eyes, her heart started to pound so hard that she felt like it would come through the wall of her chest.

She dragged in a breath and let it out, then cleared her throat.

As soon as she made that small noise, the gunman's attention riveted to her.

She licked her lips, her mouth suddenly so dry that she wondered if she could speak, but she managed to say, "Excuse me."

"What?" he snapped.

"I have to go to the bathroom."

"That's too damn bad."

"This is making me nervous. Couldn't you just let me go to the ladies' room?"

"You're kidding, right?"

"I…"

Behind him, Gallagher was moving. He held on to the rope and swung away from the building, then came flying back, feet first, the metal tips on his shoes gleaming in the sun as they aimed at the window. She heard a tremendous splintering crash as the glass broke and Duckworth whirled, his gun raised.

She was the only other person in the room who moved as Gallagher smashed through the window, flying at Duckworth like a giant bird of prey, but feet first.

Still, the gunman wasn't going down without a fight. He had a clear shot at the unexpected intruder, but just before Duckworth fired, she sprang forward and leaped onto his back, her weight pulling him down so that his gun discharged below the level of the window.

"Bitch," he shouted as he gave a mighty heave and

shook her off. She crashed to the floor as Gallagher fired back, hitting Duckworth at point-blank range.

As Gallagher landed next to the gunman, Elena pushed herself to a sitting position. Turning her head, she saw the security chief bending over the man on the floor, who lay unmoving in a pool of blood.

"He's done. It's over," he said as he got up and addressed the hostages. "Is anyone besides Miss Walters hurt?"

None of the shocked people in the room spoke or moved.

The door burst open, and paramedics ran in, heading directly for Lisa, who still lay on the tile floor where she'd fallen.

Elena watched in confusion. "How did they get here so fast?" she asked.

"You were on audio the whole time," Gallagher explained. "They came up here without making any noise, and they were waiting in the hall." As he focused on Elena, he caught his breath. Coming down beside her, he touched her face. When his hand came away, she saw blood on his fingers.

"You're hurt."

"I don't think so," she whispered, even as she struggled to figure out if it was true.

"Don't get up yet," he said when she started to stand. He inspected her carefully. "I think it's Duckworth's blood."

She shuddered.

"Come on."

He helped her to her feet and kept his hand on her arm as he led her into the hall, then a few yards away into the ladies' room, where he turned on the water in the sink and grabbed a wad of paper towels from the dispenser. Gently he washed her face and inspected her blouse.

"There's blood on your shirt. I guess Lincoln Kinkead owes you some new clothing."

She nodded numbly. Then finally the realization of everything that had happened hit her, and she felt her knees buckle.

Gallagher caught her as she started to fall, wrapping his arms around her and holding her against his muscular body as he stroked his hands reassuringly up and down her back. For a moment she let herself lean into his hard body.

"You did great in there," he said. "Just what I needed you to do."

She was shaking now, and she struggled to bring herself back under control. She should pull away from him, she knew. But she stayed in his arms. "I was scared."

"Everybody was, but you were the one who wasn't afraid to act. You didn't panic."

As she listened to the admiration in his voice, she let her head drift to his shoulder, and her hand anchored itself at his waist. A voice in her brain told her she shouldn't be so intimate with this man. She shouldn't be holding on to him as if they were lovers, but under the circumstances, she thought she was entitled to the comfort. And maybe he needed it too after what he'd done. He'd risked his life to get into that room. That couldn't be part of his job description, but he'd gone ahead and done it.

"You were brave, too," she murmured.

He answered with a rough sound, and she was fairly sure he didn't want to discuss his bravery.

"You heard everything?" she asked, changing the subject.

"Yeah. I was listening in. You told him you needed to go to the bathroom."

She felt her face heat. "I didn't know anybody could hear us, or I would have thought of something else."

"What?"

"I don't know."

"Kinkead doesn't advertise he's got the building wired for sound. And, by the way, I didn't thank you for jumping on the bastard's back. You probably saved me from being hit."

Someone knocked on the door. Before either she or Gallagher could respond or break apart, the door opened, and Bert Iverson, the assistant security chief, strode in, giving them a long, considering look as he took in Elena standing in Gallagher's embrace. There was something about Bert Iverson she didn't like, something she couldn't articulate.

Elena felt Gallagher stiffen, pretty sure he didn't much like the scrutiny, either. As he eased away from her, she reached out a hand to steady herself against the sink and realized with a start that she and the two security men were standing in the ladies' room. Truly, she didn't even remember coming in here.

"Elena had some blood spatter. We were cleaning her up, and she got a little shaky," Gallagher said.

"Yeah," Iverson answered. He flicked his gaze to the front of her blouse, then back to the security chief. "I thought you were going to get killed, bursting in there like that. I mean, dangling outside the window and then crashing through with those steel-tipped boots. And your bulletproof vest wouldn't have saved you if Duckworth had aimed for your head."

Chapter 2

"ELENA KNOCKED HIS AIM OFF," SHANE SAID, EVEN WHEN HE knew his second-in-command was right.

Iverson cleared his throat. "Maybe we should all get out of the ladies' room. I'm guessing you don't want to meet up with Kinkead in here."

Shane grimaced and ushered Elena into the hall.

He'd done a quick review of Duckworth's file, then plunged ahead with his crazy rescue plan because he'd determined it had the best chance of getting the hostages out of the HR department alive. Still, he wasn't looking forward to a face-to-face with Lincoln Kinkead now that the crisis was over. When he'd come up with the idea of going in through the window, he'd thought the S&D president was going to blow a gasket.

It had been a risky plan, but Shane had started enjoying risks since he'd realized he had nobody but himself to worry about. And when he'd spotted Elena Reyes watching him through the window, he'd been sure she was going to help him.

"Speak of the devil," Bert whispered as a tall, balding man in his late fifties strode around the corner. It was Lincoln Kinkead, wearing his usual Savile Row suit and Italian shoes. In the aftermath of the hostage crisis, his face was slightly flushed.

"Gallagher," Kinkead barked. "Are you all right?"

"Yes."

"Good." Once he heard the reassurance, he continued, "We'll talk about that stunt later."

"You want me to pay for the window?" Shane asked.

Kinkead swung toward him. "I have insurance. The window's not the issue."

Bert inserted himself into the conversation. "It was an unconventional approach, but it worked. Really, you're lucky Shane was willing to try it. All the hostages could have gotten killed."

"The usual procedure is to negotiate with the hostage taker," Kinkead snapped.

"Do you think that would have worked with Duckworth?" Iverson asked.

"No," the S&D president conceded. "We could all hear him coming apart at the seams. He was winding himself up for the slaughter—before he took his own life."

"And you would have hated the negative publicity," Bert said.

Kinkead nodded.

"This way, it's a win for the company."

"Yeah."

When he heard that dispassionate assessment, Shane dragged in a breath and let it out, relieved to be off the hook for the moment.

The S&D president turned to Elena, looking at the blood on her blouse. "And you're all right, too?"

"Yes."

"We all heard you get Duckworth's attention."

"Then she tackled him," Shane added.

"He was going to shoot Mr. Gallagher."

"Right." Kinkead's gaze flicked to Shane, then back to Elena. "That was very brave of you."

She raised one shoulder. "I guess it was instinctive."

Kinkead cleared his throat. Still addressing Elena, he said, "We have several mental health professionals on call. You might want to contact one of them tomorrow."

"What do you mean?"

"You went through a pretty rough experience. Talking to a professional about it could help put it in perspective."

She looked uncertain. "I'm okay."

"Just keep it in mind. I'm making the same offer to everyone involved. There's nothing wrong with getting some professional help."

"Okay," she agreed, but Shane was rather sure from her reaction that she didn't want to let a therapist into her head.

"The police and the press are waiting to speak to both of you," Kinkead said.

"The press?" she breathed, looking panicked.

The S&D chief gave her a reassuring smile. "You know how these things work. When there's a dangerous situation, the media are all over it. It would be almost impossible for you and Shane to get out of here without making a statement. You're both heroes."

A man with a lined face joined the group. He had a salt-and-pepper buzz cut and was wearing a rumpled tweed sport coat and gray slacks.

"This is Detective Langley," Kinkead said. "He wants to get a statement from you. Why don't we go down to my office?"

Shane nodded, staying beside Elena as they took the elevator to the second-floor executive offices.

"As soon as I heard about the blood spatter, I had my

assistant run out to Lord and Taylor," Kinkead said to Elena. "She's getting you a blouse you can wear instead of that ruined one."

"Thank you."

Shane was in the middle of explaining his surprise attack to the detective when Penny Martin, an attractive young blond, came into the office with a shopping bag and took Elena to the executive washroom.

Shane watched them leave as he continued his explanation.

"Risky but effective," Langley said, then asked some detailed questions.

When Elena came back, she was wearing a royal-blue blouse that set off her Hispanic good looks. As Shane gave her the once-over, she flushed, and he looked away. He was still remembering holding her in his arms, something he hadn't thought he'd be doing. But when her adrenaline had stopped pumping, and she'd started wobbling on those slender legs of hers, he'd instinctively reached for her and pulled her close.

After finishing with Shane, Langley got a brief synopsis of the whole incident from Elena and said he might have more questions later.

"And now the media," Kinkead said.

"What should I say?" Elena asked.

"Just tell them your role in what happened. It can be brief."

"Why were you up in HR?" Shane asked.

Her gaze swung to him. "They were having trouble with some of their computer equipment."

He nodded. He'd check that out when he had some time.

"The sooner we satisfy the press, the sooner you can get out of here," Kinkead said.

"All right," Elena agreed, but Shane could feel her tension.

Because she was nervous about being put in the spotlight, or because she had something to hide?

He gave himself a mental shake, annoyed that he was suspicious of her under these circumstances, but he couldn't help it. He was suspicious by nature. His job made him suspicious. And he couldn't help thinking that Elena Reyes might have something to do with the problem he'd been hired to solve at S&D.

They all moved to the lobby of the building, and Shane was surprised to find it had gotten dark while they'd been in the executive offices. Camera crews were standing by, spotlights were aimed at the front entrance of the building, and reporters ringed the door.

Elena gave him a panicked look, and he reached for her hand, squeezing it and feeling the cold of her fingers.

When he stroked his finger across her palm, he felt a little shiver go through her. "This isn't worse than being held hostage at gunpoint, is it?" he whispered.

She laughed. "If you put it that way, I guess not."

"So let's get it over with." He let go of her hand, and they stepped outside. Kinkead walked to the microphone and made a brief statement about what had happened, ending with:

"Thanks to the fast thinking of Elena Reyes and the courageous intervention of Shane Gallagher, the hostages were rescued quickly."

"What about the woman who was shot?" a reporter called out.

"She's in serious but stable condition," Kinkead answered.

As his boss talked, Shane scanned the crowd. In the back he could see his two partners and friends, Jack Brandt and Max Lyon. They'd met a little over a year ago when they'd all been in Miami and had all gotten caught in a drug raid at a local nightclub. Along with a bunch of drunk and disorderly guys, they'd been taken to police headquarters and held overnight at the Miami jail.

The three of them had kept order in the holding cell all night. And when they were released in the morning, they'd gone out for a beer and started talking. It turned out that Jack was a former Navy SEAL. Shane had been in the Army Investigative Service. And Max had been a detective in Howard County, Maryland.

When they discovered that they were all currently unemployed with similar skill sets, they'd come up with the idea of starting the Rockfort Security Agency. And since they were all from Maryland, they'd located the agency in Rockville, outside D.C., where they could get a deal on the rent. And they'd made a success of the venture.

Shane knew his two friends were staying at the back of the crowd because he was working undercover at S&D. Lincoln Kinkead had hired Rockfort to find out who was trying to steal proprietary information from his company, and Shane had taken the job as security chief, which put him in an excellent position to poke into all of the personnel files.

Shane's mind snapped back to the present as Kinkead said he was turning the interview over to him.

He stepped to the microphone and told about his rescue plan.

"What if you'd failed?" a reporter asked. "Wouldn't the hostages have been in more danger?"

"I didn't plan to fail," Shane answered, thinking that probably sounded too arrogant.

After taking a few more questions, he ushered Elena to the microphone. She looked pale but resolute.

"I was one of the hostages," she began and told about being held captive by Duckworth.

"And she held his attention while I came in the window," Shane added.

"Were you scared, Ms. Reyes?" someone shouted.

"Of course. But I thought Mr. Gallagher was our best chance to get out of there alive."

He stayed with her while she answered a few more questions. But he knew she didn't want to prolong the ordeal, so he cut off the interview quickly.

"Thanks for getting me out of there," she said as they went back into the building. "Well, actually, thanks for getting us all out of the HR department."

He laughed. "All in a day's work."

"Oh, sure."

She looked outside at the reporters who were still gathered around the entrance. "Unfortunately, I still have to get to my car and get out of here."

"I can retrieve your car. And you can meet me at the back of the building."

"Would you?"

"Of course. Give me your keys."

She fumbled in her purse for her keys. "It's a burgundy Honda," she told him. "About five rows from the front."

Max and Jack looked at him questioningly as he headed into the parking lot.

"I'm getting Elena's car for her. I'll meet you back at the office."

The two men departed, and he got into the Honda.

Elena was waiting for him at the loading dock.

"Thanks for doing this," she said as he climbed out of the vehicle.

"You still look worried."

"The next ordeal will be talking to my parents."

"Why?"

She shook her head. "We're from San Marcos, where it was dangerous to call attention to yourself. They're not going to like it that I was on TV."

He knew she was from the Central American country, but he pretended that he hadn't perused her personnel file.

"But it's not for anything bad. You're a hero. They should be proud of you."

"In their minds, it won't matter," she said as she climbed into the vehicle and drove away.

He watched her disappear into the darkness, thinking that he would have liked to spend some time with her—decompressing after the ordeal. Then he canceled the thought.

He was attracted to her, but that couldn't get in the way of his investigation. And because of her position in the IT department, she was high on his suspect list.

Chapter 3

"NOTHING LIKE RELAXING WITH A BEER AFTER ALMOST getting shot," Shane said as he kicked off his shoes and put his feet up on the scarred table in the Rockfort offices, conveniently located in an industrial park not far from S&D.

"I guess you weren't counting on a nutcase trying to take down the HR department," Max Lyon said dryly.

"Not hardly. But like I told Bert Iverson, all's well that ends well."

"You don't think you were taking a chance rappelling down the building and crashing through the window?" Jack Brandt asked.

Shane took another swig of beer and gave Jack a pointed look. "You mean like you were taking a chance invading a nut-ball militia group a few months ago?"

"I wouldn't do it now," Jack said.

"Because you were redeemed by the love of a good woman," Shane shot back.

"Is that bad?"

"It worked out okay for you. I got burned by my ex, and I'm not looking to repeat the experience."

"That doesn't mean all women are bad."

"It means I'm not going to get fooled again," he said, punching out the words.

When he saw Jack open his mouth, then close it, he was relieved his friend had decided to drop the subject.

Max jumped into the conversation. "Lincoln Kinkead owes you one for stopping that lunatic before he shot anyone else."

"Kinkead wasn't exactly happy about my methods. I thought he might fire me before Bert Iverson pointed out that I'd saved a bunch of lives."

"You did. What was Kinkead's objection?"

Shane laughed. "He doesn't like what he considers hotdogging. Plus I don't think he liked my calling attention to myself."

Max shook his head. "So you won't climb the outside of his building again."

"Let's hope."

"We haven't talked to you in a couple of days. Are you making any progress on your main mission?"

"There's nothing new."

S&D developed software for the business and financial community. Their biggest product was an office software package that was giving Microsoft a run for its money. But they had something in development that was rumored to be a blockbuster.

Lincoln Kinkead had come to Rockfort after one of his employees, a man named Arnold Blake, was murdered. Blake had worked in the IT department, and Kinkead suspected he'd been trying to steal the specs for the new hush-hush product. It was something called Falcon's Flight. Shane had no idea what it was, and Kinkead had kept the information to himself.

Shane was working on the theory that Blake had been murdered because he refused to turn over the material he'd stolen to the people who had hired him.

But that wasn't the end of it. Kinkead was sure that

whoever wanted Falcon's Flight was making another try for it, substantiated by evidence that someone had recently been poking into the company's product files without authorization.

"Do you think today's events are related to the Arnold Blake murder?" Max asked.

"It doesn't seem like it, but I guess I'd better check to see if there's any connection between Blake and Duckworth. The only thing I know now is that who-ever's tiptoeing around in the development files again is very skillful and very careful—and you couldn't say that for Duckworth. His style was more like clomping around in jackboots."

"You said you don't think it's someone in development."

"They're all squeaky clean."

"But that woman who saved your butt—Elena Reyes. Isn't she one of your suspects?" Jack asked.

"Yeah."

"Interesting that she got herself into the middle of that mess."

"She says she was in the HR department on business and didn't know Duckworth was going to come in wav-ing a gun."

"You're sure there's no connection between *them*?"

"What would be her motive for walking into danger?"

"To get to know you better," Max answered.

"She didn't know I was going to show up."

"She probably had a good idea you weren't going to leave a bunch of innocent people twisting in the wind."

Shane shrugged. He wouldn't discount anything, but he wasn't going out of his way to manufacture a devious scenario for Elena. Or was he?

—⁓—

Elena's stomach was in knots as she pulled up in the driveway of her parents' modest ranch house on a dead-end street in Germantown. When she saw one of the front curtains drop back into place, she knew her mother had been looking out the window, watching for her to arrive—sure that she was coming over as soon as she could get away from the media.

She had thought about going back to her apartment and changing her clothes first. Then she'd told herself that her parents would be worried and would want to talk to her.

Still, she couldn't keep her nerves from jumping as she climbed out of her car.

The front door opened as she hurried up the walk, but nobody came out. After taking a steadying breath, she stepped inside, and her mother closed the door.

Both her parents had been in the living room, which was furnished with a love seat, two low-slung side chairs, and a flat-screen television on a chest at the side of the room. It was tuned to CNN. Elena glanced from the TV to her parents. Both of them looked old for their years. Her mother's dark hair was streaked with gray, and her father had lost most of his hair, so that only a thin fringe clung to the back of his skull.

He'd been a newspaper reporter back home, and he'd been able to write some articles for a local Spanish language paper here. But he'd supported the family by taking on janitorial duties for the local school system and had worked his way up to supervisor before retiring.

"You were on television," he said in Spanish as Elena walked into the living room. "Local and national, too."

He had been careful to learn English when he came here, but he was always more comfortable with his native language.

"*No mucho*," she answered, speaking in Spanish for his benefit.

"I taught you to keep your head down. Now everybody knows you were in that office where the man shot that girl. Then he was killed."

She wished she could simply turn around and walk out of her parents' house. Instead, she crossed to one of the worn easy chairs and lowered herself to the seat.

It was tempting to ask, "Would you have been happier if I'd gotten killed?" but she kept the question locked behind her lips as she said, "I was at the wrong place at the wrong time."

Unable to drop his original theme, her father said, "Everybody knows who you are."

"Papa, this isn't San Marcos. Nobody's coming after me."

"You can't be sure."

"I had no choice. I was in the office. I had to help the man who came to rescue us."

"Shane Gallagher?"

"Yes."

"He was on the TV, too. What does he do for the company?"

"He's head of security."

Her father sucked in a sharp breath before speaking. "Like the secret police."

"No." She looked toward her mother. "I came straight here. Could you get me a glass of water?"

Her mother looked toward Papa. When he nodded, she went into the kitchen and came back with the water.

Elena took several sips, then cradled the glass in her hand, grateful for something to hold on to. "I'm all right. I came by to tell you."

"You stay away too much."

She struggled not to make a cutting remark. She stayed away because coming here was never pleasant.

"Alesandro was here," her mother said.

"How is he?"

"*Bien*," Momma answered, but there was something in her voice that made Elena wonder if her brother was truly fine. As a boy, Alesandro had been happy to come to America. He'd liked the freedom and the standard of living here, but he hadn't been able to make the most of his life in his new country.

He'd had trouble learning English, and his grades in school had been poor—not good enough for college. He'd worked a bunch of low-paying jobs. The best one was at the service desk of a rental car company. Usually he was short of money, and sometimes he tried to borrow from Elena. After she had lent him cash a few times, and he had never paid it back, she'd vowed never to do it again. That was something else her parents held against her. She should be willing to help her brother.

"Do you want to stay to dinner?" Momma asked.

"*Gracias, pero no*. I want to go home and lie down. I just stopped by to reassure you."

Her father jumped into the conversation with the kind of comment she'd grown to expect from him.

"That gunman could have been politically motivated, and the government could be watching you now."

"I don't think so."

"Don't get lulled into a false sense of security. You remember I thought we were okay. Then I got a tip that government agents were coming for us, and we had to get out of the house. We had to leave almost everything behind."

Elena nodded. She'd heard this story many times.

Her father began to ramble on about how they'd traveled north by car, then crossed the border.

She'd been young, but she still remembered the soldiers inspecting their documents, and her father lying and saying that they were going to visit relatives in Mexico. She didn't want to listen to the story again, but he was her father. He had saved her by getting her out of San Marcos, so she settled into her chair to hear the tale one more time.

If anyone had a right to be paranoid, it was Eduardo Reyes. But listening to him was exhausting, and by the time she left, she was almost too tired to think. Her father had gone on about government spies. She was more worried about the press. Had some reporter dug into her background and figured out that her parents also lived in the area? Was someone from a local television station or newspaper outside waiting to ambush her? Pausing just inside the door, she looked out into the darkness. There seemed to be no activity on the street. Perhaps the reporters had finished with her. Or they hadn't tracked down her family.

With a little sigh of relief, she crossed quickly to her car and got in. When she pulled away from the curb, she thought she saw another car pull into the street behind her, but the driver had left the lights off.

A car with its lights off at night? A reporter following her? Or what? She sped up, thinking maybe whoever was back there would let her go. Or was she seeing things because she was too tired to think straight? If she felt more comfortable in her parents' home, she might have gone back and asked to spend the night. But then she'd have to tell them why she was nervous, and she certainly didn't want to explain about the car.

———

After taking off his bulletproof vest, Shane made a show of relaxing with the other guys, but he probably wasn't fooling them. He knew he was too keyed up to unwind, and he was sure they did, too.

He left after an hour and headed home, his mind replaying the events of the hostage takedown. He was willing to bet that Duckworth was just a sideshow and had nothing to do with the reason Lincoln Kinkead had hired Rockfort Security. But he kept coming back to Elena Reyes. She might have saved his life when Duckworth had whirled around, but that didn't mean he could trust her.

He felt his chest tighten as he tried to sort through his feelings about her. She'd been in the perfect position to help him out. At the very least, that was interesting, although he wasn't sure there were any sinister implications.

He lived in one of the high-rise apartments that had been built in the first flurry of modernization in Rockville. The red-brick building was showing its age now, which was why he'd gotten a good deal on the sublet.

He parked in the garage and stopped in the lobby to get a bunch of circulars from his mailbox. Then he proceeded to the fifth floor where he unlocked his apartment and stepped inside. He'd rented the furniture—a standard sofa and a couple of chairs, plus a flat-screen TV on a stand in the living room, a small table and chairs in the dining room, and a dresser and king-size bed in the bedroom. All of it sat on oatmeal-colored carpet that had seen better days.

He usually paid no attention to the furnishings. Maybe because he'd almost gotten killed today, he stopped in the living room and looked around, trying to see the place from the point of view of a stranger. It looked like the abode of a man who didn't give a shit where he lived. Which was an accurate summation of the situation.

His previous apartment had been an entirely different matter—filled with trendy furniture, sheets, towels, and knickknacks carefully chosen by his ex-wife. If he'd wanted to take any of them, he supposed he could have. Instead, he'd let her have all the booty and all the wedding presents because he didn't need any of it around to remind him of past mistakes.

He cursed under his breath as he flashed back to the day a year and a half ago when he'd told Glenda that he knew she was cheating on him and their marriage was over. He'd been deployed to Afghanistan when the affair with Larry MacMillan started. And she hadn't even had the sense to break it off when he got back.

She'd claimed that MacMillan didn't mean anything to her. Shane had said that the cheating meant something to him. He'd walked out the door and never saw her again except for some mandatory appearances at lawyers' offices.

More than that, he'd changed his life around. He could have volunteered for a war zone. But he wasn't going to give Glenda the satisfaction of sending him into harm's way. He'd been up for reenlistment, but he'd mustered out. Then he'd taken some time to figure out his next move.

Annoyed that he was thinking about her now, he stomped into the bedroom, pulled off the running suit he'd worn for the surprise attack, and dropped the jacket and pants into the hamper. He took a quick shower, then put on jeans and a dark T-shirt, and wandered into the kitchen where he opened the freezer and examined his stash of frozen dinners. It wasn't home cooking, but it was convenient, he thought, as he pulled out a chicken and pasta dish, stripped off the wrapper, and put it into the microwave. While he drank another beer, he booted up the computer in the spare bedroom he used as an office, then brought the food to the desk.

He was tired, but he was too wound up to relax, and he might as well get some work done.

He'd told the other Rockfort agents that he couldn't help suspecting Elena Reyes. He had no proof that she'd done anything illegal, but with her access to the whole company's operations, she was in a perfect position to steal information from S&D. Not only that, but she had the skills to cover her tracks.

Or was he digging into her background so relentlessly because he was obsessed with her—and investigating her gave him the perfect excuse to get to know her better, at least in the abstract?

For a moment, he let his mind zing back to the scene in the ladies' room when he'd held her in his arms. He'd felt protective and at the same time vulnerable. Maybe crashing through that window and getting shot at had affected him more than he wanted to admit.

With a rough sound, he stopped thinking about his reactions after the takedown and went to the file he'd compiled on Elena, skimming back through the notations he'd made. Her father was a political refugee from San Marcos. He'd come here legitimately, but did Dad still have ties to his country of origin? What if he was involved in something illegal and had dragged his daughter into it?

And what about the brother, Alesandro Reyes? Elena had a well-paying job at S&D. Her brother had had the same opportunities in his adopted country, but you wouldn't know it to look at him. He worked for a rental car company where the pay couldn't be anywhere near what his sister was making. But he did have unexpected luxuries like a top-of-the-line Buick and an apartment in a high-priced building. Did he have other sources of income? Or was he forcing his sister or his parents to subsidize his lifestyle? And if so, how?

Even as Shane made a note to dig further into Alesandro's background, his thoughts went back to Elena.

Did she have a secret life that she was keeping hidden from everyone at S&D? A relationship she was hiding? And what would be the significance if she was? Could she be seeing someone who was influencing her behavior?

Was she under stress—with signs he could pick up, like moodiness and paranoia? Was she hiding financial transactions or extreme views?

He laughed. Maybe if he'd investigated Joe Duckworth for those tendencies, today's hostage situation could have been avoided. But Duckworth hadn't even been on his radar screen. He hadn't been investigating former employees.

Once again, he went back to Elena because he'd rather investigate her than Joe Duckworth. And it was too late to do anything about that bastard, anyway, besides bury him.

Shane had several pictures of Elena. One must have been from her high school yearbook. And some were snapshots that he'd gotten off the Web, like the one that went with her S&D employee bio.

He studied one of the head shots, admiring the waves in her long, shiny dark hair and the thick lashes that framed her dark eyes. She was a beauty, even though she didn't do much to enhance her looks.

Not like Glenda, who had always spent a good deal of time at the makeup table.

He clenched his teeth, wondering why he had dragged his ex-wife into the evening again.

Chapter 4

IN A MANSION IN THE TONY ACRES OF POTOMAC HORSE country, Jerome Weller picked up the remote and turned off the news.

The hostage situation and shoot-out at S&D had made CNN and Fox. But after hours of breathless reporting, the anchors had run out of anything new to say. The talking heads were just rehashing old details, which was good, from his point of view. Just the same old pictures of the S&D building. Then the news that the guy who'd held the hostages in the HR department was dead— taken down by the chief of security, Shane Gallagher.

Again Weller saw the interview with the hero of the day. Shane Gallagher. He could be a problem. He'd been very effective in the takedown. And he'd also been reckless. Not a good combination for an enemy. And he knew that was what Gallagher was going to be—unless he killed him first.

Jerome reached into the bowl on the table beside the couch, took out a butter mint, and unwrapped the candy. It was a green one, and he popped it into his mouth, sucking as he enjoyed the flavor. He'd liked the candy since he was a kid. Of course, he'd never gotten to eat them at home. His dad had been a health-food nut who'd kept sweets away from his kids. The only time Jerome had gotten sugary treats was when he was playing at a friend's house.

He'd done a lot of that as a kid. He'd never liked bringing friends home. Not only because Dad was weird. They'd also been the shabby family in the neighborhood, and he'd been ashamed to have the other kids see the way they lived.

He'd remedied that as an adult. Now his home was a showplace, with all the comforts he'd lacked as a child—including all the candy he wanted. Which hadn't done his teeth any good. But today you didn't have to worry too much about that. You could get implants—which were better than the real thing.

As he sucked on the candy, he thought about Shane Gallagher and decided that bumping the guy off might not be such a great idea right now. It would be suspicious if the head of S&D security bought the farm just after he'd done that heroic hostage rescue.

Heaving his considerable bulk out of the custom-made leather chair in his den, Jerome crossed to the bar at the side of the room and poured some schnapps into a glass. The peppermint liqueur was just the thing to go with the mint candy—with a bit more punch.

He took an appreciative swallow. It was imported from Germany. An indulgence he'd only enjoyed as an adult. In addition to banning candy from the house, Dad had also lectured extensively on the evils of alcohol.

After taking a few sips, Jerome set the glass down and paced the room, his expensive alligator shoes making no sound on the thick carpet. He was a short, stout man wearing top-of-the-line Gucci jeans and a five-hundred-dollar cashmere sweater over a soft white dress shirt, all in plus sizes. And the outsized heavy gold chain at his neck winked in the illumination from the overhead lights as he walked to the window, then back to the chair.

He glanced toward the door. He'd given his staff the night off because he wanted to be alone. Now he was thinking that he should have kept Mario around to give him a massage. That would have relaxed his tense muscles.

There was a new product in development that he had vowed to get from S&D. And he wasn't going to let anything stand in the way of him acquiring it.

He'd tried and failed once, and maybe he'd even thought about giving up. But now the newscast was like a sign winking on and off in the darkness—pointing him in the right direction. He'd set up a couple of options. Finally, he knew which one he was going to take.

Or was that plan too risky?

He picked up the glass of schnapps and took another swallow while he considered his options.

⁓

Elena lived in what was called a garden apartment. Not one of the sexy new developments north of Rockville, but an older yellow-brick complex in the less fashionable part of the city. Still, living there meant she could afford to be on her own, which was important to her.

She drove past her building and circled the parking lot, checking to see if the car she'd spotted was still behind her. Although it seemed to have disappeared, she wished she could have gotten a space closer to her door.

The lot was full of older model cars, pickup trucks, and vehicles like delivery trucks and service vans that were owned by local businesses but driven home by workers.

She parked between a van from a rug cleaning company and a pickup with a padlocked toolbox under the back window. And before she got out of her car, she took the canister of Mace out of her bag and held it in her left hand. Her keys were in her right hand as she walked rapidly up the sidewalk to the front entrance of her building. Grateful that the light wasn't out at the mailboxes as it had been the week before, she got her mail, then climbed the steps to her second-floor apartment. Once she was inside, she slid the security chain into place and breathed out a little sigh.

She stopped in the living room to straighten the brightly colored accent pillow on the discount easy chair, then turned on the kitchen light and shuffled through the mail, separating the bills from the advertisements. The bills went into a drawer in the heavy, carved sideboard she'd picked up at a garage sale. The ads went into the trash. That was the way she liked it. Everything in its place.

She listened to several messages from friends and coworkers who had heard the news and wanted to make sure she was okay.

She returned most of the calls, keeping her voice bright and cheerful even though she'd had an exhausting and frightening day.

Finally, she went into the kitchen, glad she didn't have to cook. As was her habit, on Saturday she'd gone to the grocery store and bought the ingredients for several of her favorite dishes—some from home and some popular American entrées. She'd spent a couple of hours cooking and stored the food in the refrigerator. Now she got out a casserole of chicken and vegetable stew and some of the rice and beans she'd always liked. San Marcos comfort food, she guessed you'd call it.

Scooping some onto a plate, she microwaved her dinner while she went down the hall to the bedroom to kick off her medium-heeled shoes and change into sweatpants and a T-shirt.

It was tempting to simply drape her slacks and the blue blouse over the back of the scarred straight-backed chair she'd painted a cheerful yellow, but she hung them neatly in the closet before going back to the kitchen and taking the plate out of the microwave. She brought the meal to the table, along with a glass of cold tea from a pitcher in the refrigerator.

The food was good. She'd asked Momma to teach her to make a lot of the dishes they'd enjoyed back home, and she and her mother had spent many hours together in the kitchen. Those were some of her best memories of her parents. No politics. No sibling rivalry. Just two women in the kitchen, cooking.

She should be hungry, but after making it through only half the food, she put down her fork. Knowing she wasn't going to eat anymore, she covered the plate with plastic wrap and put it back in the refrigerator.

She looked toward the living room, thinking she might turn on the television and find out if there was anything new about the hostage takedown. Then she canceled the idea. Why go through it again? And maybe if she got a good night's sleep, she'd be ready to face tomorrow at S&D.

She wouldn't kid herself. A lot more people than the friends who'd called were going to be curious about to-day's events, and she needed to think about what to say.

And think about Lincoln Kinkead's suggestion. He'd said she could talk to a therapist. It wasn't something she would have considered on her own. But he'd made the offer, and maybe she shouldn't dismiss the idea out of hand.

For the moment, she was still feeling shaky. She turned on the shower and got undressed. After standing under the pounding water for ten minutes, she told herself she felt better, although it was only marginally true.

Wrapped in a towel, she used the blow-dryer on her hair, then got out one of the long sleep shirts that she liked to wear. This one had a picture of a cat and a fawn cuddled up together, and she smiled at the picture before pulling on the shirt.

Before getting into bed, she took one of the over-the-counter sleeping tablets that she needed occasionally.

It helped her relax, but after slipping into bed, she lay rigidly under the covers. Finally she got up again and turned on the bathroom light, then closed the door so that only a sliver of illumination came through the crack. She hated that she needed the light, but after the ordeal of the day, she didn't want to be in the dark. Truly, she didn't want to be alone, but there was no one she'd feel comfortable calling this late at night.

A face drifted into her mind, Shane Gallagher's face. She clamped her hands around the edge of the sheet, ordering herself to get him out of her mind. She barely knew him, and she certainly wasn't going to ask him to watch over her.

She felt a laugh bubbling in her throat. No, she wasn't going to call *him*.

Instead, she worked the pillow into a better position

under her neck, moved her shoulders to get comfortable, and closed her eyes. Maybe the pill she'd taken had started working, because she felt herself letting go. And soon she had crossed from wakefulness to sleep.

For a few hours, that slumber was peaceful. Then a dream grabbed her. She was back at the S&D building, and it was after the hostage situation was over. Hadn't they been in the ladies' room? Instead, Shane helped her to her feet and pulled her into Mr. Perkins' office and closed the door.

Wrapping her in his arms, he gathered her close. She closed her eyes and leaned into him the way she'd wanted to but hadn't allowed herself.

"Are you all right?" he asked urgently.

"Yes." She raised her head and opened her eyes, searching his face. "Are you?"

"Yes."

She caught her breath as she took in their surroundings. They had come into Mr. Perkins' office. But that wasn't what she saw now. She and Shane Gallagher were in a bedroom, where they obviously shouldn't be.

She pushed at his shoulders, but he kept her in his arms.

"What are we doing here?" she asked in a shaky voice.

He tipped his head to the side, giving her a look that made her blood heat. "Don't you know?"

Of course she did, but she wasn't going to say it.

His words didn't quite match the look he'd given her. "You've just been through a terrible ordeal. You need to calm down."

She swallowed hard. She had been scared out of her mind a few minutes ago, and she was still off balance.

Shane massaged her tense shoulders, helping her relax. He ran his hands up and down her back the way he'd done before...but this time he went farther, gliding down to the rounded curve of her bottom, sending currents of sensation through her body.

Every lesson she'd learned from her mother about how to act with men told her he shouldn't be touching her like that. She should push herself away from him, but she didn't have the strength to do it.

"I want to kiss you," he said in a gritty voice. "And you want to kiss me."

She wasn't going to admit that aloud. When she didn't move, he crooked one hand under her chin, tipping her face up, and she saw that he was smiling down at her.

She stared into his dark eyes, watching him as he lowered his head, so that his lips brushed back and forth against hers, then settled, pressing, moving, asking her to open for him.

She did, feeling another surge of heat as his tongue dipped into her mouth, playing with the inside of her lips, then the line of her teeth.

This was more than she should allow, but she ignored proprieties. Experimentally, she moved her own tongue, sliding it against his, each stroke of that intimate contact increasing the heat coursing through her body.

She was wearing the blue blouse that Lincoln Kinkead had given her, and her breath caught as Shane began to unbutton it.

"No," she protested.

"You don't want me to do this?"

Emotions warred inside her. All the warnings

Momma had given her clashed with her own desires. "I don't know," she managed to say.

He laughed. "Don't fool yourself."

Before she could come back with a retort, he moved one hand from the buttons to her breasts.

"Don't."

He let go of the button he was holding and glided his fingers over the silky fabric of the blouse, making her nipples poke out against the silk.

What—had she forgotten to wear a bra?

Heat surged through her as he circled the tight peaks with his fingers. And this time, when he started unbuttoning the blouse, she didn't protest.

He pushed the sides of the blouse out of the way, baring her breasts.

"Don't," she protested again, but her voice had gone weak.

"You like it."

"I shouldn't."

His gaze grew more intense. "Don't deny yourself what you want."

She couldn't answer.

She might have run, but she was rooted to the spot. He took her nipples between his thumbs and fingers, tugging on them, making her body rigid with molten need. He kept one hand on her breasts, playing with them as the other hand slid down her body to the juncture of her legs.

She felt her knees buckle, but he backed her against a wall to keep her upright as his fingers separated the folds of her sex, slipping into her most intimate flesh.

He caressed her there, stroking and pressing, making her hips rock to increase the contact.

"That's it, sweetheart. Go with it," he whispered as his teeth nibbled at her ear.

An explosion gathered and flared, sending a burst of pleasure through her body. She cried out, calling his name.

"Shane."

Seconds later, her eyes blinked open, and she knew she was alone in her own bed. The heated encounter with him had all been a dream. And the memories of what she had dreamed made her face redden. Now she was glad that the room was almost dark and that she wasn't at her parents' house.

The dream had started with the terror of the hostage scene. But the terror had dissolved into sexual need, then... She didn't want to admit that her unconscious mind had brought her to sexual climax, but there was no way to avoid the reality.

She lay in bed, struggling to bring her emotions and her breathing under control.

Moments ago she had imagined making love with Shane Gallagher. Well, not sexual intercourse. She supposed she hadn't dared go that far—even in her dreams. But he had made her come.

Made her come. That's what it was called. Something nice girls didn't do. But she hadn't been able to control her dream.

She laughed out loud, the sound startling in the darkened bedroom. She'd been asleep. That was her excuse.

A long-ago scene flashed into her mind. Something she didn't like to think about. The time Momma had come into her bedroom and caught her touching herself. She'd slapped her and told her that was something forbidden.

And Elena had made sure she'd never been caught doing it again. Of course, "caught" was the operative word. It was something she didn't want to give up, and she'd just been more careful about it. That was all.

She dragged in a breath and let it out.

Back then she'd been a scared little girl, wanting to please her parents. When she'd grown up, she'd read a lot about sex. It was a natural function and perhaps a joy for married couples. But in the world where she came from, it was forbidden to anyone else.

Well, at least that was true of women. She was fairly sure that a lot of men felt entitled to disobey that rule. They could get away with it because their wives were dependent on them, for themselves and for their children, if they had any. But she would never be the kind of woman with no resources of her own. She'd dreamed of being an artist, but she'd known that was an uncertain career. She'd made sure she had a marketable skill, working with computers. That had gotten her a good job. She was perfectly capable of supporting herself. And maybe someday she'd find the right man. Someone who would love her and respect her.

Her heart squeezed. Was the right man out there? She didn't know, but for the moment, her best choice was to keep on with the life she had made for herself.

She sat up in bed, pulled her knees up and clasped her arms around her legs, rocking back and forth. Her life had been going along the way she'd planned it until a new chief of security had showed up at S&D. Shane Gallagher. She was afraid of him, but at the same time she was attracted to him, and she thought the attraction was mutual. But there were times when it felt like he had something against her, something she didn't understand, because she had no idea what she'd done to set him against her. That part was like the soldiers back home. You never knew what they'd be ordered to do—and why.

She didn't understand his moods, and right now she was praying that she wasn't going to run into him tomorrow. Not after her unconscious mind had led her to an admission she never would have made if she'd been awake. She wanted him, and she'd dreamed of him kissing her and touching her with the intimacy of a lover.

Of course, the episode had made another decision for her, as well. Lincoln Kinkead had suggested she might want to talk to a counselor. That was out of the question now, because the thing at the top of her mind would be her fantasy sex with Shane Gallagher. And she certainly wasn't going to talk to anyone about *that*.

Chapter 5

AFTER ONLY A FEW HOURS OF SLEEP, SHANE HEAVED HIMSELF out of bed and winced. He must be out of shape if a jaunt to the eighth floor of an office building made his muscles sore.

He laughed. Yeah, sure. He'd been confident of his ability to make the climb down from the roof, but now he was paying the price because he'd used muscles that didn't usually get a workout.

He did some stretching exercises, then headed to the home office that doubled as his workout room. After a punishing forty-five minutes on the elliptical trainer, he showered and headed for Rockfort Security.

Max was already in the office. Jack was probably at home, snuggled in bed with his wife. Shane wasn't going to complain about that. The guy was entitled after the rough year he'd had before stumbling naked into Morgan Rains' front yard. Quite a way to meet. But then Jack had never been the conventional type.

Part of him envied his friend for being happy and settled down. The other part knew that Jack had found a rare woman—a woman worth trusting and loving. Was that in the right order? Did you have to trust someone before you could love her? Probably it was the wiser course. He'd fallen in love with Glenda without knowing enough about her—and paid the price for his impulsiveness later.

He shook his head, then realized that his other partner, Max Lyon, was watching him.

"What?" he asked.

"You look like you're doing some deep thinking."

"Yeah, about the case," Shane lied. "I was hoping you or Jack could do some background checking for me while I'm at S&D."

"Sure, what do you need?"

"There are two guys in the IT department, Jed Lansing and Roy Newman, that I'm wondering about. I don't want to use the work computers to poke into their backgrounds, because if I did, they might find out about it."

"You mean—they might check up on you?"

"Right."

"What do you want to know about them?"

"Dig below the surface of the usual information and see if either of them has been involved in anything questionable."

"Any particular reason you're interested in them?"

"Both of them act uncomfortable around me. I'd like to know if there's a reason for it."

"Will do."

Shane thanked his partner, then headed for S&D. He had planned to go straight to his office, but as he walked down the hall, people kept stopping him to congratulate him on the takedown of the evening before and to ask questions. By the time he got to his desk, it was after ten. But the questions gave him an idea. He'd been wondering how he could bump into Elena today. It would certainly be natural for him to go over to IT to find out how she was doing after yesterday's harrowing events.

The plan lightened his mood, which he found annoying.

His relationship with her should be strictly business, yet he was pleased at the prospect of seeing her again.

He spent an hour and a half at his desk doing routine security work, looking at the logs of calls from hardwired company phones as well as running through cell phone calls made inside the building. He was sure most employees didn't know that the company could track their private communications. In fact, the system was something like what the National Security Agency had been using to monitor phone calls and emails around the United States.

He didn't have ready access to the conversations themselves, but he could see who was calling whom. So far he hadn't picked up any suspicious patterns, but that could simply mean the person out to steal company secrets was being cautious and not communicating with anyone questionable while he or she was at work.

Around eleven thirty, Shane got out of the computer program and sat for a moment, picturing the layout of IT.

There was a small reception area, then cubicles along two short halls. Elena's desk was near the end of the hall on the right.

Shane took the elevator down to IT and stepped into the department, pausing in the reception area as he pretended to get his bearings. He saw that several people noted his presence, including Roy Newman, one of the men he'd asked Max to check on.

When Shane looked in the guy's direction, Newman quickly lowered his head back to his work, which might be significant or not.

Shane continued down the right-hand hall, walking slowly on feet that were almost silent. Several of the nearby cubicles were empty, but Elena was at her desk, poring over a spreadsheet on her screen. Absorbed in her work, she wasn't aware that anyone was standing behind her, which gave him a few moments to take her in.

His gaze skimmed over the glossy black of her wavy hair and the feminine tilt of her shoulders. He could see her delicate features reflected in her computer screen.

When she realized she wasn't alone, she stiffened and looked up quickly, turning to see who was there. As she registered who it was, a mixture of expressions flickered across her features. She looked glad to see him, but at the same time embarrassed and wary.

"Mr. Gallagher," she said.

"After last night, I think you know me well enough to call me Shane."

After last night.

She flushed, and he wondered what about the hostage takedown was making her blush. "Shane," she murmured, letting the sound of his name hang between them.

He had the feeling she'd wanted to ask why he was there, but then thought better of the question and waited for him to explain.

"I wanted to find out how you were doing—after that ordeal with Duckworth yesterday."

"I'm fine."

"You answered pretty quickly."

She raised one shoulder. "Okay, it was an automatic response. But it is true."

"I'd like to get your impressions of what happened."

"I'm kind of busy."

He waited a beat before saying, "I was thinking we could get some lunch. You were planning to eat lunch, weren't you?"

"I guess."

"Let's get out of the building. There's a sandwich shop I found a few blocks from here that's very good."

She looked torn, and he felt his stomach clench while he waited for her to make a decision. When she finally agreed, the tension eased out of him.

"Give me a couple of minutes to freshen up."

"I'll meet you in the main lobby."

———∿∿∿———

Elena hurried to the ladies' room, used the facilities, and went to the sink where she inspected her face in the mirror while she washed her hands.

The woman who stared back seemed flushed and nervous, and she was sure Shane Gallagher had picked up on that when he'd come to her cubicle. Did he think she was hiding something that had to do with work? She hated to think so, but on the other hand, she'd hate him knowing the real reason why she was on edge. She'd had a very sexual dream last night, a dream where he was the star attraction. Just that thought brought more color to her cheeks, and she made a sound low in her throat.

"Stop it," she muttered to herself. "Think about something else."

She dug her comb out of her purse and swiped it through her hair, then got out lipstick and stroked on a little. Standing back to survey the effect, she hoped it didn't look like she'd gotten fixed up for him. But then what was wrong with that? An attractive man had asked her to lunch, and there was no reason not to make herself look good for him. Any American girl would do that.

Like her. Making herself into an American had been

one of her goals. On the surface, she thought she had succeeded, but she knew her values were old-fashioned by American standards.

Ordering herself not to keep going on about her reactions, she left the ladies' room and took the elevator to the first floor, where Shane was standing in the lobby, gazing out the front window.

He turned when he heard her coming up behind him. "Hi."

"Hi," she answered, hearing the breathy quality of her voice. She ordered herself to act normal, whatever that meant.

"The deli's not fancy."

"Do I look to you like a woman who needs fancy?" she heard herself ask.

That stopped him for a moment, and she felt she might have scored a point when a hint of a smile touched his lips. "I guess not."

"Good." But was she keeping score—and of what?

When they stepped out of the building and into the parking lot, she noted that he had a good space, one of the numbered ones close to the building.

His car was large. An SUV, she guessed you'd call it. Still, when they climbed into the front seat and closed the doors, she felt like the two of them were very close together. Closer than she would have chosen. She could smell the subtle tang of the aftershave he'd used, and she could see the muscles work in his arm as he reached to start the car and put it in gear. She grabbed on to the attraction she felt for him and deliberately pushed it into a corner of her mind.

Still, when he twisted to look behind the car as he

backed out of the parking space, she felt his shoulder brush hers and jumped back.

"Sorry," he said.

"That's okay. I'm just…"

"What?"

She dragged in a breath and let it out. "I was brought up not to be alone with a man. It's hard to break old habits."

When he tipped his head to the side, she heard herself explaining. "I'm from San Marcos." So what was she doing now, trying to sabotage her all-American image?

"Right. I forgot," he said, making her think that he knew very well where she was from.

"How long have you been here?" he asked.

"Twenty years. But behavior gets drummed into you by your parents. And you know…the church."

"Yeah."

"So you know what I mean?"

"Uh-huh."

As long as they were having this conversation, she decided to ask, "What did your parents drum into you?"

"Politeness, for one thing." He paused. "And honesty."

She nodded. "I got that, too."

"And they made sure I valued work."

"Were you always in security?"

"After college, when I couldn't get a job, I joined the army and went into their investigative service."

"Oh."

"It was good training."

He pulled up in the parking lot of an entertainment complex.

"It's in here."

They didn't go directly inside. Instead, she followed him around the side of the sprawling building to a restaurant that looked out over a small lake. Tables shaded by umbrellas were scattered around a wide concrete patio. Many were occupied, but there were still some vacant. When they went inside, she could see more tables with fewer people.

"It's a nicer view if you eat on the patio," he commented. "And the sunshine's good."

"Yes," she answered as she scanned the menu, which was printed on a large board above the cooking area. There were a lot of items, enough to make a decision difficult.

"My standard is corned beef on rye with coleslaw and Russian dressing. What's your choice?"

She focused on the board again and found one that met her own standards. "Tuna salad."

"And we could split some potato salad."

"Okay."

"What do you want to drink?"

"Iced tea."

It was strange to suddenly be choosing food and preparing to have a meal with the man she'd had an intimate encounter with last night—even if it had been a fantasy that he didn't even know about. The juxtaposition made her feel as though she had stepped from the real world into an alternate reality.

"Why don't you go get us a table," he said. "I'll order and bring out the food."

When she fumbled for her wallet, he waved his hand. "I'll get it."

"But…"

"You might have saved my life last night," he said. "The least I can do is buy you lunch."

She answered with a small nod.

"Get a nice table," he said, changing the subject.

Glad to get away from him for the moment, she stepped outside, feeling like she'd escaped from...what exactly?

Blinking in the sunlight as she waited for her eyes to adjust again, she looked around at the tables and chose one close to the lake. She'd brought a sweater, thinking they might be eating inside where the air-conditioning was chilly. Because she didn't need it out here, she draped it over one of the chair backs. Looking up again, she saw a mother duck in the water with eight fuzzy yellow babies trailing behind her. Glad for something to focus on besides the man buying her lunch, she went over to the waterside and bent over, watching the little family and wishing she had something to feed them.

A hand on her shoulder made her jump. Looking around, she saw that Shane had come out with the food. He could have told her that he was back. Instead, he'd touched her.

"I couldn't resist watching the ducks. But I saved our table."

"Good."

She caught something in his voice, something she couldn't quite figure out.

He had put a plastic tray on the table with the sandwiches, potato salad, and drinks.

As they sat across from each other, she emptied a packet of sugar into her tea and stirred it with the straw he'd brought. Then she unwrapped her sandwich and took a bite. "This is good."

He kept his gaze on her. "How do you rate tuna sandwiches?"

She laughed. "This one doesn't have too much mayonnaise. The tuna is good quality, and it's seasoned with pickle relish—which I like."

"An interesting analysis. I'll keep it in mind."

"What do you look for in a tuna sandwich?"

He shifted in his seat. "I guess I think of tuna salad as lady food."

"Oh."

"I forgot to ask what kind of bread you like. Is the whole wheat okay?"

"It's fine."

They bit into their sandwiches and chewed, and there was a moment of silence during which she wondered if they were both trying to think of something to say that didn't involve the food.

"I'm guessing they don't have the same dishes in San Marcos," he said.

"No. They weren't into sandwiches at home. More like meals based on rice and beans. Sometimes with meat. Chicken or fish."

"And not canned tuna fish, I'll bet."

He was trying to make her relax with the small talk, but she wondered if she'd ever be able to relax around him.

"No. I got to like it at school. Imitating the other girls in the cafeteria."

"You went to school around here?"

"Yes. In Germantown. It was a good place to grow up."

"Why did you like it?"

"There was a mix of people. I could fit in."

"What did you do for fun?"

"Sky diving."

He blinked.

"That was a joke."

"Right."

"I liked to read."

"What?"

"Everything. Mystery. Science fiction. Romances. What about you?"

"I was more into sports. Depending on the season. Football. Basketball. Baseball."

"I did that too. I was on a softball team."

"Really?"

"Yes." She laughed. "I was a good pitcher."

He gave her a considering look. "You?"

She managed a mischievous smile. "I don't look like a pitcher?"

"I'll take your word for it," he said with a grin. "And you stayed in the area after high school."

"My family's still here. I didn't want to move too far from them, in case my parents needed help."

"They're getting old?"

"They're still doing all right."

"But you worry about them?"

There was a lot she could say. She settled for a little nod.

"You've been at S&D a while."

"It's a good working environment."

She had let him lull her into letting down her guard, but the relaxing small talk ended abruptly with his next question.

"Do you know about an employee in the IT department who was murdered?"

Chapter 6

ELENA'S HAND TIGHTENED ON THE SANDWICH, SQUISHING THE bread, and she deliberately eased her grip as tuna salad oozed out from between the slices.

"You mean Arnold Blake?"

"Yes. Any insights into what might have happened?"

"You're the security chief."

"It was before my time, and the police don't have any leads."

Her mouth had gone dry, and she took a sip of tea. "I didn't know him well," she managed to say.

"Did he seem suspicious to you?"

That might be an opening to say something about the emails Arnold had sent her. But then what?

"No," she responded as she turned her sandwich in her hand, wishing she could get up and walk back to work. Shane Gallagher had put her on edge as soon as he'd started talking to her today. Then he'd fooled her into relaxing before springing a question about Arnold Blake. Or maybe she shouldn't put it that way.

Maybe he saw that he'd spooked her because he leaned back in his chair, focusing on his sandwich for a while and eating some of the potato salad. She took some of the salad, too.

She finished most of her sandwich, saving the edges of the bread. She was annoyed with herself for acting nervous around him. He didn't know about her damn dream. And she wasn't going to talk about Arnold Blake.

Arnold had been in his early sixties when he died. He had been friendly to her when she came to S&D. She'd thought of him as a mentor because he'd shown her the ropes in the IT department. And she'd come to him with questions when she was finding her way.

He was married, and she had no intention of getting involved with him outside of work. But he'd started a correspondence with her that wasn't strictly work related. He'd sent her little jokes, and he'd been into puzzles. He was designing them, calling them SIMon Sez, and sometimes he'd run answers by her. But that was about as far as it went with them.

Because her mother had made her superstitious about discussing the dead, she didn't want to talk about any of that with Shane. Instead, she walked to the edge of the lake and broke the bread crusts into pieces, throwing the bits into the water. The mom duck paddled over, and the babies followed. Smiling, she fed the little family, watching them scrabble around for the food.

Shane came up beside her, and to her relief, he didn't ask any more questions about Blake.

"You like animals?"

"Yes. That's one of the things I miss in the States. There were lots more animals around back home. I loved to watch the babies with the mommas." She looked at her watch. "This was a nice break, but I should get back to work."

"I'm sorry if I kept you from something you needed to do."

"It's fine. I'll just stay a little late."

"Sorry," he said again.

The conversation had petered out. For a little while, she'd felt closer to him. Now she reminded herself that she had no business thinking about him as anything but the company chief of security. They drove back to the S&D building without speaking.

"Thanks," she said as she got out at the front door and hurried back to her desk.

As soon as she was out of his sight, she was angry with herself for being so off balance. She wanted to be a normal, self-assured American woman. She'd reached that status in her work. Now she had to do the same with her personal relationships. But she didn't have a personal relationship with Shane, she reminded herself. Just a fantasy relationship. That silent observation made her snort.

Shane dragged in a breath and let it out as he watched Elena hurry into the building. She'd been on edge with him, and he needed to know why. Because she was deep into something illegal that she was afraid the security chief was going to discover? If that was the case, she could be in danger, which gave him another reason to find out what had prompted her reaction to him.

Or was he just looking for excuses to maintain contact with her because that's what he secretly wanted?

He spent the rest of the afternoon working on background checks, putting in extra time because he felt guilty about…something. He wasn't sure what.

Elena had told him she might work late, too. When he finally made his way down to the parking lot, she was standing beside her car, looking around with a disturbed expression on her face.

Wondering what was wrong, he hurried over. By the time he reached her vehicle, she was inside again, trying to start the vehicle, but the sound told him she wasn't having any success.

Leaning down, he rapped on the driver's side window of Elena's car.

Her head jerked up. When she saw it was him, she rolled down her window.

"Shane. What are you doing here?"

"I was working late, too. It sounds like you're having problems."

She tightened her hands on the wheel. "My car won't start."

"I can take a look."

She gave him a grateful look as he walked around to the front of the vehicle.

"Open the hood release," he said.

As he leaned in and looked at the engine, he could see her watching him through the crack between the hood and the bottom of the window. The worry in her eyes made his chest tighten because he was thinking this might give him an opportunity he'd been looking for. He clamped his teeth together as he reached to touch a few engine parts, then shook his head. "I guess I don't know what's wrong."

"I'll have to call a tow truck."

He looked around the almost empty parking lot. "It's late, and I don't want you hanging around here by yourself. I'll wait with you."

He saw her consider the offer.

"I don't want to put you to any trouble. You probably want to get home."

"Why don't you let me drive you home, and you can take care of the problem in the morning?"

She thought that over, then finally nodded, climbed out of her car, and locked the door behind her.

"Do you have a tissue?" he asked. To emphasize his problem, he rubbed his thumb across his fingers.

She was instantly contrite, making him feel even guiltier.

"You got your hands dirty. I'm sorry." Digging into her purse, she found a tissue pack and gave him one. He wiped at his hands, but of course he couldn't get all the grime off.

"Where do you live?" he asked as they walked back to his car. Did he see a vehicle at the edge of the parking lot with its lights on? A car pulled the wrong way across several spaces. As he looked in that direction, the driver started the engine and drove off.

"Luckily, not far," Elena was saying. She gave him directions to a downscale garden apartment complex only a few miles from the S&D office. "I probably could have walked."

"Not a great idea." As he turned into the complex, he looked toward the side of the road. "There are no sidewalks here."

"There are—in front of the buildings."

"Which one is yours?" he asked as he made the turn off the main road. He hadn't been to the location before, and he thought he'd categorize it as lower middle class. The yellow-brick buildings looked to be at least fifty years old, each with a metal balcony. Some had a couple of plastic chairs on them. Other balconies were obviously being used for excess storage. And some sported bicycles.

She glanced up, maybe judging his reaction.

"It's not fancy."

"It probably doesn't matter once you get inside."

She directed him to a building at one end of the complex. When he pulled up, she immediately reached for the door handle.

"Do you think I could come in and wash my hands?" he asked.

When she answered, "Of course," he got the feeling that she wished he'd simply drive away.

Instead he turned into a nearby space and cut the engine.

They both got out, and she turned rapidly away, leading him toward the front entrance, where she stopped to get her mail, then took him up a flight of concrete steps to the second floor.

"A good location," he remarked. "I mean, better than the basement for safety—and not so far to climb as to the top."

"But I do sometimes hear people in the apartment above me walking around." She gave him a quick smile. "And of course, it's possible a guy on a rope could swing down from the room above and crash through the window."

He laughed. "Yeah, but unlikely."

After unlocking the door, she switched on the light, and they both stepped inside. She walked a few paces away as he looked around, then breathed out a small sigh as he made a professional judgment. If she was pulling in extra money because she was stealing information from S&D, it didn't look like she was spending it on herself.

The furnishings were inexpensive, probably even secondhand. Some of them were like the furniture he'd rented for his own apartment. But there was really no comparison. He hardly noticed or cared about his surroundings. She obviously wanted to make her living space into a real home, and she'd worked hard to do it on a budget. She'd found some unusual pieces, like the carved sideboard, and added a lot of touches, like bright throws and pillows that gave the place an unexpected warmth.

But he wasn't simply admiring the decorative effects. He was also looking for a place where he could leave the bug he'd been carrying around, thinking he'd use it if he got the opportunity. He might have put it in her office at S&D. But he hadn't thought there was much chance she'd talk out of turn there. Her apartment was a much better bet.

Elena saw him taking the place in, and the expression on her face told him that she cared what he thought about her efforts.

"This is charming."

"Thanks." She raised a hand and let it fall back to her side. "I'm paying off some student loans. The decorating style is early cheap."

"But you've done a good job with it. It looks like you have a flair for design."

"Thank you," she said in a low voice. He was fairly sure she wasn't comfortable with him being there. And he was thinking that the sooner he left, the better, before he did something he shouldn't. And what would that be, exactly? He managed to keep his mind from going there.

He held up his still-dirty hands. "Which way to the bathroom?"

"Down the hall."

He looked in the direction she'd indicated, still thinking about the bug in his pocket. If he got her to fix him something to drink, he could probably plant it then.

"Do you have a rag I can use?" he asked. "I don't want to get grease on your towels."

She brought him a piece of terrycloth, then left him alone to soap his hands.

He looked around while he worked on the grime. It was a standard apartment bathroom, but she'd given it a lot of personality—with a rainbow-colored shower curtain and small ceramic figurines on a wicker shelf sitting on the toilet tank top.

He got most of the grease off and wrung out the towel, then draped it over the edge of the tub.

He was just fumbling in his pocket for the listening device when a loud rap at the front door made him go still.

Glancing at his watch, he saw that it was after seven. So, who was dropping in on Elena this evening? Not someone with a key.

He heard her walk to the door and hesitate a moment before opening it. She stepped rapidly back as someone barreled into the apartment.

A sharp male voice spoke. Shane could tell by the inflection that a question was being asked. But he didn't know what the guy had said because he'd spoken in Spanish.

Chapter 7

SHANE STEPPED OUT OF THE BATHROOM, STILL LISTENING TO the Spanish conversation and picking up only a few words here and there. He arrived in the living room to see Elena confronting a dark-haired man who looked to be in his early thirties. His narrow lips were set in a grim line, and his angry, deep-set eyes were focused on her.

When he saw Shane approaching, he turned his attention to him and switched to English that was much more accented than Elena's.

"Who are you?" he demanded.

"Who are *you*?" Shane countered.

The guy's hands went to his hips in an aggressive stance. "I said who are you? And I'd like to know what you're doing here."

Elena answered quickly. "This is Shane Gallagher. He works at S&D. My car broke down, and he gave me a ride home—after he tried to see if he could fix the car. He got his hands dirty under the hood, and he came in to wash them." She looked from the newcomer to Shane and back again. "Shane, this is my brother, Alesandro."

Neither of them said, "Glad to meet you," but the brother relaxed a fraction.

"I was just leaving," Shane said, wishing he had an excuse to stay for a few more minutes. He hadn't accomplished his main mission in coming here, but it was instructive to observe the relationship between brother and sister. The guy seemed overprotective. Or was "protective" the right word?

Shane didn't have much experience with cultures where the men ran roughshod over the women, but he had wondered if that was the case with Elena's family. She'd talked about them a little, but now he had a better idea of where she was coming from, as the phrase went.

The brother stepped out of the way, and Shane exited the apartment, hearing the door close firmly behind him. He had to fight the temptation to stay where he was and press his ear to the door to find out what was going to happen in there now. But he could picture Alesandro pulling the door open again and discovering the Good Samaritan was a snooper.

With a sigh, Shane walked rapidly down the steps and out to his SUV. Too bad he didn't carry around equipment like a directional mike. Of course, they had probably switched back to Spanish, and the effort would be wasted.

He looked up at the lighted window that he now knew was Elena's and waited a couple of minutes. Finally, he drove away, wondering why the guy had shown up in the first place. Had he followed them from work? Or was he just making a social call on his sister? It didn't exactly seem like it. He'd been angry or upset when he came in.

Shane thought about the two people in the apartment as he drove home. Elena spoke almost as if she'd been born here. Her brother, not so much. But he'd been older when his parents emigrated. That could have made the difference, or maybe he hadn't put as much effort into assimilation.

———

Elena stood facing her brother. He looked upset. Because of Shane, or was it something else?

"I don't like coming over and finding a guy in your apartment," he said, switching back to Spanish.

There were a lot of things she wanted to say. Like— that's none of your business. Or—are you checking up on me? Or—how dare you decide who I can see. But she pressed her lips together. She'd been taught respect, and she wasn't going to throw that away because her brother was acting like a jerk.

Instead she said, "You haven't visited in a while." As soon as the words were out of her mouth, she hoped they didn't sound like an accusation.

"Sorry. I've been busy," he said in an apologetic voice.

"Did you eat dinner yet?"

He turned one hand palm up. "I'm fine."

Maybe if he was referring to food. But from the tone of his voice, she thought that wasn't entirely true. Something was wrong.

To give herself a little breathing room, she asked, "Do you mind if I eat something? It's been a long day."

"Sure. Go ahead."

She was glad for the chance to turn away from him as she opened the refrigerator and got out the dinner portion of rice, beans, and chicken she'd barely touched yesterday.

She covered the bowl with wax paper and put it into the microwave.

When she looked up and saw Alesandro watching her, she asked, "Can I get you something to drink?"

"You got any hard stuff?"

"No. Sorry."

"Wine?"

"I don't really drink."

"Yeah, right. Okay, you got soft drinks?"

"Ginger ale."

He wrinkled his nose but let her put ice in a glass and pour some of the fizzing liquid over the ice.

He fiddled with the glass, then sat down at the table. When the rice dish was heated, she put a mug with water and a tea bag into the microwave.

She sat across from her brother and ate a few bites of her dinner, then glanced up as he shifted in his chair.

She could let this go on for a few minutes, or she could find out what was going on.

"Why did you come over?" she asked.

"I'm in trouble, and I hope you can help me," he answered, surprising her with his bluntness.

Elena put down her spoon. "What's wrong, and how can I help?"

He gave her a look that said he wasn't happy about providing an explanation, but he knew she wasn't going to cooperate unless he did.

"I've gotten into some stuff I can't handle," he clipped out.

"Like what, exactly?" she asked, feeling as though she were prying a piece of hardened gum off the bottom of her shoe.

"I was making a delivery."

"At the rental car agency? What does that have to do with anything?"

"Not the car agency." He stopped and shifted his

weight from one foot to the other. "It's better if you don't know."

She waited for more information.

"Someone's got the goods on me. They can have me arrested big time if they want. But they told me there's a way out. If you can get me some information from S&D."

"What are you trying to say?" she asked in a voice that hardly sounded like her own.

He leaned across the table toward her. "There was a guy who died. Arnold Blake."

There was the name again. She hadn't thought about Arnold Blake in months, and now both Shane and her brother had brought him up.

"What about him?" she managed to ask.

"He took some information from S&D. He was supposed to turn it over to a guy, but he didn't do it. That's how he ended up dead."

"I don't understand. What do you want me to do—exactly?"

"Find out where he hid the material, and bring it to me."

Chapter 8

ELENA MOISTENED HER DRY LIPS. "WHAT INFORMATION? What are you talking about?"

"I don't know what it is. I only know it's my ticket to freedom."

She tried to take in the reality of what he was saying. "You're asking me to steal something that belongs to S&D?"

He waved his hand dismissively. "No."

"Then what?"

She heard the exasperation in his voice. "Just find where Blake put it, and give it to me."

"Alesandro, you know I can't do that."

"You want me to get beat up real bad? Maybe killed?"

"No. Of course not. But I thought this was about not getting arrested."

"It is. It was." He made a low sound. "The bastards set me up. They can turn me in to the cops, or they can make me wish I was in protective custody."

She gasped, trying to understand but not really getting it.

"Think about helping me. But don't think about it too long because I don't have much time."

"What if I get caught?" she blurted out.

"Blake took the information months ago. They won't link you to him."

"What you're asking could get me fired."

"They won't know you did anything."

She couldn't believe he'd said that so casually. He was asking her to do something immoral, and he wasn't worried about it at all.

"I'd better go," he said, standing up abruptly.

She jumped out of her chair. "Wait, you can't just drop something like that on me and leave."

"I have to go. They could be tracking me. I have to keep moving."

He strode out of the dining area, down the hall, and out of her apartment, where he carefully closed the door behind himself.

She stood, rubbing her hands up and down her arms to try and ward off the sudden chill that had gripped her body.

When she looked at the food still on the table, she knew she couldn't choke down another bite. Mechanically, she picked up the dish, carried it to the sink and scraped the rest of the meal into the sink, then ran the disposal and washed the mess away. Looking back at the table, she saw the glass of ginger ale she'd set in front of Alesandro and poured that down the sink, too, then stood with her fists clenched.

Damn him.

It was easy to get rid of the evidence that he'd been in her apartment, but not so easy to figure out what to do.

For a split second she thought about calling Shane Gallagher. He'd know how to handle this. But then she'd have to explain about her brother's gambling and about what he'd asked her to do.

Not stealing, he said.

She didn't know if she agreed with that interpretation,

but whatever you wanted to call it, it was wrong. And she didn't even know if her brother was lying. He said he wanted the information from S&D to settle a gambling debt. But that might not even be true. It might just be a story he'd told her.

She pounded her fist against the counter, hating Alesandro for putting her in this position.

———

Shane knew if he went home and tried to relax, he was only going to let the scene with Elena and her brother keep spinning around in his mind. Instead he stopped for a small pepperoni pizza and took it back to the S&D office to eat at his desk.

While he ate, he checked his email. There was a message from Max reporting that Jed Lansing and Roy Newman were both on record as complaining about not getting adequately compensated for new products they had developed for S&D. Did that mean one or both of them would be willing to get back at Kinkead by stealing from the company? He didn't know, but it left him with a feeling of relief. Maybe it was one of them—and not Elena.

The sound of footsteps in the hall made him switch from Max's message to a Google search of camera equipment that he could put on the screen if needed.

Glancing at the clock in the lower right-hand corner of the screen, he saw that it was nine thirty. Late for someone to be in the building, besides the security guards.

When he looked up, he saw the bulky form of Bert Iverson standing in his office doorway.

"You're working late," his second-in-command said.

"I could say the same for you."

"I had a few things to finish up."

"Me, too."

"I was about to leave. Then I saw the light on in here. You need any help?" Bert asked.

"No. You go on home. I'll be leaving soon."

He watched the big man head for the elevator, then reread the email from Max on Lansing and Newman.

Next he checked their office emails, looking for patterns that would clue him in to suspicious activity. When he found none, he went back to another office email account—that of Elena Reyes. At first he found nothing interesting. But when he scrolled back to a year ago, he stared at the screen. There had been a fair amount of correspondence between Elena and Arnold Blake.

A lot of it had been work related, with the new employee running questions by the old hand. She could have mentioned that at lunch. She could also have mentioned that Blake had sent her jokes and asked for advice on puzzles that he was working on. He'd called them SIMon Sez. There had been quite a lot of back and forth between them, so she'd known Blake better than she'd let on.

Could the puzzle stuff be some kind of code he was sending her? Why? And a code for what?

Shane made note of the puzzle queries and saved them into a work file.

Then he pushed his chair away from the desk and leaned back with his hands laced behind his head.

Was he looking at evidence of suspicious behavior on the part of Elena and Blake? Or was he looking for more reasons to question her? Translated—spend time with her.

With a snort, he shut down the computer and got up, thinking about his next move in the game they were playing. Or maybe he was the only one actually playing, and she was perfectly innocent.

But he knew that he couldn't stay away from her. She might be a suspect, but it had been a long time since he'd found a woman so appealing. Maybe it was the combination of innocence and strength he sensed in her. Or was he making up the innocent part?

He'd asked her to lunch. What if he asked her to dinner?

Would she go with him? Or make it clear that there wasn't going to be anything personal between them?

Chapter 9

ELENA CALLED A CAR-REPAIR SERVICE THE NEXT MORNING, took a cab to work, and met the auto mechanic in the S&D parking lot. She'd expected that he'd have to tow the car away, but after looking under the hood, he fiddled with some stuff and told her to try and start the car.

It started right up, and she was grateful that the problem had been easy to solve.

"You had a couple of loose spark plugs," he said.

Not knowing much about cars, she answered with a small nod.

"Kind of an uncommon problem."

"What do you mean?"

"It doesn't usually happen spontaneously."

When she didn't answer, he asked, "Could anyone have fooled with your vehicle?"

She felt the hair at the back of her neck bristle. Why would anyone fool with her car? But she only answered, "I don't think so."

Of course, Shane had fiddled with her car, she reminded herself. But that was only after it wouldn't start.

Still, the mechanic's assessment was unsettling.

Could someone have arranged the incident? And why?

She flashed back to a few days ago when she'd thought she'd seen a car following her. Was this related? And were there security tapes that showed what was happening in the parking lot? It crossed her mind to ask Shane—or was that a good idea?

She hadn't intended to get involved with him again. In fact, she'd intended to stay away from him for a lot of reasons, including last night's talk with her brother, which she was trying to push to the back of her mind.

But her life had a way of changing rapidly these days, starting with the hostage situation in the personnel department. That had thrown her into contact with Shane. The next day he'd asked her to lunch. And today he came to her office again.

She looked up in surprise when she saw him.

"I was wondering what happened with your car," he said in the deep voice that set her nerve endings tingling.

"It's okay."

"What was wrong?"

"The mechanic said it was loose spark plugs. He said that was unusual."

He kept his gaze on her. "Do you have any reason to think someone could have…tampered with your vehicle?"

She'd wondered the same thing, but she only said, "I hope not."

"I've been thinking about you," he said. "Not just because of the car."

"I have, too," she heard herself say, then blushed furiously. "I mean—about you."

"I was hoping we could go out to dinner," he said.

She had wondered if he was going to make another move. She'd thought she'd make up an excuse if he did, but she heard herself saying, "All right."

"Are you free tonight?"

"Yes."

His face lit up like he'd been worried about her answer, and she had the feeling that this wasn't all that easy for him, either.

"What's a good time for you?"

"Maybe seven."

"I'll pick you up at your apartment."

As soon as he walked away, she had the impulse to call him back and say she'd changed her mind. But she didn't do it. What was she supposed to say—that she'd remembered a previous engagement?

Besides, she was in a mood that felt strange. Perhaps even unique. She'd focused on her career goals for so long that maybe she'd forgotten the reason for them. What was the point of getting ahead in the world if your life was all work and no play? Hadn't she imagined that she'd get married some day and start a family? And raise her children differently from the way her parents had raised her.

She pulled herself up short. Shane Gallagher had asked her out to dinner—and she was already entertaining fantasies about marrying him.

That was certainly getting ahead of herself. But she wanted to spend time with him, and there was nothing wrong with doing it. Yesterday she could have told herself that and believed it. But then her brother had shown up and asked her to do something so totally at odds with her moral code that she could hardly wrap her head around it. And now she was going out to dinner with the head of security?

She forced thoughts of her brother out of her mind and focused on work until she left the office promptly at five. She rushed home, where she took a shower, brushed out her hair, and stood in front of her closet, trying to decide what to wear. She should have asked where they were going. Then she'd have a better idea of what outfit to choose. Not something she wore to work, she decided. Instead she picked a royal-blue sundress she'd bought on sale. It was almost the color of the blouse Lincoln Kinkead had given her. And that had looked good on her.

As seven o'clock approached, she stood in front of the mirror, wondering if she should change into something more buttoned up. When she heard a knock at the door, she knew it was too late for second thoughts.

She walked down the hall in the wedge sandals that she'd chosen to go with the dress, then looked through the spy hole before opening the door.

Her heartbeat picked up as she saw Shane standing there, even though his image was distorted by the lens.

When she opened the door, her breath caught. Obviously he'd done something similar—gone home and changed into an outfit that he hadn't worn to work. In this case, it was a blue-and-white-striped, short-sleeved shirt and a pair of dark slacks.

They stood looking at each other for a long moment, each of them seeming a bit uncertain.

"Nice dress," he said. "The blue looks great on you."

"Thanks." She turned back to get her purse and a shawl, in case it was chilly in the restaurant.

"Where are we going?" she asked, as he led her downstairs to the SUV.

"I made a reservation at the Fire Station. I guess I should have asked first."

"I haven't heard of it."

"It's a fun place in Silver Spring. A combination restaurant and brew pub in a former firehouse that's almost a hundred years old."

"That does sound like fun."

They drove to the restaurant, which had been remodeled into a bar and two-story dining area. Instead of a podium, there was a desk made from the front of an old fire engine. A statue of a Dalmatian dog sat on the floor beside it.

"I asked for a table upstairs where it's quieter," Shane said as the hostess led them past a bar where the lights in the barrel-vaulted ceiling kept changing color. They ascended a set of wide steps with openwork metal railings to a large balcony room overlooking the main floor.

As Elena had at lunch, she ordered iced tea when the server asked what they wanted to drink, and Shane got one of the beers on tap.

"They make great battered onion rings," he said. "We could share some for an appetizer—unless you don't like them."

"I do," she answered, thinking how strange it was to be sitting here with this man. She'd known her parents wanted her to marry someone who'd come from San Marcos. She'd never explicitly said no, but she knew that wasn't what she was picturing for herself. She wanted to be in the mainstream of American society, with… She stopped herself from finishing the thought, then looked up and found Shane watching her. What was *he* thinking about *her*? Was he thinking relationship? Or was he going to start asking her about Arnold?

She ordered seafood risotto for dinner, and he ordered a rare rib-eye steak.

"How are things at work?" he asked as he sipped his beer. Was he being casual, or was he probing?

"Good. There's nothing urgent on my desk right now," she answered. "How about for you?"

"I'm settling in."

The onion rings arrived, and they each reached for one. When their hands collided, they each drew back quickly.

"Sorry," he murmured.

"I think we're both hungry," she said, then wondered if the words had a double meaning. Focusing on the rings, she took a couple of bites.

"These *are* good."

"You told me you like reading. What else do you do for fun?" he asked.

"You already saw my apartment. I like going to garage sales and picking up finds. I guess that goes back to my roots, where you always bargained in the marketplace." She took another bite. "What about you?"

"I guess I'm a movie buff."

"Action adventure?"

"Only if there are characters I can get into."

"Did you see *Avatar*?"

"Yeah, I liked the way they translated traditional values to that planet."

"Pandora," she supplied. "I loved the way the good guys won—and they weren't the humans."

"Yeah. What's your favorite music?"

"Well, I don't understand why people think rap is music. I like the oldies. Creedence Clearwater Revival."

He hummed a little of "Proud Mary." "How did you get into that?"

"Music was a way to understand America."

"A good way. If you don't take everything you hear as gospel."

She wanted to know more about him and asked, "How did you hear about the security chief job?"

He hesitated for just a moment. "Networking at a conference. I ran into Ted Winston, and he said he was retiring."

Was that truly how he'd heard? Did that hesitation mean he had some reason to fudge his answer? But why would he?

"Do you think Bert Iverson was mad when he didn't get the position?"

He gave her a steady look. "I don't think so. Bert likes being number two and not having so much responsibility. Why do you ask?"

She took a bite of onion ring and swallowed, wishing she hadn't brought up the subject of the assistant security chief. Finally she said, "I was just wondering. I mean, if I'd been at a company for a few years and someone from the outside was hired for a job I'd been qualified for, I might be…"—she paused for a moment, then chose the word—"resentful."

"He's always been helpful to me. In fact, he showed me the ropes when I came on board."

"That's good."

Shane shifted in his seat, and she knew her comment had made him think about Iverson—perhaps in a different light. "Did you hear anything about his being unhappy about my taking the security chief spot?"

"No. I was just relating to how *I'd* feel," she answered, taking a chance and letting him know what her reaction would have been.

"Some people don't want added responsibility."

"I like it when people rely on me."

"Do you have aspirations to be head of IT?"

She gave him a startled look. "Me? I'm much too junior."

"But you must have plans."

"I always thought I'd work for a while—then get married." She stopped short, wondering how that sounded on a first date. If this was actually a date.

She was glad when the server chose that moment to arrive at the table with their food.

The young woman set the risotto in front of Elena and the steak in front of Shane.

"Is there anything else I can get you?" she asked.

"I think we're fine," Shane answered and glanced at Elena for confirmation.

She nodded in agreement.

After she'd taken a few bites, he asked, "How's the risotto?"

"Good. Do you want to try some? Or is it lady food?"

He laughed. "I'm not one of those guys who won't eat quiche, and I like risotto, but not as a main dish. I'll see how it tastes, if you'll take some steak."

They exchanged some of the food, both of them saying they liked the other's meal. Elena was thinking she'd never done this with a guy before. It was strangely intimate.

Shane cut a piece of steak and ate it before asking, "I was thinking about your car. Could anybody have disabled it to harass you?"

"Why would someone do that to me?"

He shrugged. "Well, you were on television. Maybe somebody made you a target because of that."

"Does that make sense?"

"As much as anything else these days." He kept his gaze on her. "Or is there someone who might have a more personal reason to go after you?"

She felt a little shiver climb up her spine. "I don't think so. Why would they?"

"Are you having problems with anyone at work? Or anyone in your family?"

The question came too close to home, and she wished he hadn't opened the subject. Could the car incident have something to do with her brother? And then there was that car she'd thought was following her.

"You're thinking about who it might be," he said. It wasn't a question, but a statement.

For a split second, she thought about mentioning her brother. Then she warned herself that was a bad idea.

"It's nothing I want to talk about," she said quickly.

"Okay. Forget I mentioned it."

They finished their meal, and he asked, "Do you want some dessert?"

"I shouldn't."

"The banana split is good."

"What is it?"

"You've never had a banana split?"

"No."

"The one they have here is half a banana, vanilla ice cream, caramel syrup, whipped cream. It's good. We could share one."

"You're tempting me."

"Then let's indulge."

"Okay," she agreed.

If she'd thought having a bite of dinner was intimate,

sharing the dessert was a lot more so. Each of them dipping their spoons into the gooey concoction and taking bites, then coming back for more.

"This *is* good," she murmured. "I didn't know banana and ice cream went so well together."

"Way before your time—and mine—drugstores had soda fountains where they sold drinks and ice cream dishes. The banana split was invented by an apprentice pharmacist at a drugstore in Latrobe, Pennsylvania, in 1904."

"How do you know?"

"I was curious about who came up with the idea and looked it up. You can find anything on the Web these days."

"Uh-huh," she answered, thinking she wouldn't find out about her brother's problem there.

"Traditionally it had chocolate, vanilla, and strawberry ice cream. And often walnuts."

"I like this one better."

"So do I."

She watched him enjoy the confection, letting him have some of her portion and thinking that he was like a kid who'd been given an unexpected treat. He scraped up the last of the melted ice cream and looked at her.

"You let me have more than my share."

"We'll both have to work it off. I'll bet you've got exercise equipment at home."

"And you don't?"

"What would you recommend for a lady who doesn't want to spend too much?"

"Free weights. I could show you some toning exercises."

"Okay." When would that be? she wondered.

Shane paid the bill, thinking he'd had a good time this evening—even when they'd talked about stuff like Bert Iverson.

"Thanks for dinner," Elena said as they reached his car. "I enjoyed it."

"Yes."

They both climbed into the front seat, and as he drove back toward her apartment, neither of them said much. He could feel tension crackling inside the vehicle as they approached her parking lot. Both of them were wondering how the evening was going to end.

He knew what he'd like to do. Not what you did on a first date with a nice girl. Particularly one from a very conservative culture.

Had it been a date? He wasn't exactly sure of the definition in the early part of the twenty-first century.

He should simply drop her off and leave, but he was thinking that he wanted to prove to himself that she wasn't having an effect on him.

Slowly he pulled up in front of her building and cut the engine, feeling his tension mount. Should he drive away? Or reach for her. He watched as she unbuckled her seat belt in preparation for exiting. Her next move might have been to thank him for a nice evening and exit the car quickly, but when he unbuckled his own seat belt and put his hand on her arm, she went very still, then turned toward him, a questioning look on her face.

He could have told her he'd see her the next day at work. Instead he slowly pulled her closer, ready to let her go if she did anything to tell him she didn't want the contact. Instead of drawing away, she came easily into his arms, and he folded her close.

"Elena."

"Yes." Was she simply answering to her name or giving him permission? To do what—exactly?

When she tipped her face up, he lowered his head, touching his lips against hers. He had been prepared to leave it at that, perhaps a chaste good-night kiss on a first date.

But as soon as his mouth touched hers, he knew he'd been fooling himself all along. He wanted to kiss her. And more. He increased the pressure, brushing his lips back and forth against hers, and feeling the contact send little sparks to his nerve endings.

He nibbled at her lips, increasing the pressure, silently asking her to open for him. She resisted for a moment, then opened her mouth, and he caught the sweet scent of her breath before his tongue slipped inside so that he could play with the interior of her lips and the line of her teeth. She made a small sound of approval low in her throat and angled her body so that her breasts were pressed against his chest. As he absorbed their twin pressure, he wanted to reach between them and cup one, but he resisted the urge because he was fairly sure from her response to him that she didn't have a lot of experience with men.

Still, he couldn't stop himself from sliding his hand along her arm and over her back, and finally combing his fingers through her thick dark hair. He'd wanted to touch that hair all evening, and she didn't stop him from doing it now.

He could feel her breathing accelerate—and his

along with it. He stroked his tongue along the side of hers, loving the intimacy. He had known she would taste wonderful. And he had been almost sure that she would respond to him. Now the reality of what was happening between them was like a whirlwind swirling through his senses.

He wanted to go inside with her where they could have the privacy he craved. He wanted to take off her clothing and stroke his hands all over her body, concentrating on the sensitive places and watching to see the effect he was having on her.

For long moments he contented himself with holding her and kissing her while his body clamored for more.

Chapter 10

FINALLY, SHANE EXERTED ENOUGH WILLPOWER TO BREAK the kiss, knowing that he was going to have to stop while he was still thinking clearly.

Her eyes blinked open, and she stared at him, looking dazed and aroused. The arousal almost tipped the balance for him, but he managed to say, "You should go in." He could hear the thick quality of his own voice and knew he was close to the edge of doing something he'd be sorry for about five minutes after he did it.

He watched her tongue flick out and stroke across her lips.

"Yes."

"I want to see you again," he said, hoping she didn't think he'd been taking advantage of her.

"Yes."

What else would she agree to, if he asked? He wanted to find out, but at the same time he knew he was walking very close to the edge of forbidden territory.

She turned away from him and reached for the door handle. He watched her climb out and close the door, then walk slowly toward her apartment building on unsteady legs.

The impulse to follow her was almost too great to resist, but he stayed where he was, watching her enter the building. There was a large window in the front of the stairwell, and he could see her climbing to the second floor.

When she reached her landing, she turned and looked back. Seeing his car, she raised her hand and gave a small wave. He waved back and watched her turn to her apartment and unlock the door.

———

Elena stood for a moment at the top of the stairs. She was far enough away now that she could turn and face Shane, looking at his car through the window. She raised her hand and gave him a little wave. He waved back, then backed out of the parking space and drove away. She'd dreamed about kissing him—and more. The dream had been erotic, but the reality had been so much greater that she could hardly deal with it.

She was aroused, but that was only part of what she'd felt—a connection to him that she hoped was the start of something new and good in her life.

But what had the kiss meant to him? He'd looked at her as though he wanted to eat her alive. That should have frightened her. Instead, it had made her heart leap inside her chest. She'd been afraid that the attraction was all on one side. Now she knew that he felt something for her. But she wished she understood the depth of those feelings. Her thoughts circled around as she tried to make sense of the kiss. She knew he wanted to make love with her. And she was quite sure he felt more than just the physical attraction. Still, that didn't mean he wanted to marry her.

She made a scoffing sound. One kiss and she was thinking about marriage again. But that was what her upbringing forced her to think about. Women from her culture who slept around were considered sluts. And she wasn't able to get her early training out of her head. If this was leading nowhere, she should tell him she wouldn't see him again. But why do it so quickly? She could be pushing him away when he was still making up his mind as to what kind of relationship he wanted.

———

Shane forced himself to breathe deeply and get his body back under control. He'd never wanted a woman more, even though he'd vowed that he wasn't going to get involved with anyone after the sting of his divorce. His relationships over the past year had been few and far between—and casual. He liked it that way. Sex with no strings, because he didn't have to think about the future with anyone he took to bed.

But this evening had confirmed his suspicion that a casual relationship was the wrong way to go with Elena. For a whole lot of reasons. He suspected she was a virgin. Not because most women her age would be, but because of the culture she came from and the way she'd kissed him—with enthusiasm but not a lot of skill.

If he wanted to keep seeing her, he'd have to think carefully about where they were headed. And not only because she'd mentioned marriage when he'd asked her what she was planning for her career. There was another factor as well. He still had the problem that she was a prime suspect in the S&D case. And if their relationship was going anywhere, he'd have to satisfy himself that she wasn't into something illegal.

But did he have to stay away from her while he figured it out?

He snorted. What was he hoping—that he could act

serious, then catch her with her hand in the cookie jar, giving him the perfect excuse to congratulate himself on making a timely escape?

——◌◠◠◌——

Elena pulled her keys out of her purse, unlocked her front door, and stepped inside her apartment. She'd been wrapped in the rosy glow of the kiss. Suddenly she was back to reality, and she didn't like what she saw. The first thing she noticed was that the light she'd left on beside the sofa was off. The second thing she noticed was a strong coppery odor that smelled like it had nothing to do with her apartment. She was about to back out the door when she saw the figure huddled on the end of her sofa and stopped short.

It was her brother.

"Alesandro." He had her key, and after she hadn't answered the door, he'd let himself in.

When he made a moaning sound, she rushed toward him and went down on her knees in front of him. As soon as she saw him, she knew that the odor she'd smelled was blood. His nose was bleeding, and one of his eyes was black. Bruises and abrasions spread across his face, and the collar of his dress shirt was torn. He looked like he'd been in a fight and lost badly.

"*Madre de Dios.*"

He raised his head and squinted at her through his good eye. "You came home. Finally."

"What happened to you?" she gasped.

He made a sound deep in his chest. "It's what I told you." He gave her a direct look. "Where were you?"

She felt the question thud against her. "Out to dinner

with a friend," she answered, holding her breath for him to ask who she'd been with, but the answer seemed to satisfy him. Or maybe he wasn't in good enough shape to focus on her social life.

"What you told me?" she asked, trying to understand what he was talking about.

"The guys who want that information from S&D. They want me to persuade you to get it. And they gave me some extra incentive."

His flat words made her feel like he'd knocked the breath from her lungs, but she managed to ask, "How did you get involved with them?"

"I did some work for them. Easy jobs. Like taking a car from a particular parking space."

"Stealing a car?"

"I'm not sure it was stealing. But that's not the point. They want more now. They beat me up as a warning. Next time they'll kill me—unless you get me that thing from S&D."

Her head was spinning as she tried to work her way through what he was asking.

"I don't even know what I'd be looking for."

"Something Arnold Blake stole from the company. Information about a new product that isn't on the market yet. But it's a big deal. He got it, but then he held out for more money and didn't turn it over."

"You said they killed him."

"Yes."

She shook her head in confusion. "How were they supposed to get what they wanted if he was dead and couldn't tell them where he'd hidden it?"

Her brother raised one shoulder. "They're violent men.

They beat people up to get what they want. But maybe what they did to Blake was a mistake. Maybe they leaned on him too hard. Did too much internal damage or something. They could have done that to me tonight—and I wouldn't be here begging you to help me."

She felt her throat close. He was right. He looked awful, and he was lucky he'd gotten here under his own power.

"Would they do something to my car?" she asked suddenly.

"Like what?"

"It wouldn't start, and the mechanic said the spark plugs were loose. He said that was unusual."

"They might have done it."

"Why?"

"To make you worry." He gave her a sharp look. "Stop asking questions about your damn car. You have to get that thing for me."

"I don't know what it is," she repeated, trying to make him understand that she was in no position to do what he wanted. "And why would it still be there? Wouldn't they have cleaned up his work area?"

"No. It was left alone."

"How do you know?"

"They have inside information. They told me his office hasn't been touched."

"Not even by the police?"

"Of course by them. But they didn't take anything away."

"How do you know?"

"I just do."

When she started to object, he rushed on. "If it's not the truth, then I'm a dead man."

Her brother reached for her arm, squeezing his fingers into her flesh. "Blake must have left it somewhere around his work area. You have to check through his stuff."

"Why his work area? He could have taken it home."

"If he had, the guy who wants it would already have it."

"We can get help."

He gave a mirthless laugh. "If you tell anyone about this, I'm dead."

Her stomach clenched. She felt like she'd stumbled into an alternate universe where nothing was as it seemed.

Still trying to be logical, she said, "But someone would already have checked Blake's work area."

"And they didn't find anything," Alesandro insisted, a note of desperation in his voice. "But it's got to be there."

Feeling like they were going around in circles, she asked, "How do you know?"

"Because the men wouldn't be asking me to get it if it didn't exist."

His logic didn't make perfect sense. Someone was making impossible demands, yet she wasn't going to waste her brother's energy by arguing with him. Instead, her mind was racing as she thought in detail about what he wanted her to do.

"There are security cameras at work. I can't just go into the building and up to Blake's desk."

"You can go into the building. You can go to your office. Then you can go to Blake's office."

"But…"

He reached into his pocket and brought out a

rectangular object that looked something like a smart-phone, only a little smaller. "This will jam the cameras."

She made a moaning sound. "But they'll know some-thing's wrong."

"Then you have to be quick."

"Alesandro, *por favor*. I can't do this."

"You have to. Now."

"Now?" she echoed.

"This is the perfect time. Pretend you forgot to do something at work. Go into the building, and go up to your office." He held up the device he'd shown her. "It's preprogrammed. You press these buttons. It will disable the cameras in that area."

She wanted to say no. She wanted to scream at him that she couldn't do what he was asking.

But after handing her the device, Alesandro slumped back against the back of the couch, his face contorted with pain.

"Go now," he said. "Please. For me."

"What am I looking for? Something on a piece of paper?"

"No. Something with data in electronic form."

"And what if they figure out the information is miss-ing?" she dared to ask.

"It's already missing. Blake took it before he died."

While she was turning that over in her mind, he reached into his pocket again and took out a pair of rub-ber gloves. "You should wear these."

She winced. She hadn't even thought about finger-prints. But of course she needed the gloves.

"Give me a minute."

Feeling as though she were trying to lift her feet through quicksand, Elena walked into her bedroom.

After taking off the sundress and carefully hanging it up, she pulled on a dark blouse and a pair of slacks.

Then she came back to the living room, marched past her brother, and fled her own apartment. A few minutes ago, she'd been happily thinking about what the future might hold with Shane Gallagher. Now she knew a future with him was an impossible dream.

Chapter 11

As Alesandro watched his sister leave the apartment, he felt elation bubble inside his chest. The excitement came with pain, but he ignored that part and focused on his victory.

She was such a goody-goody that he hadn't been sure she'd do it. But he knew her family ties were strong. He'd convinced her that she was his only salvation, and now she was on her way to get the information Blake had stolen. And he was on his way out of trouble.

"Thank you, Lord," he said in Spanish, then added, "I know I've done bad things. I know I could have been a better man. But now I promise you that I'll turn myself around. I'll stop doing shit to earn extra money. And I'll get a better education, like my sister has."

He wasn't sure that he believed in God. But if there was one, it couldn't hurt to ask for an important favor and to make promises for the future. As for the past, he knew his parents had always favored him. When he was a little boy, that had made him feel good. But since he'd become an adult, he'd come to envy his sister.

He could see she was determined to make something of herself. She'd studied hard, and she'd gotten a good job. Not that their parents even noticed. To them, she would always be second best, while Alesandro knew in his heart that he was the one who truly fulfilled that role.

Was he screwing up her future? He hoped not. But he

wasn't going to call her back. He needed her to get him out of the shit pit.

He moved his shoulders, wincing at the soreness, then felt his nose. It had bled, but he didn't think it was broken.

The thugs had worked him over, but he knew that they could have done much worse. This beating had been intended to cause him pain. But it had also been for show—to make Elena realize that her brother was going to end up dead if she didn't do the job. He winced. That was no joke. They really would kill him if she didn't do it. But she was on her way, and he'd be home free soon. And then he would mend his ways. No more little jobs for the mob that had a way of turning into bigger jobs. He had to get out of that trap because if he went on like he was going, he'd end up in a Dumpster in an alley somewhere.

Elena paused at the entrance to her apartment building and peered into the darkness. Were the men who had beaten up Alesandro out there, watching to make sure she did what she was supposed to?

She shuddered, remembering that she'd thought a car was following her a few days ago. Could it be those same men? Staking her out? Was that what they called it?

She made a sound low in her throat, hating the position she was in. All her life, she'd tried to do everything right. And it had felt like it was working. And now this.

Her hands clenched and unclenched as she walked to her car and got in. She had to do what Alesandro had asked—to keep him from getting killed. Or maybe her brother was wrong, and Arnold Blake's office had been cleared out, leaving nothing to find. Then what? She'd fail and they'd kill her brother? Or would they realize they'd given her an impossible task?

She answered that question with a hollow laugh. If they thought that, she wouldn't be driving to S&D right now.

She felt like she was moving through a nightmarish landscape as she pulled up at the S&D building.

The lot was almost empty, and she was able to park close to the entrance.

In the lobby, she was relieved to see that the security desk was empty. She knew there was supposed to be a guard on duty, but apparently he'd stepped away from his station for a few minutes. That was good, because maybe he wouldn't come rushing upstairs in the next few minutes when the cameras went off in the IT area.

Quickly she crossed to the elevator, keeping her head down but feeling the camera on her. Unfortunately, she couldn't do anything about that.

On the IT floor, she walked down the hall to her own office and stepped inside, knowing the security cameras were still following her progress. For a long moment, she stood without moving. Then she pulled out the device Alesandro had given her and pressed the buttons he'd indicated. Nothing seemed to happen, but she had to believe that the cameras were temporarily off. If it hadn't worked, someone would be coming up to ask her some leading questions.

She was about to leave her own work area when she realized she needed to have a reason for coming back to work so late if anybody figured out she was here. She opened her filing cabinet and took out a folder with instructions for using the new version of the word-processing software that she'd been issued. It was something S&D had developed, and it wasn't on the market yet.

After tucking the folder under her arm, she hurried down the hall to Arnold's office and stepped inside. With the door shut, she turned on the light and looked toward the desk, zeroing in on the nameplate that she had half expected wouldn't be there. "Arnold Blake" in gold letters on a polished wooden strip. It looked as though the man had only stepped out for a few minutes and was going to walk back in.

When she moved around to his side of the desk, she saw a picture of his family at one corner. Arnold with his wife and a teenage boy and a girl. They all looked happy, unaware of what was going to happen.

His technical books were on the shelves behind the desk, and the computer was on the el at right angles to the desk. She started to reach toward it, then remembered the rubber gloves and pulled them from her purse. They were a size too big for her, but she pulled them up as far as she could.

Even though everything was here, she couldn't believe that nobody had searched for the information she'd been sent to get. Or maybe nobody at S&D knew that Arnold Blake was a thief. Yes, that could be right. They knew he'd been killed, but they had no idea why. Of course, Shane had mentioned him. And she didn't know why. Did he suspect something?

She sat down in Arnold's chair, telling herself she'd better hurry and trying to figure out where he could hide something. And all the while she kept her ears tuned for someone coming down the hall to ask what the hell she was doing here.

She pushed that imagined confrontation out of her mind and tried to focus on what she'd come here for.

If he'd hidden something, it would have to be in plain sight, because if anything was suspicious, someone would have examined it.

Hesitantly she started opening drawers. She found pencils, pens, paper clips, and an old-style cell phone in the middle drawer. He'd obviously gotten a new smart-phone and left the old one here. She felt the underside of the drawer and also the underside of the desk above the drawer but found nothing of interest.

Another drawer had vertical files, and she riffled through them, even though her brother had said she wouldn't be looking for paper.

On the bottom right was a small bottle of Scotch, which she hadn't been expecting. She hadn't known that Arnold drank at work. Under the bottle were some stacks of computer printouts that he'd just shoved in the drawer.

She kept searching, finding other things that made her pause—like a small stuffed bear with the logo of a software company on his chest. She felt over the fur and probed at the stuffing inside the body, but as far as she could tell, it was just a toy. When she found a program from his son's school graduation, she felt her stomach knot. She remembered Blake talking about his son. The boy was going to Princeton, and his father was so proud of him. Had Blake needed extra money for school tuition? Was that why he'd stolen from the company? She wished she had understood him better.

She kept looking and found nothing that could be a storage place for information Arnold intended to take out of S&D. Getting up, she began pulling books out of the shelves and riffling through them.

But she kept thinking about the phone in the middle

drawer, lying there in plain sight. And some of the things Blake had said in his emails kept circling in her head.

"If you have any doubts, phone me." And what had he called his puzzles, "SIMon Sez"? Simon Says was the name of a game kids played in the States. She'd played it at some birthday parties when she was little. The person running the game would say, "Simon says, 'Lift your hands.'" And you were supposed to do it. There would be several similar directions. Then the game leader would quickly say, "Lift your hands," without adding the "Simon says" part first. And if you did it, you were out.

It was a good name for a game. But it didn't exactly fit what Arnold was doing. Why had he used that name?

She'd thought it was odd—along with his direction to "phone me."

Her mind made a leap to an idea, and her heart pounded as she opened the drawer again, pulled out the phone and flipped it open, looking at the blank screen.

SIMon Sez.

She pried off the back of the phone, looking inside at the tiny subscriber identity module card. It was an integrated circuit, designed to store information about the phone. Once SIM cards had been as big as credit cards, but now they were much smaller—about the size of a dime. But what if this one only looked like a regular SIM card? What if it didn't have anything to do with the phone and was being used to store other data?

There was no sign on the phone saying, "This is it." And on the face of it, the idea might seem unlikely, but the more she thought about it, the more she thought that it made sense. Particularly since Blake had given her

two clues. SIMon Sez. Like for SIM card. And then he'd
said to use the phone when he had no reason to do it.

But why her? Because he knew he was in danger, and
he wanted *someone* to have the information?

She looked at her watch, seeing that she'd been in the
office twenty minutes. She had to get out of here before
anyone figured out what she was doing, and the phone
seemed the best bet for a clandestine storage device.

She stood up and started to slip the instrument into
her purse. No, maybe that wasn't such a great idea. But
where to put it? She finally tucked it into her bra, thinking that would be a dead giveaway that she was doing
something shady if anyone found it.

She was about to leave when she remembered to
take the folder she brought along. Snatching it up,
she exited Blake's office and headed back toward her
own workstation. But as she rounded the corner, she
saw the light come on over the elevator. Someone was
coming up here, probably to find out what was wrong
with the camera.

She looked around quickly, saw that the ladies' room
was only a few steps away, and sprinted inside. Then
she crossed to one of the stalls and used the toilet, flush-
ing the rubber gloves and praying they would go down.
When they disappeared, she clicked the buttons on the
device her brother had given her.

She thought about throwing the phone away. But then
she wouldn't have the information she'd come to get.
If it was truly in the phone. But what about the thing
that had turned off the camera? She shouldn't keep that,
should she?

Still unsure that she was doing the right thing, she

kept the phone in her bra and wiped off the camera remote control before stuffing it in the bottom of the trash can. Then she took a deep breath and let it out before exiting the bathroom. As she stepped into the hall, she almost bumped into one of the security guards who was standing there, staring at the bathroom door. She stopped short, trying to look normal.

"Ms. Reyes?"

"Yes. Is something wrong?" she managed to say.

"We were having a problem with the security cameras up here."

"Oh."

"Did you notice anyone in the building who shouldn't be here?"

"I'm sorry, no," she said, managing to keep her voice even.

"Did you sign in when you came in?"

She put her hand to her mouth. "Oh, I'm sorry. I guess I should have done that."

His walkie-talkie crackled, and he pulled out the device and put it to his ear.

"The cameras are operating properly now," a voice said.

"Okay, thanks." He continued to stare at her. "Let's go through correct procedures. You need to come down and sign in, then sign out."

"Fine," she answered. What was she going to do now? The camera in the lobby would have recorded her time of arrival. Which meant that she'd better not lie about that.

"What do you have there?" the guard asked, looking at the folder tucked under her arm.

"It's instructions for the new word-processing program, and there are things I don't understand. I mean, the program should do all the same functions, but I can't get some of them to work," she said, thinking that she was babbling. She ended with, "I wanted to study them at home."

"And that was an emergency?"

"No. I just wanted to get ahead of it," she answered, wondering if that sounded lame.

They walked back to the lobby, and she signed the in-and-out sheet. While she did that, the guard picked up the folder and riffled through it, but he only found the word-processing instructions.

"Don't these usually come with the program?" he asked.

"Yes, but I printed them out." Which was the truth. "Sometimes it's easier for me to deal with stuff on paper than on the computer screen."

He gave her back the folder.

"Do you mind if I check your purse?"

"Of course not," she said.

She put the purse on the counter and stood with her heart pounding as she watched him riffle through it, glad that the camera controller wasn't inside. When he was finished, he handed her back the purse, and she exited the building, thankful to have escaped. But as she stood in the cold night air, she couldn't stop herself from having second thoughts about what she'd done. She'd always been an open and honest person. Now she was breaking the law. Well, maybe not technically, but morally.

—⁓—

Lincoln Kinkead was watching *Notorious*, an old movie with Ingrid Bergman and Cary Grant that he pulled out every few years. They have a spy operation going, only she doesn't know that the bad guys are on to her and are slowly poisoning her. He loved the story and loved the young Ingrid Bergman. Such a stunning actress. And her scenes with Grant were beyond hot. He had watched the movie so often that he knew every line of dialogue before the actors spoke.

Just as Cary Grant figured out that Ingrid Bergman was in terrible danger, Lincoln's phone rang, jerking him out of the spy drama. He looked at the clock on the desk in his den. Who was calling at this time of night? When he crossed to the instrument, he saw from the caller ID that it was the security desk at the S&D building.

This better be good, he thought as he snatched up the receiver and demanded, "Is there a problem?"

The man on the other end of the line was apologetic. "I'm not sure, sir, but I wanted to call you."

"What is it?"

"The cameras on the IT floor went off a while ago, and when they came on, we saw one of the employees coming out of the ladies' room."

"Who?"

"Elena Reyes."

"What was she doing in the building so late?"

"She said she had come to get some information on her current word-processing program. That sounded strange, and she looked nervous, like she was up to something she shouldn't be. But maybe she just doesn't like dealing with authority."

Lincoln thought about the scenario. The camera coming back on just as Elena Reyes walked out of the bathroom on the IT floor. How likely was that? Had she really gone to her office, or had she done something else instead?

"Where did the cameras go off?" he asked.

"Just in the IT area."

"Would she know how to turn them off?"

The guard answered promptly. "In my judgment, not without help. Unless she's got a lot more training and special equipment than she needs for her job."

"Okay," Lincoln answered. "I'm coming in. I want to look at the security tapes. Have them ready for me."

"Yes, sir. And should I call Mr. Gallagher?"

Lincoln considered the question and answered, "He should be in on this, but I'll get in touch with him."

He hung up, thinking about what Elena Reyes might have been doing in the building after hours, and he came back to something he'd been on edge about.

Falcon's Flight, the software from Alex Rosenbloom. Although Alex had never understood its true worth, Lincoln had immediately seen it as a gold mine. He'd known it could make him millions—from sales of the product and from the hidden potential he had no intention of sharing with the public.

He'd been worried all along that someone might try to steal it out from under him. And when it looked like Arnold Blake had tried to get his hands on it—and gotten killed in the process—Lincoln had hired Shane Gallagher to make sure that the software stayed where it belonged.

Was this thing with Elena Reyes connected? What if she'd been working with Blake and biding her time until she thought it was safe to—do what? He didn't know, but he wasn't going to take a chance.

Chapter 12

THANKFUL TO BE OUT OF THE BUILDING AT LAST, ELENA walked to her car. She thought she had the information her brother so desperately needed. She had taken a big chance getting it, and she should be relieved to have accomplished her mission. But as she unlocked the vehicle, she couldn't help having second thoughts. Could she really drive back to her apartment and turn over something so vital that a man had been killed because of it?

She'd gone to Arnold Blake's office to get the information. Then she'd had a confrontation with a security guard. And now she was feeling sick to her stomach. Not only because she'd almost gotten caught. Something Alesandro had said was rattling around in her mind, and now she understood the implications. If Blake had been holding the information, nobody had done anything with it yet. But if it came on the market from another company, someone was going to be blamed. And S&D security would remember this incident.

And now that she was thinking straight, the idea of stealing from Lincoln Kinkead made her sick. He'd always been straight with her. He'd given her a good job with good possibilities for advancement, and she couldn't knife him in the back.

She pulled her phone out of her purse and called her home number. The phone rang, and she thought

Alesandro wasn't going to pick it up. But finally after five rings he did.

"Do you have it?" he asked immediately.

"I think so."

"Then bring it to me."

The words were hard to speak, but she said, "I can't."

"What the hell are you talking about?"

"I can't do it. You'd better get out of my apartment and find somewhere to hide until I figure out what to do."

"Where are you going?"

"To Shane Gallagher."

"That guy I met?"

"Yes."

"You *puta*!" he screamed at her.

"That's what you think—that I'm a whore?"

"When you're killing me. I need that information. I need it to be safe."

"I'm sorry," she said and hung up because she couldn't stand the fear in his voice or her disgust with him. Or with herself. Alesandro had gotten her to do something she never would have done on her own. Not in a million years, and now she had to put it right.

Instead of heading home, she used her phone to find Shane Gallagher's address and drove to his apartment building.

Shane was relaxing in his boxers, sitting at his computer when the phone rang. The caller ID said it was Lincoln Kinkead. He looked at his watch. Eleven o'clock. What did the head of S&D want at this hour?

"Something wrong?" Shane asked.

"There may have been a breach of security tonight."

"What happened?"

"One of the security cameras went offline, and when it came back on, Elena Reyes was coming out of the ladies' room on the IT floor. There's no record of what she was doing before that."

"Shit."

"Indeed."

"I'll be right over." He clicked off the phone and charged into the bedroom where he grabbed a pair of jeans and a shirt. After putting them on, he pulled on socks and shoved his feet into running shoes. He was just heading back to the front of the apartment when someone knocked at the door, and he stopped short.

His Sig was in his desk drawer. He got it out and took it with him to the door. When he looked through the spy hole, he saw Elena Reyes, of all people. She was the reason Kinkead had called, and now here she was. But why? She was standing stock-still, but with the distorted image of the fish-eye lens, it was impossible to read her expression.

"Elena?" he called out to see her reaction.

She jumped.

Pulling the door open, he found her standing in the hallway, looking pale and upset—and also with an expression he hadn't seen on her face before. He decided it was steely determination.

He'd just been talking to Kinkead about what she might have been doing in the building. Strange that she was standing at his door looking like she was in the middle of a mess. But maybe the lunch and dinner and helping her after her car broke down had made her trust him.

"What are you doing here?" he asked.

She shifted her weight from one foot to the other, apparently having second thoughts about this midnight visit. "Maybe I shouldn't get you involved."

"But you're here now, and you must have had a reason. Come in."

When she stepped into the apartment, he closed the door and turned the lock, making her jump.

"Something bad happened," she whispered, reaching out to touch his arm.

"Okay."

She didn't continue, only stood in the short hallway looking sick.

Unwilling to let her back away from her mission, he prompted, "Something bad happened?"

"My brother…"

"The guy I met at your apartment?"

"Yes. He said they were going to kill him. That's why…" Her voice trailed off.

He ignored the last part and asked, "Who?"

"Bad men."

"Can you be more specific?" he asked, wishing she would just lay it all out.

She swallowed hard. "He said he had done some work for them. Then they must have found out about me. That I worked at S&D. They beat him up, and he came to me. He said there was something I could do—to save his life."

When she stopped short again, he kept his face hard. "That isn't making a lot of sense. How were you supposed to save his life?"

"He said Arnold Blake had stolen something from

S&D, but he hadn't given it to the men. He was holding out for more money, only they killed him when they were…questioning him."

Shane thought back over the events at S&D. Everything she was saying could be true. "And what— exactly—is your involvement?"

"My brother sent me into the building to search Arnold's office. And I'm pretty sure I found what he wanted me to get." She gulped. "But I didn't take it to my brother. I came here instead."

He pinned her with his gaze. "Why not?"

She raised one shoulder. "I couldn't…"

"What did you find?" he demanded.

"A phone in his desk."

Shane snorted. "And that's supposed to prove anything?"

"Why would he leave it there? You don't leave your phone at work, do you? And if you were going to steal something and keep it around, maybe you'd hide it in plain sight. Like in that Edgar Allan Poe story I read in school." She snapped her fingers. "Wasn't it called 'The Purloined Letter'?"

She kept talking, giving him reasons why she thought the information her brother had asked her to get was hidden in the instrument. And as she spoke, what she was saying began to make sense. That was interesting, because Shane had ordered Blake's office left the way it was—as a trap. In case someone went there looking for whatever Blake had presumably stolen.

"In his emails Blake specifically told you to phone him? And he called his game SIMon Sez? With the first part of 'Simon' capitalized?"

She nodded.

He hit her with a fast question. "Were the two of you into something illegal together?"

"No! Would I be here if that were true?"

"I don't know," he answered honestly. "You could be trying to throw me off the track after you got caught in the building."

Panic bloomed on her face. "I thought you could help me. I guess I was wrong."

She had just finished speaking when a knock sounded at the door.

Both of them went rigid.

"Who is it?" Shane called.

"S&D security."

"What are you doing here?"

"We have reason to believe you are sheltering Elena Reyes, and we want her for questioning."

Shane thought about that. Kinkead had asked Shane to come in, not hold her at his apartment. And how would Kinkead even know she was here?

"Hold up your identification."

The demand was greeted by several low pops as holes appeared in the door, inches from where they were standing.

Bullets from a gun with a silencer.

Shane pulled Elena back and around the corner moments before the door burst open and two men rushed in. Pulling his gun, Shane got off a shot in their direction, making them dodge and giving himself a moment to consider what to do. He wondered if the neighbors would call in the incident to the cops. Or would they figure they were just hearing a loud television shoot-'em-up show?

But he couldn't count on the police coming to the rescue. That meant he was in a very awkward position, caught between goons with guns and a woman he didn't trust.

He already knew she'd done something unethical, if not strictly illegal. But she'd apparently had second and maybe third thoughts and come to him instead of bringing the phone to her brother. That seemed to count in her favor, but it could be a ploy to get herself out of trouble.

Taking a considerable chance, he decided to trust her—for the moment.

When he turned to her, he saw she was thinking she'd gotten herself into more trouble than she'd bargained for.

"Too bad I didn't bring my climbing equipment home."

She nodded.

"There's a back way out of the apartment," he said. "The kitchen door. Lucky for us, it's around the corner from the main entrance here." He gestured toward the door where the thugs had crashed inside. "And it opens into the hallway near the stairwell. You go out that way and down to the garage—on the level below the lobby. You know my car, right?"

"Yes."

"It's in space 52 about halfway from the stairs to the main door." He sighed as he fished his keys out of his pocket and handed them to her. "Drive it up to the stairwell door, and wait for me."

"And you'll come right after me?"

"As fast as I can."

He was trying to get her to safety. But was it safe to send her into the hall at all? Did the gunmen know about the back exit? Or had they come here on the spur of the moment without any preparation?

He risked darting back to the kitchen, opening the door a crack, and looking out into the corridor. "All clear. Go. The stairs are to the left."

He saw the fear, but also the determination in her eyes as she followed his directions.

Movement in the apartment's front hall had him rushing back and getting off a shot as one of the gunmen came around the corner. But Shane couldn't keep shooting at them. Shots inside the building were eventually going to attract attention, and if one of the residents came to investigate, they could get hurt.

He had to give Elena time to get downstairs. Looking around for a way to keep the bastards busy, he spied the metal office trash can that he'd left by the back door when he'd taken out the rubbish.

Working quickly, he snatched up two dish towels and dribbled water onto them from the faucet before stuffing them into the can. Then he set a wad of paper towels in on top of them and lit the towels with a match from the box he kept in one of the kitchen drawers. The paper flared up, but when the fire burned down to the dish towels, they started smoldering and giving off smoke instead of more open flames. Excellent. Because his aim wasn't to set the apartment building on fire.

From inside the kitchen, he used a broom handle to push the smoking can toward the front door, coughing as he inhaled some of the fumes. He gave it a shove, and it scooted across the floor toward the front of the apartment where he could hear the other guys coughing, too.

"What the hell?" he heard one exclaim.

"Get out if you don't want to get fried," he shouted back.

Then he ducked out the kitchen door and quietly crossed the hall, following the route Elena had taken. When he was in the stairwell, he started running, taking the steps as fast as he could without tripping over his own feet. With a sigh of relief, he reached the garage level and snatched open the door.

In a hurry to catch up with Elena, he burst into the open area, then stopped dead when he saw a man grab her and hustle her into the backseat of a vehicle.

Chapter 13

PANIC SEIZED ALESANDRO. HE'D SCARED THE *MIERDA* OUT of his sister, then sent her over to S&D to get the information he needed. All the time he'd been waiting in her apartment, he'd thought she'd done it.

But the *puta's* nerve had failed.

That left him up shit creek in a wire canoe, an interesting American phrase that fit his present situation well.

He channeled his panic into anger at Elena for double-crossing him. Jesus, if he'd known she was going to screw him, he would have gotten the hell out of her apartment hours ago. With his heart almost blocking his windpipe, he pushed himself off the couch, wincing as his injuries protested.

Waiting a moment until he was steady on his feet, he started moving, heading for the door. The climb down the stairs was agony, and he cursed Elena for living in an apartment without an elevator.

Outside, he paused for a moment on the stoop to catch his breath and make sure the coast was clear. To his relief, he saw no one lurking in the shadows. He was almost to his car when two tough-looking men stepped up, one on either side of him. One was tall and muscular, the other shorter but also in good shape. He knew who they were—enforcers for the man who had given him the assignment of getting the information from S&D.

"What?" he gasped, fighting the sudden sick feeling in his chest that made breathing almost impossible.

"Give me your keys," one of them demanded.

He looked wildly around the parking lot, hoping someone would show up and interrupt the scene, but there was no one around but him and the ruthless thugs. They must have been outside all along, waiting to see what would happen. Which meant it wouldn't have done any good to leave earlier.

"Wait. My sister will be here soon."

"You lying piece of shit. We had a directional mike on her apartment. We heard you talking to her on the phone. She's not coming back. Now give me those keys."

Struggling to control his shaking fingers, Alesandro dug out his keys. The man snatched them away and hustled Alesandro to the back of his car, where the man clicked the lock on the trunk.

"What…"

One of them held his arms. The other punched him in the stomach, making him double over in sudden pain. Another punch to the jaw made him literally see stars. He was fighting to stay conscious, for all the good that was going to do him.

Dimly he heard them talking.

"The boss said to make sure he arrives with his cell."

More of his senses returned as one of the men fumbled for the phone at his belt and unclipped it. Then they dumped him into the trunk and folded his legs so he'd fit inside, the awkward position adding to his misery.

"No, please," he managed to gasp.

Before he could say more, the trunk lid slammed shut, leaving him in darkness. He clenched his teeth, trying to think. Was there some way out of here? Like if he broke a taillight, could he stick his hand out and attract someone's attention?

"Christ."

Shane couldn't let them take Elena out of the garage. Determined to cut them off, he ran for his SUV, then realized he didn't have the goddamn keys. He'd given them to Elena.

Cursing, he thought his only option was to rush the other car on foot. Then he spotted something on the cement floor where the thugs' vehicle had been moments earlier. The keys. She had dropped them, maybe on purpose, knowing he was going to need them.

As the car with Elena headed for the garage door, he scooped up the keys and ran back to his vehicle. Once inside, he whipped out of his parking space, almost crashing into a pickup in the row behind him.

As he gunned the engine, he could see the car with the bad guys ahead of him. There were two men inside — in addition to the ones who had come into his apartment. An impressive strike force. Apparently whoever had sent them wasn't taking any chances.

One of the thugs was driving, and one was in the backseat with Elena to keep her under control. She was sitting up, which he hoped meant she hadn't been drugged, and she'd be able to run when he needed her to.

The lead car slowed as it approached the mesh door at the garage entrance. The driver must have acquired the code for the garage door and an automatic opener to go with it. As the door wheezed upward, Shane barreled forward, intent on escape, but there wasn't enough head room to exit immediately.

Taking advantage of the momentary delay, Shane pressed the button on his own automatic opener clipped to the sun visor. The wide door made a grinding sound and reversed directions, coming down just as the other car sped forward. Taken by surprise, the driver crashed his car into the barrier, and the vehicle bounced back toward Shane.

The driver leaped out of the car and whirled, firing his automatic pistol at Shane. But Shane had already opened the door of his SUV. Using it as a shield, he returned fire, and the guy went down and lay unmoving on the floor of the garage. As Shane advanced on the car, he could see Elena in the backseat struggling with the other man, who had his attention focused on her.

The thug yanked her long, dark hair, whipping her head around so violently that Shane was afraid her neck might snap. The guy was hauling back his other hand to smack her when Shane pulled the door open, jerked the guy out, and slammed him onto the ground, hearing his head crack against the concrete. Elena raced out after him, crunching her shoe on his gun hand. He screamed and let go of the weapon. Shane kicked it a few feet away, then kicked the man in the face. He went still.

Grabbing the extra weapon, Shane fired a bullet into the car's engine before hurrying Elena to his car.

"Are you all right?" he asked as they both climbed inside.

"Yes."

"You dropped the keys."

"I was hoping you'd find them."

"Yeah. Thanks."

He worked the controls on the garage door again, lifting the metal barrier just as the stairwell door in back of them burst open and the men from upstairs stormed out.

He gunned the engine, making it out of the garage as he heard bullets whizzing past.

They sped into the night.

Elena had twisted around. "They're getting in the car I was in."

"I don't think it's gonna start."

She was still looking back as they exited the apartment development onto Rockville Pike.

"Did you kill that man?" She asked. "The one you shot?"

"I don't know."

"Shouldn't we call the police?"

"I don't think so."

"Because?"

"Because those goons found you at my apartment. They could just as easily find you at the police station. Or maybe they even have contacts *inside* the police department, for all I know."

"*Madre de Dios,*" she whispered, then asked, "Where are we going?"

"To a safe house where we can hole up while I find out what's really going on."

"I told you about my brother."

"But there's more to it. I mean, who wanted that information, and why?"

—∿∿∿—

Jerome Weller made a fist with his left hand and pounded it into his right. He wanted to spit out a stream of curses, but he knew that wasn't going to do him any good. He'd thought everything was under control, but then it had all blown up in his face because Elena Reyes had had a stab of conscience.

That was the trouble when you dealt with people who thought they had a moral code. He'd had no problem like that with Arnold Blake. The guy might have once cared about right and wrong. But he'd given that up when he'd found out he could get more of the luxuries that his wife insisted she wanted and that were impossible to procure with his salary from S&D.

Blake had agreed to steal a valuable piece of software under development, something Lincoln Kinkead called Falcon's Flight. That was only a code name, of course. The product had nothing to do with birds. It was just designed for people who thought of themselves as high fliers, and apparently Kinkead had enjoyed the little joke.

Jerome had always maintained legit business interests to cover his other activities. He'd gotten wind of Falcon's Flight at a software conference in Las Vegas. He'd stumbled on it by accident in a bar when a guy named Rosenbloom, who should have been keeping his mouth shut, was bragging about his hotshot son, the computer whiz.

As soon as Jerome found out about the product, he knew it was worth a fortune. He could use it, but even better, he'd found a client who would pay big bucks for the program.

Jerome had researched S&D for vulnerable employees and found Blake. He'd arranged to bump into the guy at the public golf course where he played and got to talking with him. After several conversations, he'd come around to the subject of the software, and Blake had been interested in working out a deal. Jerome had been sure the IT guy would deliver it to him. But after they'd come to an agreement, the little worm had held out for more money. His mistake.

Too bad he'd croaked under torture. That put Jerome back at square one. But he'd figured out another way to get what Blake had stolen. He'd gone back to his list of employees in the S&D IT department and started doing background checks—not just on the individuals, but also on their relatives. That had led him to Elena Reyes. Her loyalty to her family was supposed to get him what he needed. Only she'd double-crossed her own brother and taken the information to the S&D security chief instead.

He snorted. Although he hadn't counted on that little twist, he'd scrambled to have her intercepted her at Gallagher's place.

Unfortunately, his guys had come up against some serious problems. And why had she run to Gallagher? Because she trusted him? Or because she was sleeping with him? He should have checked that out more carefully.

Now one of his men was dead, and Reyes was in the wind. But there was still a good chance of getting her back.

Jerome's cell phone buzzed, and he looked at the number. It was one of the men he'd sent to Reyes' apartment.

"We're here with the brother."

"Good work."

"Where do you want him?"

"In the interrogation room downstairs. No point in letting him think that we're going to make him comfortable."

The man on the other end of the line laughed.

"And you got his cell phone?"

"Yes."

"Keep it handy. I'm betting that his sister is going to call to find out how brother boy is doing. And she's going to be upset when she finds out where he is and what's been happening to him."

The man on the other end of the line made a sound of agreement.

"Strip him and strap him down on the table. I'll be right there," Jerome said, feeling like things were looking up. Elena Reyes might have double-crossed her brother initially, but how was she going to react when he started pleading with her to save him?

Elena turned toward Shane and kept her gaze steady as she punched out her words. "I told you what's going on."

"I want to hear your story again."

The way he was looking at her made her cringe. "It's not a story. It's the truth."

"Start at the beginning. Did you and Arnold Blake have some kind of scam going?"

"No."

"Okay. You found something in his desk," he prompted, seeing if he would get the same story from her that she'd given him in the apartment.

"An old cell phone. I think he transferred the information he stole to the phone's SIM card. The way you could put it on a memory stick. Only it wouldn't be obvious."

"You think so because?"

"Because of the emails he sent me. About SIMon Sez."

—◈—

Lincoln Kinkead sat down at the monitoring station and looked at the two uniformed security guards from the night shift. Philip, the one who had called him, was in his late thirties with thinning brown hair. He had been with the company for five years. The other one was Charles, who had come on board six months ago. He was younger, with blond hair a beat too long for Lincoln's taste. Both were very reliable.

"Let's go over what happened step by step," Lincoln said.

He kept his gaze on the guard's face as Philip repeated the story.

"I was in the can when she came in. But I saw her on the monitor when I rewound. She took the elevator upstairs, just before the cameras on the IT floor went off."

"You have the camera feeds?" Lincoln asked.

"Right here, sir," Charles answered, apparently not wanting to be overlooked.

He pressed a button, and the view showed Elena in the lobby crossing to the elevator. He switched screens as the camera in the car showed her going up. Then a camera in the hall took over, and he saw her walking into her office.

There was no camera in the actual IT offices. When Charles switched back to the hall camera, the screen was blank.

"Can you account for the lapse?" Lincoln asked.

"No, sir."

"Okay. Let's see the rest of it."

"Can I fast forward through the blank part?" Charles asked.

"Yes."

Just after the camera came on, Elena was stepping rapidly out of the ladies' room.

"She looks like she was in a hurry."

"Maybe she had—you know—a tummy ache."

"Or maybe she heard me getting out of the elevator," Philip suggested.

"That's a good point." He looked from one guard to the other. "Go up and search the ladies' room."

"What are we looking for?"

"I'm not sure. You'll know it when you see it."

When the men had disappeared into the elevator, Lincoln looked at his watch. Where was Gallagher? He'd said he was coming right in. He should be here by now.

Shane kept his voice even. "Tell me again what you and Blake were doing together."

He saw Elena suck in a sharp breath. "Nothing. I didn't even know him outside of work."

"But you say he was emailing you, and he trusted you enough to give you valuable information."

She lifted one shoulder. "I can't explain that. All he was to me was a nice man who showed me the ropes at S&D. Then he kept up an email correspondence with me." She dragged in a breath and let it out. "He and I had a lot in common at work."

"Right." He shook his head. "And then it just happened that your brother needed your help to recover what Blake had stolen."

She turned her hand palm up. "I can't explain that, either."

He snorted, then ordered himself not to jump to conclusions about her. There was no reason why she had to come to him. She could be on her way out of town by now. And she'd certainly been in trouble when she'd come to his apartment—and later when he'd gotten her out of that car.

To get her reaction, he said, "Of course, Kinkead knows you were in the building and that the cameras in the IT section were off."

She sucked in a sharp breath. "*Madre de Dios*."

"I assumed you turned the cameras off. How did you manage that?"

She clenched her teeth, then deliberately relaxed her jaw before answering. "My brother gave me this thing to use."

"What?"

"Something that looked a little like a smartphone. It had a numeric pad. I guess he got it from the men who wanted me to search Arnold's office," she said, jumping ahead to anticipate his next question.

"And where is this thing now?" he asked, punching out the words.

"I stuck it in the bottom of the trash can in the ladies' room."

"Jesus!"

"What?" she asked in alarm.

"You think they're not going to find it?"

"They might have found it on me. They looked inside my purse before they let me leave the building."

"How did you get the cell phone out?"

She flushed. "I stuck it in my bra. And with that other thing, there's no proof I was the one who brought it into the building."

"Fingerprints," he muttered.

"I had on rubber gloves."

"Oh, did you?"

"My brother gave them to me."

"You were seen coming out of the bathroom. That's when the camera started working again. They'll check to see what's in the trash now. And they'll know the night cleaning crew emptied it shortly before you went in there."

"I wasn't thinking about that."

"Or a lot of other things, apparently."

She looked like she was working hard not to cry, and he told himself to ease up on her. At least for now.

"Where did you leave your car?"

"On the street outside your building."

"How do you suppose those four men knew where you'd gone?"

"I guess they could have followed me to make sure I went to S&D."

"Or they could have had a tracking device on your car. This looks like a high-tech operation. They supplied you with something to turn off the cameras. And they had an opener for the apartment's garage door."

Before he could say anything else, Shane's cell phone rang. He looked at the number, then at Elena, then back at the phone and sighed.

"It's Kinkead."

She grabbed his arm. "Don't answer it."

"I have to. When he found out you were there after hours and there was something funny with the cameras, he called me to come in. He has to be wondering why I'm not there trying to figure out what happened.

Don't say anything," he ordered, then pressed the screen.

The voice on the other end of the line was angry. "Shane, where the hell are you?"

"Something's come up."

"What?"

"Elena came to my apartment after we spoke."

Beside him, she drew in a startled breath.

"And you're bringing her here?" Kinkead asked.

His answer was immediate. "Actually, I don't think that's a good idea."

"Listen here, Gallagher, I make those kinds of decisions, not you."

"There were gunmen at my apartment a few minutes behind her. The police are probably there now. And the fire department, since I started a fire in a trash can to make a smoke screen."

"Jesus."

"And if you want, you can go over and see the bullet holes in the walls and my front door. And the mess in the garage."

"What mess?"

"I had to shoot our way out."

He heard Kinkead's shocked exclamation on the other end of the line. But the man's words were calm. "Come in. This isn't something you can handle alone."

"I'd do it if I were alone, but I don't think it's safe to bring her there," Shane said.

"We can protect her."

"I'm not betting her life on that."

"Gallagher…"

Shane clicked off, then pulled to the side of the road.

Getting out on the shoulder, he dropped the phone onto the gravel and ground it under his heel. Then he got back into the car.

Elena was staring at him.

"Why did you do that?"

"Because we can be traced through the GPS in my phone. Yours, too." He held out his hand.

"But we won't be able to call anyone."

"Inconvenient." He kept his hand out.

She dug into her purse and pulled out a phone, which he subjected to the same treatment as his own.

Then he drove away, wondering if he was making the wrong move.

He switched on WTOP all-news radio and waited through an announcement of sports scores.

The next item was what he was thinking he would hear. "A shoot-out at a Rockville apartment complex has left one man dead."

Elena's breath caught. "They're talking about what happened at your apartment, aren't they?"

"Yeah. And we'd better listen."

"Shane Gallagher, head of security at S&D Systems, and Elena Reyes, another employee of the high-tech firm, are wanted for questioning regarding the murder."

Chapter 14

BESIDE SHANE, ELENA'S EYES WERE WIDE. "HE'S DEAD," she gasped out.

"Because he came after us and started shooting at me. One of us was going down, and I wanted to make sure I walked away."

"What are we going to do?" she asked.

"My plans haven't changed. I mean I'm not turning around and going back there. And I'm not turning you over to Lincoln Kinkead."

"Why?"

"It's a bad idea," he answered, unwilling to share his reasoning.

She apparently wasn't going to leave it at that. "But we're wanted for questioning. And shooting that man was self-defense. You have to tell that to the police."

"We're going to lose a lot of time if we go to the cops."

Her voice had gone high and strained. "But we didn't do anything wrong. Well, I mean at your apartment."

He snorted. "Haven't you seen how things get twisted around in the legal system? People go to jail for years for things they didn't do. Or they get off for something they did do."

She gave a small nod.

He took his eyes from the road for a moment and gave her a hard stare. "You should have thought twice before you went into the S&D building to get that stuff from Blake's desk."

She looked like he'd slapped her, then firmed her lips. "Right. Too bad I didn't come to you first." She stared ahead of her, and he could see wheels turning in her head. Swinging back to him, she said, "I asked you how you found out about the job as chief of security at S&D. Did you tell me the truth?"

"Why are you asking?"

"Because of the way you hesitated before answering and because of how wound up you are with this case."

"Any chief of security would be wound up with a theft at their company," he clipped out.

"That's all it is?"

He sighed.

"What are you really—a cop?" she asked in a flat voice. "No, that doesn't make sense. You wouldn't be wanted for questioning if you were a cop. Or maybe they'd say that if they didn't want people to think so."

He heard her snort as she finished working her way through that twisted logic. He wished they hadn't gotten into this conversation, but on the other hand, he didn't see much point in stonewalling. "Okay, I work for Rockfort Security. After Blake was shot, Kinkead hired us to find out who was planning to steal proprietary information from the company. And here you are."

She winced. "I didn't steal anything."

"What would you call it?"

"He'd already stolen it. I took it out of his desk."

"Yeah, right."

"You think I'm lying?"

"I wish I knew what to think," he answered, this time keeping his eyes on the road.

--~~~--

Elena hated the flat tone of Shane's voice as she huddled next to him in the car. She cut him a sideways glance, thinking that he wasn't much like the man who had kissed her so passionately. Was that why she had come to him—because he'd made her trust him? Or because she'd thought he was the only one who had a chance of getting her out of the mess she'd gotten into.

She was alone with him, going God knew where. She'd followed him out of the garage without question—not that she'd had much choice. The men who'd captured her had been tough and determined like Shane. But they'd had a sinister quality that had set her teeth on edge. And if they were connected to the men who were after her brother, then she absolutely understood why Alesandro was afraid for his life.

When Shane volunteered nothing else, she endured the silence for long moments, then finally whispered, "I got you in trouble by taking that phone, then coming to your apartment."

He still kept his eyes on the road, but his voice softened a little. "It's better that you came to me instead of taking the information to your brother."

"That doesn't exactly sound like a vote of confidence."

"Sorry."

Again they lapsed into silence, and she kept her own face forward, casting him sidewise glances as he drove into the night.

As they fled the D.C. metro area, she couldn't help

thinking that her life had gotten tangled up with his rather quickly. Maybe because he'd been stalking her, she thought now. Well, not stalking, but he'd probably been looking for suspects at S&D, and she'd been at the top of his list because she was in the IT department. And then he'd found out she'd had some dealings with Arnold.

But she still didn't know much about Shane Gallagher, beyond what she'd learned in the past few days. Especially the past few hours.

He'd already proven that he could handle himself in a tight spot. And for that matter, he'd also proven that he cared about her, beyond simply thinking of her as a suspect. He had risked his life to save her in the garage. She had no doubt of that. Still, she wished she was sure that they'd come out of this mess okay.

Her vision had been turned inward. When she saw an overhead highway sign for the Bay Bridge, she asked, "We're going to the Eastern Shore?"

"Yes."

"Why?"

"It's an isolated area. You have to go to some trouble to get there."

Was that truly going to help them? She didn't ask, looking for the seven-mile bridge that spanned Chesapeake Bay.

"You've driven here a lot of times," she ventured.

"Yeah. What about you?"

"My parents took us to Ocean City a couple of times for short vacations." She glanced at him. "The bridge is so high. It scared me."

"The bridge gets to a lot of people. Some drivers freeze up, and the cops have to come and get them."

"Truly?"

"Yeah." He gestured into the darkness. "It's easier at night, actually. You can't see much."

"Okay."

She saw Shane swing his gaze toward her and tried to relax her jaw. It wasn't just the height, of course. He had said he was taking her to a safe house. All she knew was that he was taking her *somewhere*. Somewhere isolated where she would have no chance to get away or call her brother. She was sure she had put Alesandro in danger, but she hadn't been able to make herself do what he'd asked, either. Now that they were leaving him in the lurch, she was sick with worry about him. And worried about herself, if she was honest.

Lincoln Kinkead pushed his chair back from the security console and stood up. Struggling to keep his breathing even, he paced the length of the lobby and came back to where he'd been sitting.

Something was going on here. More than he'd bargained for. Was Gallagher lying about men shooting up his apartment? To buy himself time? That was easy enough to check.

He glanced at the clock and saw he'd missed the evening news. But there was an all-news station in D.C. He could pick up the broadcast at the guard station.

He tuned it in, then waited tensely through a weather report. When the news reader started talking about a fire at a Rockville apartment complex and a dead man in the garage, he cursed. Gallagher wasn't lying about that. He was wanted for questioning, but apparently he'd decided to run instead of turning himself in.

"Shit."

Lincoln shook his head. His security chief—the man he'd hired to find the rotten apple in S&D—had just gone rogue. He'd known there was some chance of that. He'd spent a lot of time going over Gallagher's record before he'd given him the assignment. And spent a lot of time digging into other cases Rockfort had handled. He'd found out they didn't always follow accepted procedures. But they got results, which was what he was counting on.

Now this.

He stopped and looked at the two security guards, who were watching him with interest.

He ordered himself to relax because he wasn't going to let them know that the situation was spinning out of control.

"Get me Bert Iverson on the phone," he said.

A minute later, a sleepy voice came on the line. "Yes?"

"I need you to come in to S&D."

"What's up?" his assistant security chief asked.

"A big problem. I'll explain when you get here."

Max Lyon looked at his partner, Jack Brandt. They both had police scanners at home, and they'd both been listening when all hell had broken loose at Shane's apartment. Both had dropped what they were doing and rushed to the office, where they waited for a call from Shane. It didn't come.

"He's gone underground," Max muttered. "Because he doesn't want to get us involved. At least not yet."

"I think he'll call if he thinks it's safe."

"Otherwise we may be able to follow the trail of mayhem he leaves in his wake."

"That bad?" Jack asked.

"I hope not."

<hr>

After they'd crossed the bridge, Shane continued up Route 50. He'd been thinking about what they were going to do when they got to their destination. Elena was probably wondering about that, too. But he wasn't going to share anything with her until they got to the safe house.

Leaving Route 50, he took a winding road toward one of the small towns that dotted the area. Turning in at a driveway, he drove fifty yards further until he came to a gate, where he opened the car window and punched in the security code. When the gate swung open, he took the access road into the darkness, through the woods and into a parking area in front of what had once been an old farmhouse.

"We're here," he said.

When he opened his door and got out, Elena did the same. He crossed a short stretch of gravel and climbed the three steps to the wide porch where he stopped at the front door to punch in another security code.

He didn't look behind him, but he heard his companion climb the steps. When he opened the door, she followed him inside.

The house had been gutted to make a great room with

a leather sofa and chairs at one side and a kitchen on the far wall, with a dining area between. He walked across the room and turned on a couple of lamps on end tables, keeping the lighting low. Then he went to the keypad on the kitchen wall and checked all the alarms. When he was satisfied that nobody could sneak up on them, he walked around, drawing the shades.

When he turned, he found Elena watching him.

"We're staying here?" she asked.

"Yeah. There are three bedrooms upstairs, each with its own bath. The one to the right of the stairs is for female guests."

"Okay."

He watched her look around.

"Isn't it expensive to keep this place vacant?"

"It's part of the cost of doing business."

"You mean this belongs to S&D?"

"No. Rockfort Security. Sometimes we need privacy—and security."

When she nodded, he said, "Give me the cell phone. The one you think has the information Blake stole."

"Okay," she said in a low voice. Turning slightly, she unbuttoned the top button of her blouse, and he wondered if she was trying to get his mind on another track. But she was only retrieving the cell phone from where she'd said she put it. She reached inside her bra, pulled out the instrument, and held it out in her hand.

He took the phone from her, feeling the warmth of the plastic that had been next to her skin. Conscious that her gaze was fixed on him, he stepped to the kitchen counter and turned on a fluorescent light so he could see what he was doing. Using a knife, he pried the back off the phone and examined the inner workings. Carefully, he took out the SIM card and held it up.

"This could be nothing more than an ordinary card," he said.

"I know. But I think the clues Arnold gave me argue that it's something else."

"Let's hope so."

He looked around the room, evaluating his options. "I'm going to put this in a safe place."

"Where?"

He waited a beat before saying, "I think it's better if I don't tell you."

She swallowed hard. "Maybe that's right."

He clicked the case back on the phone and shoved the knife back into a kitchen drawer.

"Be right back."

When she nodded, he went to the basement stairs. Of course, a basement was an unusual feature on the Eastern Shore, but Rockfort had found a house with one.

After turning on the light, he descended and looked back the way he'd come. Elena was nowhere in sight, and unless she had some kind of reverse periscope, she wasn't going to see what he was doing.

He walked to the tool bench. There was a small gap where one of the table legs was attached to the top, and he shoved the card into the space, then used a screwdriver head to push it far enough in so that it was invisible. If you didn't know it was there, you wouldn't be able to find it. After replacing the screwdriver, he returned to the first floor to find Elena standing where he'd left her, looking lost and uncertain.

He'd been intent on taking care of the evidence. Now

he suddenly thought of everything that had happened to her during the past few hours and had to fight the impulse to reach for her and fold her into his arms. She looked like she needed holding, but he thought that was a bad idea, considering the passion that had flared between them when he'd kissed her in the car after their dinner together.

As he'd held her then, he'd thought about asking if he could come inside with her. If he had, he would have bumped into her brother waiting for her. That thought helped him keep his objectivity. And also brought up another point. What if he'd confronted the brother earlier? Could the last few violent hours have been avoided? Would he have known by looking at Alesandro that something bad was about to go down? Or would he have simply thought that the brother was being hostile to a guy who wanted to sleep with his sister?

He tried to dismiss that last thought and return to the subject of violence. He was used to it, but Elena wasn't. And because he wanted to help her cope with her recent ordeal, he said, "You should drink something."

"You mean liquor?"

"I was thinking water. We both should."

He opened the refrigerator, took out two bottles, and handed her one. He unscrewed the top from the other and lifted the bottle to his lips, drinking deeply.

She did the same.

"Now what?" she asked.

"I'm going to contact Rockfort Security and tell them what happened."

"Okay."

He considered it a good sign that she agreed.

"Do you think your brother is still at your apartment?" he asked.

"No." She gulped. "After I double-crossed him, he would try to get away before those men caught up with him."

"You didn't double-cross him."

"That's how he thinks of it."

"He asked you to get involved in something unsavory, and you realized you couldn't go through with it."

She clenched her fists at her sides. "I should have come to you first instead of going to the S&D building."

"Why didn't you?"

She unclenched her fists, then clenched them again. "Family loyalty. And...I didn't know if I could trust you."

"Because?"

She lowered her head, and the posture made him reach for her. When he pulled her into his arms, she melted against him, and he pulled her close. It felt good to hold her, like the two of them were in this together— and they could get out of it together. Family loyalty had gotten her into a mess. She could have flat-out refused, but she hadn't done that. It made him wonder what it would be like to have someone so totally committed to him that they'd do anything he asked.

"You're a tough guy. And ruthless, like the soldiers back home."

"That's how you see me?"

"I'm sorry."

"I have a tough exterior," he muttered and was glad she didn't ask him what he was really like. Did he actually know? Or had the past year changed him into someone he didn't recognize? Instead of revealing anything more than he wanted to, he said, "We could both use some rest."

"Yes," she murmured.

He eased away from her, wondering if the situation was going to look better in the morning. He didn't think so, but maybe Max or Jack could do some investigating in Rockville and find out who had come after the brother.

"I don't suppose you know who demanded that your brother send you over to S&D on that unfortunate mission," he said.

"No."

"And Alesandro's probably not going to tell you."

"Maybe he doesn't even know who's really behind it."

"That's possible," he conceded, wondering if it could be true.

He had just downed another swallow of water when an alarm started to ring and he knew the situation had just gotten a whole lot worse.

"Shit."

He'd brought Elena here because he thought it was safe—at least for the time being. Apparently he'd been wrong. Hopefully not dead wrong.

Chapter 15

TURNING, SHANE CHARGED INTO THE SAFE-HOUSE OFFICE and looked at the monitor.

Elena followed him. "What's happening?"

"We've got company."

"How?"

He kept his gaze fixed on her. "I'd like to know. Did you have something on you that would lead them to us?"

"No," she said in a shaky voice, then more firmly, "No. I mean, what would it be?"

Scenarios spun through his mind as he strode to the control panel and clicked off the alarm, then crossed the room and did the same with the lamps he'd turned on, plunging the room into darkness. It sure hadn't taken long for the bad guys to arrive. It looked like they'd come down from Rockville right behind him and Elena. A nasty thought struck him. What if the thugs had put a transponder on *his* car—just in case? If he managed to get Elena out of town, they'd know exactly where the two of them had gone. That scenario made as much sense as anything else.

The kitchen held a lot more than food preparation equipment and dishes. He hurried back and took a pair of night-vision goggles from a drawer. With them in hand, he killed the lights, then crossed the darkened room to the side of the window. When he looked out, he could see men coming up from the road, slipping through the tall grass and shrubbery, and silently advancing on the house.

"I see five men out there."

She closed her hand over his arm. "This is my fault. Let me help."

"It's not your fault," he answered automatically.

"It is. And maybe I can get us out of it."

"How? You're not going to give them that SIM card."

"No." Her alternative suggestion came so fast that he knew she'd been trying to come up with a plan.

"I could go out and pretend to surrender. While they're focused on me, you could circle around in back of them."

He thought about the dangerous plan for a couple of seconds. If he didn't care about her, it was a reasonable approach. Instead, he said, "No."

"Why not?"

"You could get killed or captured."

"I could anyway."

He gave a harsh laugh. "Yeah. But you've got a better chance of getting away if you stick with me."

"What are we going to do?"

"Get out the back and head for the river." He looked at her purse. "Leave that here."

"Why?"

"I don't know how those guys got here. They didn't follow directly behind us. I was checking for a tail, but your brother could have put a transponder in your purse. Was he alone with it at any time?"

"When I was changing my clothes." She swallowed hard and laid the pocketbook on the counter. "I wasn't thinking about anything like that."

He went back and took a remote controller from the drawer where he'd gotten the goggles. At the side window again, he noted the position of the invaders, then pointed the device toward the front yard and pushed several buttons. Along the driveway and across the lawn, small explosions erupted.

"Surprise," he muttered as he saw rocks and dirt fly into the air, along with one of the men who had been too close to one of the detonation points. He came down hard, while the other invaders ducked for cover in the tall grass and shrubbery.

Shane didn't wait to find out how many of the bad guys he'd put out of commission. At this point, his goal was to slow them down enough to give himself and Elena a little more time to get the hell out of there.

He pulled his gun as he hustled her to the back of the house. There was no back door as such, but a large window had been designed to serve the same purpose. He looked out, sweeping the gun in a semicircle, not sure if any of the thugs had circled the house. In the moonlight, he saw no one.

"Looks like we're okay, but wait until I make sure it's safe," he whispered as he pulled up the sash. He exited quickly, waiting for a bullet to slam into him, but apparently nobody had covered this side of the house, perhaps because there was no back door. After dropping a couple of feet to the ground, he turned and motioned for her to follow. Elena climbed out, wavering on her feet as she hit the ground. He caught her in his arms and steadied her.

He moved to the corner of the house, then pushed the buttons on the controller again—creating more explosions in the yard, this time on the back side of the property. He didn't shoot because that would alert the men that he and Elena were out of the house.

As he waited for rocks and dirt to stop falling, he heard cursing, then low voices discussing what to do. The men didn't know if he had more charges planted and where they were. In fact, there weren't any more hidden land mines between them and the invaders.

While the invaders were regrouping, he led Elena down the path to the dock.

There was another gate where the pier met the land. He opened it, then closed it behind them as she followed him down the dock to a waiting speedboat.

He ushered her across the gap between the dock and the boat. "Get down."

As she crouched in the rocking craft, he untied the mooring line, then moved to the front of the vessel and pressed the starter. The motor sprang to life, and they pulled away from the pier. But more shots came from the bank and also from out on the water.

Too bad. Apparently the attackers had been ready for an escape attempt from the rear of the property and had gotten at least one boat into position before mounting the attack on the safe house.

"We can't get away," Elena gasped as she saw the other boat closing on them with more speed than their own craft could muster.

"Can you swim?" Shane asked.

"Yes."

"Okay, then. We're going into the water," he said. "Head for the left shoreline, where we came from."

"What are you going to do?"

"I'll head the boat across the river. If we're lucky, they'll think we kept going, crashed into the bank, and got out on that side."

He slowed the boat's speed. "Go."

Without any argument, she did as he asked, sliding over the side into the water. As soon as she was off the craft, he increased the speed again, heading for the far shore. When he was halfway across the river, he bailed out, hitting the water hard as the boat continued its wild ride through the dark water. Hopefully it wasn't going to crash into anyone out for a midnight cruise.

Clear of the boat, he dove and swam underwater for several yards, then came up and struck out for the shore opposite where the boat had been headed.

He could hear more than one group of searchers in the water, circling around and shouting to each other. One craft followed the speedboat and the other stayed in position near where he'd gone over the side, ready to shoot if the men spotted him.

Diving again, he continued for the shore where they'd come from. When he surfaced, he didn't see Elena, and he couldn't call out to her. Maybe he wasn't going to find her.

That thought make his chest tighten painfully. After taking Arnold Blake's phone out of his pocket and dropping it toward the bottom in the river, he kept swimming toward the bank, following the same method of keeping mostly underwater. Finally his feet touched the muddy bottom, and he crouched low as he waded ashore.

––––––––

Elena had learned to swim at the neighborhood pool when she was in grade school. It was another skill she'd thought of as "American." But now she was thankful she'd insisted on lessons.

She ducked below the surface, striking out for the shore where they'd come from. When she needed air, she surfaced, looking around for the men who had come after them. It seemed like the chase had passed her by, but she was still cautious as she made for the edge of the river. When her feet finally touched the bottom, she crouched low, staying near the surface of the water, moving along the shoreline, and wondering where Shane was going to come up. Teeth gritted, she struggled to stay calm.

But that was difficult when she considered Shane's dangerous maneuver. And the men chasing them. Men who had shown they would shoot first and ask questions later.

When her brother had come to her, he'd said he was in trouble. At the time, she hadn't really understood how much trouble. She'd thought he might be exaggerating his predicament. Now she knew that the truth was far worse than she could have imagined. Alesandro was in a terrible spot, and she had to figure out how to help him—without betraying Shane. She'd put him in the middle of her problems, and she had to help him break free. Or them, actually, because she couldn't kid herself. She was way out of her league.

Frustrated, Shane searched the water's edge. Elena had bailed out first. Hopefully she had already reached the shore, but which way would she go? Downstream made sense because it was easier to move in that direction, and he didn't think she'd head back toward the safe house that had only offered the illusion of safety.

"Good move coming down here," he muttered to himself. He'd thought that putting distance between them and S&D would buy them some time. It hadn't, and now they were in the river.

He looked back, seeing the boats in the water searching for him and Elena. Sometimes he still heard voices, but not close enough for him to make out what they were saying.

Trying to get out of their range, he kept heading downstream, keeping to the shoreline. Sometimes it was reinforced with barriers of large rocks to hold the soil in place. And sometimes there were marshy areas with cattails and other reeds.

Then he heard a low-pitched voice coming from a patch of marsh. He stopped short, turning in that direction.

"Shane."

His name floated toward him from out of the reeds.

"Elena," he answered, relief flooding through him as he changed directions and sloshed toward her. When she came out of the foliage, looking bedraggled but unharmed, he reached her and folded her in his arms. The air was mild, but he felt her shivering and stroked his hands up and down her back, trying to reassure her.

She'd done what he'd asked without question. And to tell the truth, he hadn't known how it was going to come out. He kept his hold on her.

"Are you all right?" they both asked.

"Yes," they both answered.

"I was worried about you," she murmured.

"Same."

"What are we going to do?" she whispered.

He eased away from her and looked around. "We can't spend the night in the water."

"Is it safe to get out? Won't they come down the shore looking for us?"

"First, the explosions and the firefight at the safe house would have attracted attention. There are probably police all over the area now. Which means the bad guys will get out of here. And if they do stay on the river, they'll find that the shore is lined with multimillion-dollar estates. They'd have to come onto private property to follow us. And if they did, they'd probably get shot."

"Isn't the same true for us?"

"Not if we do it right."

He waded into the reeds and looked toward the nearest mansion. A few lights were on, which he hoped would discourage the goons from approaching. At the same time, he was hoping that the house was actually vacant, and the lights were set on a timer.

He came back to Elena and motioned for her to follow him along the water's edge.

A hundred yards farther on, he found what he was looking for, a dock where a large cabin cruiser was moored.

"Wait here," he whispered.

She huddled in the water by the edge of the pier while he climbed out. He looked around for signs that he was being followed or that anyone in the house had spotted them. When he saw and heard no one, he climbed a ladder onto the horizontal planks, staying low as he crossed to the cabin cruiser and climbed onto the long back deck lined with bench seating. At the far end was a custom-made brown tarp with snaps closing the entrance to the interior. He figured it wouldn't be closed from the outside if someone was in there.

Still, he was cautious about entering. After pulling a couple of the snaps open, he stuck his head and shoulder inside, waiting for his vision to adjust to the moonlight coming through the windows. Inside was a spacious and comfortable cabin with teak paneling and leather sofas. If it was any indication of the level of luxury in the house, these people were quite well off. And hopefully rich enough to use this property as a vacation escape, not a permanent residence. He saw stairs at the far end of the room, which he assumed led to staterooms.

Ducking back out, he returned to the dock and looked around again to make sure nobody was watching. After several moments, he returned to the ladder where he found Elena still standing in the water, shivering as she wrapped her arms around her shoulder.

"Come on. And stay low when you get up here."

When he gestured toward the ladder, she climbed up, and he led her toward the yacht, then onto the rear deck. After they were both on board, he crossed to the tarp where he opened more of the snaps.

"Go in."

"Is this okay?"

He repressed a laugh. "You mean are we trespassing? Yeah, but that's the least of our worries."

She ducked through the opening, and he followed, pulling the tarp closed behind him and securing it with an interior hook at the top right edge.

"I can't see much," she murmured.

"We can't turn on any lights. We'll have to wait for

our eyes to adjust. There's some moonlight coming in through the window."

He waited until he could see a little, then walked around her to the companionway, taking the stairs carefully in the dark. He felt his way along the narrow passage to one of the cabins and called softly. "Come on, and watch the stairs. They're steep."

The windows let in more light down here, and he looked around the small cabin, seeing a wide bunk with storage drawers underneath. He began opening them and found various items of clothing.

When he heard Elena come in behind him, he looked up. She was trying to keep her teeth from chattering and not succeeding very well.

"We need to get out of our wet clothes. There's stuff we can wear in here. Nothing that fits well, but it will do."

He rummaged through the items and found T-shirts and sweatpants for both of them.

"We passed a head on the way down the hall."

"A what?"

"That's what they call a bathroom on a boat. You can change in there," he said, handing her a set of clothing.

When she took them from him and turned back the way she'd come, he watched her leave, thinking that he hadn't planned to spend the night in the same room with her—and certainly not in such close quarters. There were other staterooms on the craft, but he didn't want to be separated from her now. For a lot of reasons.

He was trying to protect her, and at the same time, he didn't entirely trust her. After all, she'd gone into S&D to take something that didn't belong to her. On the other hand, she'd brought it to him. And then she'd offered to grab the bad guys' attention while he circled around in back of them. All that had to count for a lot, he told himself.

———

Max and Jack had stayed in the office, hoping for a call from Shane. When he failed to check in, they got out their statewide police scanner. It was all routine stuff, until they caught excited chatter about explosions and a firefight in St. Stephens on the Eastern Shore.

Max gave Jack a long look as he turned up the volume.

"That's where one of our safe houses is located," Jack said. "I'm betting that Shane went down there with Elena Reyes. He probably thought they'd be out of the line of fire, but it looks like they ran into trouble."

Jack's expression hardened. "And I don't think we can do anything about it."

"From the police chatter, I think he got away," Max said. "At least there was nobody on the property."

"Or the bad guys scooped them up," Jack added in a low voice.

"Let's assume he got away," Max said. "Too bad we have no idea where he went after that."

"And if we go down there and get stopped by the cops, we're going to have to answer a bunch of questions." He got out his cell phone and stared at the blank screen, willing their partner to call—like that was going to do any good.

———

Elena retraced her steps, looking along the hallway and finding the bathroom that Shane had mentioned.

She slipped inside and started to close the door. But that left her in total darkness, so she cracked the door again and began tugging at her wet clothing, the blouse and slacks she'd put on for her trip to S&D earlier in the evening.

Quickly she pulled the wet blouse off. Her bra was wet too, and she unhooked it, which left her naked from the waist up. The cold had contracted her nipples, and she looked down at them before reaching for a towel on the rack and drying off the upper part of her body. She thought about taking a shower, but the river water seemed okay.

When her torso was dry, she pulled on the T-shirt, which was a size too big for her. Then she slicked off her wet slacks, panties, and sandals and dried her bottom half before pulling on the sweatpants. When she got the pants on, she pushed up the legs, then draped her wet clothing over the shower rod.

It felt weird to be wearing a T-shirt and sweatpants with nothing underneath. Trying not to think about that, she turned to get a look at herself in the mirror. The room was too dark to see much, but she used the towel to dry her hair as best she could, then finger-combed it back from her face, thinking that what she looked like when she was escaping from trained killers shouldn't matter. But apparently she wasn't strictly using logic.

Conflicting emotions surged through her. She wanted reassurance that everything was going to be all right. And at the same time, she wanted Shane to know that the current danger had made her admit that her feelings for him ran deep—as deep as she'd suspected.

Which left her where—exactly? She'd been taught

all her life that good girls waited for marriage to sleep with a man. Now she thought that was asking too much, given the circumstances. She and Shane had almost gotten killed. Maybe they still would.

Back at her apartment with Alesandro, she'd told herself she had no future with Shane. Probably that was still true, but they had *now*. She focused on that thought as she returned to the stateroom.

When she didn't see Shane there, she went stock-still. Then she heard footsteps behind her and turned.

"Where were you?" she asked.

"Setting up an alarm system. If anyone tries to come through the tarp, they're going to ring the bell I hung there."

"Okay. Good."

He gestured toward one of the windows. "It's a tight squeeze, but we can get out that way."

She nodded, switching her attention back to him. He had put on the other pair of sweatpants, but he was standing bare-chested at the side of the room, wiping off his gun with another T-shirt.

Probably he'd gotten rid of his wet briefs, the same way she'd discarded her own bra and panties. Knowing she shouldn't be thinking about his underwear or her own, she focused on the gun.

"Will that fire now?" she asked.

"I think so."

"But you don't know?"

"I can't be sure, but it will be more reliable when it dries off."

She came up behind him, trying not to think too much about what she was intending to do. She'd tried to turn

herself into a real American woman. And in many ways
she'd succeeded. But a lot of her mother's values had
stuck, which meant she didn't have a lot of experience
with men, the way most women her age would. And
what her father had taught her about the value of a son
versus a daughter wasn't exactly reassuring.

Maybe Papa had thought he wasn't broadcasting his
preferences, but the way he favored her brother had
been obvious to her. Alesandro had picked up on it,
too, and had always acted superior, even when he'd
come to her demanding that she find what Arnold
Blake had stolen. Both her father and her brother had
little regard for the person she was. But Shane had
seemed different from the first. She'd been attracted to
him, and she hadn't known where that attraction was
leading. Or she knew what she wanted, but she wasn't
sure he had the same goals.

But if you stuck to the moment, she was surer of his
feelings. At the end of their date, he'd aroused her with
his kiss. Then later he'd saved her life, because she had
no doubt that those men intended to kill her after they
found out where Blake had hidden the information they
wanted. Just the way they'd killed *him*. Maybe that was
what they were planning for her brother after they got
what they wanted.

She didn't want to think about that now. She wanted
to focus on the man in front of her. She'd had a vivid
dream of making love to him. The dream had embarrassed her when she'd seen him the next day, and she'd
tried to deny what she felt for him. Not tonight. At the
safe house he'd held her in his arms. That had to mean
something. Now she was alone with him after their

perilous escape, and she was going to take advantage of that.

"Shane?"

When he turned to face her, she reached for him, pulling him close. She felt him go very still.

"That's not a good idea."

"Why not?"

"I almost went too far with you earlier in the car. Well, not in the car, exactly. I was thinking about taking you in to your apartment."

The frank words shocked her, but she managed to laugh.

"If you had, we would have stumbled over my brother, and we could have prevented a lot of chasing around."

"Yeah, I was thinking about that earlier. He wasn't going to tell me why he was there."

"But you would have seen from his face that something was going on, and you would have gotten him to admit what it was."

"You're sure about that?"

"You're very persuasive."

She heard him swallow. "You've just had a bad experience, and you're reacting."

She kept her voice low. "And you're trying to protect me from myself."

Although she was clasping him to her, he kept his hands at his sides. His voice sounded gritty when he said, "I'm trying not to do the wrong thing."

She didn't let herself examine that too closely, even though she was rather sure she knew what he thought was wrong, under these circumstances.

Instead she said, "Maybe the bad experience has let me admit what I truly want."

Chapter 16

ELENA HAD NEVER THOUGHT ABOUT SEDUCING A MAN. SHE wasn't even sure of her moves. But she knew that Shane wanted her, even if he wasn't prepared to admit it. She also knew he felt protective of her, which was probably part of the conflict he must be feeling.

Before he could come up with another objection, she cupped the back of his head with her hands and brought his face down as she raised her own head toward him.

She hadn't been sure what would happen. Or perhaps she'd been afraid that he'd wrench himself away from her. But the danger must have affected his emotions as well as her own. When their lips met, it was as though someone had tossed a match into a pile of gasoline-soaked kindling. Invisible flames rose as heat flared between them.

She heard him growl her name and felt him gather her closer as he kissed her with purpose, running his hands up and down her back.

The heat coming off him made her dizzy. She should be afraid, but she kept kissing him, letting him feel all the passion that she'd held inside herself for so long.

Opening her lips, she invited him to explore her mouth, then did the same with him, absorbing his taste and the way the mouth-to-mouth contact sent shock waves to every part of her body.

His hands slid down her back, cupping her bottom,

pulling her against him so that she could feel a hard shaft pressing against her middle. When she realized what it was, her breath caught.

He must have wanted her to understand where they were headed. When he caught her reaction to his arousal, he dropped his hands and lifted his head, looking down at her with a mixture of smoldering passion and icy control.

"You know that you're playing with fire?" he asked.

"I know what I want."

"You want that inside you?" he asked, and she knew he was trying to end this encounter by making her aware of reality.

Her mouth had turned so dry that she could hardly speak, but she managed to say, "Yes."

"Then take off your clothes."

Again, a dose of reality. Was she ready to get undressed in front of him? Or was she going to back away—the way he hoped she would.

She wouldn't give him the satisfaction of scaring her off. Not because she was trying to score any points, but because what she wanted hadn't changed, even if he was trying to make her take a step back.

She did step back, but only a few feet. She kept her gaze on him as she reached for the hem of the T-shirt and pulled it over her head, then let it drop on the floor so that she stood before him naked to the waist, her nipples puckered and her eyes defiantly on his.

When she started to slick down the sweatpants, he made a sound low in his throat and reached for her, folding her close and rocking her in his arms, his naked chest against her breasts.

"Sorry," he whispered.

"I understand."

"You understand what?"

"That you want me, but you think that making love with me is wrong, so you were trying to…scare me off by acting…tough."

He answered with a low laugh. "Yeah."

"I'm not going to back off."

"And you think we're safe here?"

"You think so."

When he started to say something else, she raised her face again and brought her lips to his once more, trying to tell him with the kiss that this was the right thing to do.

They swayed together in the center of the room, both of them unsteady on their feet, maybe from the gentle rocking of the boat.

He scooped her up in his arms, carried her to the bed, and stood looking down at her before joining her on the horizontal surface.

She pressed her face to his shoulder and opened her lips, wanting to taste him.

"Weren't you taught that nice girls don't end up in bed with a man unless they're married to him?" he asked in a gruff voice.

She'd been thinking that same thing earlier. Now she said, "Nice girls don't steal secrets from the company where they work."

"You didn't steal from the company."

"That's a technicality. And it was the wrong thing to say, anyway. I want to think about how you're making me feel, not what I did at S&D."

"How am I making you feel?"

She considered the answer. "Like all my nerve endings are on fire. Like I want more, but I don't exactly know how to ask for what I want." She swallowed. "Or maybe I do."

Shocked by her own boldness, she reached for one of his hands and placed it over her breast.

The light pressure against her taut nipple made her breath catch. It caught again when he began to move his hand, cupping her roundness and stroking against the puckered peak.

No one had ever touched her like that, and she wasn't prepared for how wonderful it felt or for the dart of heat that shot downward through her body and found her center.

"Oh."

He rolled toward her, using both hands now, inscribing circles around her taut nipples, drawing closer and closer to their edges, making her tingle with anticipation. As he did it, he watched her face, and the intimacy was almost more than she could bear. She might have turned her face away, but this was Shane touching her, and she wanted to focus on the man as well as the sensations.

The effect on her was incredible, and when he took her nipples between his thumbs and fingers, tugging and twisting gently, the heat ratcheted up beyond imagining.

She kept her gaze on him as he lifted one hand, stroking the hair back from her face before lowering his head, taking one distended nipple in his mouth, and sucking on her as he continued to play with its mate.

She could barely catch her breath as the incredible arousal spread through her. Then he slipped his hand inside the waistband of her sweatpants, stroking downward through the triangle of dark hair at the juncture of her legs and into the folds of her most intimate flesh.

She had dreamed of him touching her there, but the reality almost took her breath away as his hand traveled a sure path to her vagina. He dipped inside and circled with his finger. When he brought it up again to her clit, she involuntarily rocked her hips.

Her eyes had closed, and she heard him whisper in her ear, "Look at me."

When she did, he asked, "Are you sure this is what you want to do?"

"Can't you tell?" she asked in a shaky voice.

"I want to hear you say it."

"I want to make love with you."

"Even though you've never done it before?"

She felt her face heat. "How do you know?"

"I can tell. Answer me."

"Yes."

"Why?"

"You're asking too many questions."

"I'm trying to make sure I'm not taking advantage of you."

Long ago, she'd heard her brother talking with his friends. Using their whispered conversation as a guide, she reached out and cupped her hand over the rigid flesh at the front of Shane's pants.

He sucked in a sharp breath as she pressed her palm against him, then grasped him through the knit fabric.

With a muttered curse, he raised over her and tugged her sweatpants down and off, before doing the same with his.

Then he reached for her, folding her close and pressing his body to hers. She thought he would plunge inside her then. Instead, he moved against her, stroking her with his penis the way he had stroked her with his hand, increasing her arousal to a point where she knew she was going to fly into a million pieces.

Orgasm grabbed her, rocked through her. And as she felt herself coming back to earth, he changed the angle of his body, thrusting inside her.

There was a moment of pain, but it was over quickly. She clung to him, feeling his strong thrusts before he went rigid above her, calling out as he joined her in ecstasy.

He was still for several long seconds, then rolled to the side, taking her with him.

She nestled against him, hardly able to believe what they had done.

"Are you all right?" he asked.

"Better than all right."

"Did I hurt you?"

"Only a little," she whispered. She was thinking that he had known exactly what he was doing. But she kept the words locked behind her lips.

He held her, stroking back her dark hair and trailing his lips against her cheek, and she loved this part, too. The part that came after making love. She drifted on her feeling of contentment for a few more minutes, until she felt him ease away. "You should sleep."

"What about you?"

"I should keep watch."

"I thought you set up an alarm."

"Yeah, but I want to make sure nobody sneaks up on the boat."

She wanted to keep him with her, but he climbed out of bed, and she felt a sudden chill as the warmth of his body left her.

"You should put your clothes on," he said. "In case we have to make a quick getaway."

She nodded, thinking that making love with him had been glorious. Beyond anything she could have imagined. He'd made her forget about the bad guys who were after them and about her brother. He'd made her forget about everything but the two of them making love. Now he was back to business. And maybe that was the right thing to do, from his point of view. Or was he trying to distance himself from her? Not only physical distance but emotional distance. Or maybe he really was concerned about keeping watch.

When he turned away to pull on his sweatpants, she picked her borrowed clothing up from the floor and pulled on the T-shirt before the sweatpants.

Then she walked stiffly out of the room and down the hall to the small bathroom.

Jerome Weller waited for news from the team that had gone out to take care of Gallagher and Reyes. He wanted Gallagher dead, especially after the confrontation at his apartment. But he needed Reyes alive because he had to find out what she'd done with the information from S&D. Of course, that left plenty of room for screwups.

When the phone finally rang, he looked at the caller ID, then snatched up the receiver. "Did you get them?"

There was a hesitation on the other end of the line.

"Jesus Christ. Spit it out."

"They got away."

"How?"

He listened to a jumbled account of how they'd taken a boat and then faked out the pursuers.

"So they could have swum to safety."

"Or they could have drowned," his man said.

Jerome managed to hold back a string of curses. "Are you looking for them?"

"Not a good idea," the man said.

"And why is that?" he asked in a dangerously quiet voice.

"In the first place, that firefight and the explosive charges he set off brought the cops running. If we're on the road tonight, we could get caught. And it's worse along the river. We'd have to dock and check out every estate. And that makes it likely someone would see us."

Much as he hated to admit it, Jerome had to agree. All they needed was police involvement.

"Stay in the area and lie low until it looks like things have calmed down," he said.

"Will do."

⁓

Feeling torn in two, Shane watched Elena walk out of the room, presumably heading for the bathroom. He wanted to jump up and pull her close. He wanted to stroke her and kiss her and tell her she was the best thing that had happened to him in eons. And at the same time, he felt as though he was doing the right thing by backing off. Or repairing a mistake. She'd deliberately seduced him, and he'd let her do it because, under the circumstances, his defenses were down. Dammit.

He'd been attracted to her since the moment he'd set eyes on her, but he'd told himself that a personal relationship with her was off limits while he was working for S&D. Then he'd practically pulled every trick he could think of to make sure he was going to do the wrong thing. Now she was probably thinking that he was sorry that they'd made love. And he was confused enough to wonder if he was.

—⁓—

After stepping into the bathroom, Elena looked over her shoulder to make sure Shane hadn't followed her down the hall. She still had to leave the door open to see what she was doing, but when she was sure she was alone, she took off her pants again and used a wad of toilet tissue to wash herself off, seeing the mixture of blood and sticky liquid. Proof that the scene between them hadn't been another dream.

She flushed the evidence, then put her pants back on. She knew he'd be watching her when she came back to the bedroom. Truly, it would be easier to walk off the boat and disappear into the night. But she knew that wasn't a good idea. And she knew she couldn't let her insecurities drive her.

Shane had wanted her. He'd taken good care of her when they made love. But now he was probably having second thoughts. She'd just have to prove to him that he hadn't made a mistake.

With that in mind, she walked slowly down the hall and into the bedroom. Her gaze went to the bed. Of course Shane wasn't there. He was sitting in the corner, cradling his gun in his lap. She wanted to go to him and hug him, but his posture kept her on the other side of the room.

A few minutes ago, he'd asked her if she was okay, and she'd said, "Better than all right."

He'd made wonderful love to her, but as she looked at him, she was surer than ever that he was thinking he'd made a mistake by giving in to temptation.

Maybe she should silently climb into bed and pretend that she could sleep. Instead, she stayed where she was.

"Are you angry with me?" she asked, her own voice startling her in the silence of the room.

He sat up straighter. "Of course not."

She wondered if it was an automatic response.

"Then what?"

"Like I said, I have to keep watch."

"Uh-huh."

"I don't want them to get their hands on you."

She answered with a tight nod. She stood where she was for a few more moments, then lay down and closed her eyes enough so that she could peer out from behind the screen of her lashes, watching Shane's granite profile and wishing she knew what he was truly thinking.

He didn't move, and finally she really did close her eyes, knowing it would be better if she got some sleep, since she had no idea what they would be facing in the morning. Somehow she managed to drift off, but her slumber was marred by dreams of her brother. Men were chasing him, catching him, doing things to him that made her gasp.

And it was all her fault.

She struggled toward consciousness and woke in the gray light that gathers before the sun comes up.

Everything that had happened the day before came back to her in a rush. The good and the bad.

Making love with Shane had been more than she could have imagined. Then he had turned away from her, and she'd felt as though a piece of herself had been torn away.

She glanced over at him. He was sleeping in his chair, his gun still in his lap. She wanted to go to him. But she'd woken up feeling like she'd stabbed her brother in the back. She was praying that he was all right, but she had to *know*. She was sure Shane wouldn't want her to call Alesandro. But she had to do it if she could.

Could she sneak out of the boat and get back before Shane woke up?

She had to try.

Chapter 17

ELENA EASED QUIETLY OFF THE BED, STOPPING TO CHECK that she hadn't wakened Shane.

When he didn't move, she breathed a small sigh and crossed the room. From the hall, she stopped again to check on him, then made a stop in the bathroom where she put on her sandals. They were still damp and stiff, but better than walking barefoot on the rough boards of the dock.

In the main cabin, she searched the countertops and drawers, looking for a phone and making a frustrated sound when she didn't find one.

Shane had been watching Elena through slitted eyes. He hadn't trusted her from the start, and now she was practically proving that she was up to something sneaky. Unless, of course, she was only getting up to go to the bathroom and didn't want to wake him.

But he wouldn't bet she was doing something innocent, not from the look on her face. The moment she went down the hall, he got out of his chair and quietly crossed to the doorway. He could hear her moving around in the main cabin, opening drawers and cabinets—apparently looking for something—but he stayed well back, out of sight. He heard the bell that he'd set up as an alarm give a hollow clank, presumably because she was holding on to the metal.

He cautiously made his way to the back of the boat in time to see her climb through the opening in the canvas. Once she was out of the cabin, he crept forward, watching her cross the deck and stand for a moment before starting toward the side where the boat was tied to the dock.

On the dock, Elena looked around, trying to get her bearings. About fifty yards away was a massive red-brick house. A mansion in what she recognized as colonial style, like at Williamsburg. It had a large center structure and smaller wings on either side. If anyone was home, there was no sign of them. Maybe they were so rich that they could afford to keep a house where they only came on weekends.

If she tried to get into the main building, she'd probably set off an alarm. But to her right was a swimming pool, and beside it was a building that was big enough to be a family home. She suspected that it was only a guesthouse or a pool house. Maybe there was a phone in there.

She hurried down the pier to a path made of stepping-stones. It led to the main house, so she turned off onto the lawn. Running across the open space, she made it to the smaller building and moved to the side away from the main house, where she looked in a window.

She saw a large room with a ceramic tile floor and comfortable sofas and chairs that looked like they were covered in fabrics that wouldn't be ruined by the pool water. There was a fireplace at one end of the room. At the other end was a kitchen area. And on the counter was what she'd been looking for—a phone. A landline, which she hoped meant the phone was in working condition and didn't need a battery charge. But could she get in there?

She started moving around the house, testing doors and windows. There were two bedrooms in the back with sliding glass doors that were locked, as were the windows. Then she came to one that seemed to give when she pushed at it. She worked it up and down, feeling it loosen more. Finally the upper sash came free, and she felt some of the tightness in her chest ease, thankful that she didn't have to break a window to get in.

After pushing the sash all the way up, she climbed inside. She was in a room that had a television and several video-game controllers.

The main seating area was down the hall, and she hurried there, then crossed to the kitchen counter. Relief flooded through her when she picked up the phone receiver and heard a dial tone.

She knew she couldn't talk long. Someone might be able to trace a call if they had time. She'd just make sure her brother was okay and then hang up. She punched in Alesandro's cell number and waited with her heart pounding as the phone rang. One, two, three, four rings. Was something wrong? Finally he picked up, and she let out the breath she was holding.

"Alesandro."

"You finally called. *Gracias a Dios.*" His voice sounded strange, like it hurt to move his lips.

"Where are you? Are you all right?"

"No, I'm not all right, *estúpida,*" he said, his tone turning hard and derisive.

She caught her breath at the way he'd addressed her, then struggled for calm. He was like this when he was upset.

"What's wrong?"

"Thanks to you not doing what you said you'd do, those men have me." He made a strangled sound, and she could hear the pain in his voice now. "They've been beating the crap out of me, and it's all your fault."

"No."

"Oh yes. They want that thing you took from Blake's office. They're going to kill me if you don't turn it over."

She caught her breath again.

"Where are you?" he demanded. "They can send someone to pick you up."

Before she could answer, the receiver was yanked from her hand and slammed back into the cradle. She had no idea who was behind her. The homeowner? The thugs? All her muscles tensed as she prepared to defend herself as best she could. Or perhaps to explain why she was trespassing.

When large hands spun her around, she saw that Shane was standing behind her.

His eyes glittered with anger. Anger at her and maybe at himself as well. When his hand tightened on her arm, she winced. "I knew I couldn't trust you," he growled. "Too bad I couldn't stay awake."

"You can trust me," she said weakly.

He answered with a harsh laugh. "Then what the hell are you doing, sneaking off the boat so you can tell them where we are?"

She swallowed hard. "I wasn't going to tell them that."

"But you were trying to make sure I didn't know you were leaving the boat."

She answered with a little nod.

"I'd love to hear exactly what you think you're doing," he said, punching out the words. He kept his hand on her, but he took his eyes from her face for a few seconds to scan the grounds outside the guesthouse.

She fought the need to wrap her arms protectively around her shoulders. Lifting her head, she said, "I woke up worried about my brother. I was worried those men had gotten him, and he told me they had. They hurt him. Badly, I think." She dragged in a breath and let it out. "I have to take that SIM card back to him, or they'll kill him."

"And what do you think will happen then?"

"I'll save him."

Shane snorted. "It sounds like that card is the only thing keeping him alive—and you and me, for that matter. I mean, come on. As soon as they get what they want, they'll kill us all."

"No," she whispered.

"We're witnesses."

She didn't answer, but now that she'd had a chance to think about it, she was afraid he might be right.

She saw his eyes narrow.

"What are you thinking?"

"I'm wondering if they can trace us through that phone call."

She sucked in a sharp breath. "I wasn't going to talk long. I didn't talk long."

"You were in the middle of what sounded like a long conversation when I got here."

She closed her eyes and opened them again. "He sounded awful. I…"—she raised one shoulder—"made some mistakes. I'm sorry."

"Which mistakes were those? Sleeping with me—or making that phone call?"

"The phone call," she answered, but she couldn't help wondering about her foolish seduction the night before.

Shane shook his head, trying to decide what to believe. He'd caught her in a compromising position, but she could be telling the truth about her motives. The trouble was, he was too emotionally involved to figure that out. But one thing he knew, if he let her get away from him now, she was going to get herself killed.

"I was worried about my brother," she said again in a low voice.

"Is he worth it?"

"I don't know. But he's my family."

Shane snorted. "I'm pretty sure he wouldn't put his life on the line for you."

Her expression turned sad. "I think that's right."

"Then why risk getting killed for him?"

She answered quickly. "My values aren't the same as his. I have to be loyal to him."

Even as he made a dismissive sound, Shane knew what she meant. At least about loyalty. His wife had pulled the rug out from under him, proving she didn't give a damn about their marriage. He'd been soured on the whole human race until he'd met Max Lyon and Jack Brandt under pretty trying circumstances. That night in jail had been a shortcut to getting to know their characters. He'd seen they were both determined and sure of their values—which appeared to be the same as his. And over the months they'd been together, he'd come to know them better than anyone else he'd ever met.

Their lives meant something to him. Too bad he couldn't say the same thing for Elena's brother. From what he'd seen of the sorry-assed guy, he was a user who didn't give a damn about anyone but himself.

Which brought Shane's thoughts back to his own ex-wife. Probably, she'd never really loved him. Probably, she'd seen him as glamorous and a good catch. But before long, she'd started stepping out on him when she thought he wouldn't find out. On an intellectual level, he knew all women weren't like her. But it was hard to trust one of them again. He'd let down his guard with Elena last night. It looked like that had been a mistake.

He knew she was looking at him, waiting for him to decide what to do. He turned toward the main house, scanning the facade. So far, it appeared that no one was home. But there was no use taking chances.

"I want to make a phone call," he said. "Go outside— where I can see you through the window. But not on the side where you can be seen from the pool deck."

"Who are you calling?"

"If I wanted you to know my business, I'd let you stay inside," he clipped out.

He watched resignation bloom on her face. "Okay," she whispered.

Turning, she exited the guesthouse. Staying on the side away from the mansion, she stood where he could see her, staring in through the window.

He kept his gaze on her as he crossed to the phone, picked it up, and made a call.

The man on the other end of the line picked up on the first ring.

"Glad I caught you."

"Shane?"

"Yeah."

"Are you all right?"

"Basically."

"What happened?"

"I'll tell you when I see you. Can you pick me and Elena up?"

"Of course. Tell me where you are."

———

Elena waited outside, watching Shane punch in a phone number. She tried to imagine whom he was calling. And why. Was he going to turn her over to Lincoln Kinkead? Or maybe he was calling someone at Rockfort Security, the company where he actually worked.

She thought about that as she watched him—just as he was watching her. She saw he was waiting for someone to answer. Then she saw when the person on the other end of the line picked up. She could tell he was relieved to have gotten through, and she tried to decide what that meant. Was someone coming down here to get them? Or were they going to another meeting point? Their car was back at the safe house—unless the police had taken it away—but she didn't think they'd go back there to get it, not after the thugs had found the location.

Her tension mounted as she watched him talking. Luckily, the call was short. Shane hung up the phone and motioned for her to come back into the house.

She didn't like the speculative look on his face as he

studied her. She wanted to ask, "Now what?" but she kept the question to herself. What she truly wanted was for him to put his arms around her and pull her close. She wanted to know that she hadn't totally messed up their relationship by sneaking out to make the phone call, but she couldn't say any of that. And she had to wonder at her own motivation.

She'd trusted him with her emotions enough to make love with him. But she hadn't trusted him with her fears about her brother. That made an interesting contrast.

She saw him cross to the kitchen area and start opening cabinets and the full-sized refrigerator. He found a carton of milk, opened it, and made a face before putting it back. Instead he gestured toward several cans of soft drinks. "The milk's bad, but these should be okay."

She took a Coke, popped the top, and took a few swallows while he took several boxes out of the cabinet. Cookies and crackers.

She munched on some, watching him do the same.

"We'll go back to the boat and get rid of the evidence that we were there. Of course, the owners might wonder where some of their clothes went," he muttered under his breath, "unless they've got so many that they won't miss them."

Again, she wanted to ask who he had called, but she kept the question locked behind her lips.

After their unorthodox breakfast, he wiped down any surfaces they might have touched. Then he closed the window where they'd both entered. Finally, they exited through the side door, and he led the way back to the boat, where he started straightening up the bed. "Get your clothes," he ordered.

She retrieved them from the bathroom and brought them to the cabin.

Shane held out a plastic bag. "Put them in here."

When she'd finished, he added his clothing from the night before, then gave her a long look. "Are you going to get into trouble if I leave you for a few minutes?"

"Of course not."

"Then stay here while I deep-six these."

She watched him get off the boat, pick up some rocks from the shoreline, and put them in with the clothing. After making some holes in the bag, he went down to the end of the dock, slung the bag around in a circle to give it momentum, and threw it far into the water, where it quickly sank below the surface.

When he returned, he looked at his watch, which was apparently still functioning after their late-night swim. "Still too early to leave."

"Where are we going?"

"Away from here."

"Shane…"

"Yeah?"

The look on his face made it clear that he didn't want to have a conversation with her. Instead, he sat down and picked up a fishing magazine from the table in the main cabin and began reading it.

She wanted to talk to him. She wanted to explain what she'd been thinking. But he looked so closed up that she couldn't get any words out.

Seeing him deliberately ignoring her made her stomach clench, but she struggled to keep her own expression neutral as she took a seat opposite him and tried to focus on one of the gossip magazines there. When she found herself reading the same page over and over, she gave up and looked at the ads.

Chapter 18

JEROME WELLER TOSSED RESTLESSLY IN HIS BED. FINALLY, he heaved himself up and staggered to the window where he looked out at the early morning scene. He had not slept well, for obvious reasons. When he'd first said he could deliver the S&D information to an interested buyer, the project had seemed easy. He'd only had to study the personnel files and zero in on Arnold Blake.

Blake had been a spectacular failure.

Yesterday everything had been on track again. But now he thought he had only a fifty-fifty chance of getting that information. And if he didn't? Unfortunately, he'd made it sound like he could deliver, and he'd already taken a down payment. What would the buyer do if he thought he was being stiffed? Jerome tried not to think about that eventuality.

Instead he pictured Alesandro Reyes downstairs in the torture room. The guy was in bad shape because Jerome had taken out his frustrations on the weakling. And when this was over, Alesandro was going to be dead. Jerome was going to make sure he didn't end up the same way. He'd been thinking that if he had to, he could take his money and disappear. He'd always known it might come to that one day, and he already had several false identities set up. It was only a matter of putting those plans in motion. But if he could avoid leaving the comfortable surroundings he'd cultivated for so long, he was going to do that.

He took his time showering, shaving, and picking the shirt and slacks he wanted to wear. When he was a kid, most of his clothing had been handed down from his older brother. When he went off on his own, he'd vowed that he'd only have new clothing—and the best that money could buy. In this case, shirts, slacks, and jackets from a London tailor who had his measurements on file.

Finally, he was satisfied with his appearance, but he was too edgy to eat any breakfast, only coffee with heavy cream and a lot of sugar—his favorite way to drink it. Taken that way, it was almost like candy, but he barely tasted it this morning. Setting down the mug, he went out in the garden and walked the pebble paths of the boxwood maze.

Around nine, he finally got the call he'd been hoping for.

"We know where Gallagher and Reyes are holed up."

"Spit it out," he demanded.

"They're on an estate a couple of miles down the river from where we lost them."

"And they're not going to slip out of your grasp again, right?"

"Right," the man on the other end of the line said, his voice firm.

"You'd better hope so," Jerome said, knowing he was transferring some of his own anxiety to the caller.

Shane tried to read the magazine he'd picked up, but his attention kept swinging back to Elena. She was slumped in her seat looking miserable. If this had been a normal situation, he would have pulled her into his lap and cuddled her against his chest while he stroked his hand through her hair.

Lord, she'd been so sweet and giving in bed. Could a woman fake such tender emotions? He didn't know, and he didn't want to make himself vulnerable to her again.

She might look miserable, but she was the one who had gotten herself into trouble. Repeatedly. Well, he amended that assessment. The hostage situation hadn't been her fault. Unless there was something going on there that he didn't know about.

He checked the time again. He hated sitting here with nothing to do—with a woman he didn't trust as far as he could throw her, if you wanted to use a cliché. If he hit her with a bunch of questions, could he get the truth out of her? Or was that a waste of time?

He shuffled his feet, wanting to get moving. It would be a good idea to check out the area where they were being picked up to see if there was adequate cover—in case they ran into trouble. After that, he could walk back to the safe house and see if he could find any evidence of who had been there.

And while he was there, he could get some gun oil and work on his weapon to make sure it wouldn't give him any problems. But he couldn't do any of that because he had no idea what the woman sitting across from him would do while he was gone.

When he saw that she was looking at him, he dragged in a breath and let it out. "If you want to take a shower, go ahead," he said.

"Can I?"

"Yeah. We never did get that river water off." *And you can't get off the boat without my knowing it*, he added silently.

She stood up, glancing at him as she walked by, then disappeared from the room, and he heard water running in the head. She was back in twenty minutes, wearing the same clothes, her hair towel-dried.

"If I shower, will you run off?" he asked.

"I'll be here."

He wasn't sure how much mischief she could get into while he was getting cleaned up, but he took a two-minute shower, then wrapped a towel around his waist and looked into the main lounge, relieved that she was sitting where he'd left her.

Satisfied that she hadn't run out on him, he went back to the cabin where they'd spent the night and pulled a windbreaker and a pair of jeans out of the drawer under the bunk. The jeans had a tight waistband, suitable for carrying his Sig. And the jacket would cover the weapon. He donned the jeans and put the sweatpants back, then returned to the main lounge, where Elena gave him an anxious look.

"We're going to wipe this place down, then get out of here," he said.

"Every page of the magazines?"

"We can take them."

After they wiped the surfaces they'd touched, he said, "Let's go."

"Where?"

"Not far," he answered, unwilling to share even the smallest amount of information with her. With the magazines tucked under one arm, he exited the boat.

She had to be curious about who was picking them up, but she simply followed him off the boat, up the pier, and along the road. He didn't walk on the crunchy gravel but stuck to the woods at one side, and she did the same, staying in back of him as he wove his way through the trees and around brambles.

In the woods, he tossed the magazines into a swampy area and pushed them out of sight with a stick.

As they approached the highway, he picked a spot well in the shadows that would give him cover.

Elena stayed close to Shane, silent and cooperative. Apparently the meeting place was close to the main road. But she still didn't know who was coming for them. Maybe it was one of the men he worked with at Rockfort Security. She and Shane had apparently arrived early. Or maybe their ride was taking longer than expected to get here. After about twenty minutes, she saw a gray SUV pull off the highway and turn onto the access road to the estate.

Her heart started to pound because she thought she recognized the vehicle. That must mean it didn't belong to one of the other men in the security company.

"Who did you call?"

He didn't answer.

She gulped. "Are you sure this is someone you trust?"

"Yeah."

When he started to step out from the trees, she put a hand on his arm.

"Don't."

He turned toward her questioningly. "Why not?"

She gave him a pleading look. "I have a bad feeling."

"You mean—like maybe you're going to jail?"

"No. It has nothing to do with me."

Again he only answered with a snorting sound. The feeling of dread increased when she saw the man who got out of the car.

It was Bert Iverson, who had been assistant security chief at S&D when she'd arrived and who hadn't tried for the head job when Ted Winston retired. She'd never liked Iverson, and she didn't trust him. She couldn't explain why, but she'd had that impression the whole time she'd been at the company. If she had to put a label on his behavior, he came across as sneaky. And he had shown up unannounced a lot of times when she was working late. Of course, maybe that was standard operating procedure for a security guy. She might even say the same about Shane.

"Wait," she whispered.

Shane spared her a glance. "Why?"

"I don't trust him."

"Yeah, he was probably on your case." He answered carelessly, as though he didn't credit her judgment. And really, he was right in making the assessment. He'd worked with Iverson, and she'd had only cursory contact with the man. Before she could say anything else, Shane stepped out from behind the tree where he was hiding.

Chapter 19

ELENA'S NERVES TINGLED AS SHE KEPT HER GAZE ON THE assistant security chief. His arm twitched, and she saw him pull a gun. Because she'd been ready for some kind of duplicity, she pushed Shane to the side. And because he wasn't expecting an attack from the rear, or anywhere else, he lost his balance. As he went down, a bullet thunked into the tree where he'd been standing moments earlier.

Knowing he needed time to recover from the tumble, Elena shouted, "Over here."

"What the hell do you think you're doing?" Iverson growled as the gun swung toward her. More bullets thunked into the tree, but she had already ducked to safety.

Meanwhile, Shane rolled back into the shadows as two more bullets hit the ground where he'd been lying.

He found his footing and scrambled up.

"Come on." He led them farther into the underbrush, back toward the river.

There were no more shots from Iverson, but she heard him moving through the woods. When they came to a duck blind, Shane stopped.

"Sorry," he whispered. "How did you know?"

She turned a hand palm up. "I've always had a bad feeling about him. I can't explain it."

"He was always friendly to me. He showed me the

ropes at S&D. I thought he was relieved not to take on the top security position."

"I guess that was part of his job. Or his jobs."

"Yeah."

There was no more time for conversation. Iverson was coming through the underbrush, trying not to make any noise. But it was impossible to move silently through the woods, especially since he obviously wasn't alone. He'd brought backup, and other men were spreading out, covering more territory.

Elena tensed for a confrontation. Then something totally unexpected happened. She heard a shot—followed by a man's shrill cry. It was Iverson. "Jesus. What the hell are you doing?"

"You did the first part of your job," another voice said. "Thanks for finding Gallagher and the woman. Too bad you couldn't finish him off."

A sick feeling rose in her throat as she heard another shot.

"They…"

"Killed him," Shane finished. "Which gives you a good idea of what kind of men we're dealing with. But I think we already knew."

She knew something else, too. They intended to kill Shane, but not her. They wanted her alive because they thought she knew where the SIM card was, although she didn't, not anymore, because Shane had hidden it. But she was sure they would never believe that. If they captured her, they'd try to torture the information out of her—the way they were torturing her brother.

When she drew in a sharp breath, Shane cupped a

hand over her shoulder. "Yeah." The one word told her
that he'd followed her logic.

She could ask him where he'd hidden the card, but
she wasn't going to do it. Right now, it seemed better
if she didn't know. Of course, that left her brother in
danger, but since the phone call this morning, she was
determined not to do anything that would make Shane
think she'd been part of a plan to steal from S&D.

She moved closer to him, watching the woods and
listening for the sound of footsteps coming toward them.

"What are we going to do?" she whispered.

"I'm thinking. I'd like to know how many there are."

The men began to move again. "There are at least two."

"Yeah."

"They won't kill me," she said.

"We know that," he clipped out.

"What I mean is, if I draw their attention, you can get
around behind them."

She watched him consider the idea.

"I don't like it."

"Do you have a better plan?" she pressed.

She saw him scrambling for an alternative.

Finally he said, "No."

"Then how should we work it?"

"Give me five minutes to get into position. Then call
out and tell them you're surrendering. Tell them you
want to be sure you're safe before you come out of hiding. Tell them I held you captive overnight. That I got
angry when I caught you talking to your brother. They
know that part's true," he added in a gritty voice.

She didn't dispute the last comment. Instead she stuck
to present reality. "And where do I say you are now?"

"Dead. One of those shots got me, and I bled out while we were trying to escape."

"Will they believe it?"

"I hope so." He turned to her and gave her a long look. "You're sure you want to do it?"

"Do we have an alternative?"

"Not a good one."

"Then go."

Shane gritted his teeth and did what he had to do. His side hurt, but he ignored the pain. Staying down and moving through the woods more quietly than their pursuers, he circled around to get in back of the thugs who were stalking them, the thugs who obviously worked for the man who'd taken Elena's brother captive and beaten the crap out of him.

Of course, the brother wasn't the main event. They were simply using him to get to Elena, and as Shane got himself into position, he could understand why she'd felt obligated to go along with their plans. He didn't like it, but he understood. What if someone were torturing Jack or Max? He'd do everything in his power to rescue them.

Now he considered his own problems. He'd taken a job with S&D thinking he understood the situation, but he hadn't counted on Iverson being in on the scam to steal from the company. There was a kind of twisted logic to it. Iverson had had the run of the place, and he'd probably spent a lot of time looking for what Blake had stolen. And even though he hadn't found it, he had been a source of inside information for the thug who wanted the program.

Iverson had taken a lot of risks, and he'd obviously expected to be well paid for his trouble. Instead he'd ended up lying in the Maryland woods with a couple of bullets in him. The first one had been to take him down, so he'd know he'd always been expendable. That was a particularly nasty tactic, probably on orders from the boss.

All that went through Shane's head as he moved from tree to tree. As he circled around behind the attackers, he prayed that he was right in his assessment of the situation. He was counting on them not killing Elena. But what if they seriously injured her?

That possibility made his gut clench. He could admit now that he'd misjudged her, but all he could do was keep moving until he was behind the enemy.

Once he was in position, he wished he could signal her when to act. But that was impossible now. All he could do was wait tensely for her and silently shout at her, *Now, now*.

Or had something gone terribly wrong back at the duck blind?

When he finally heard her call out, he breathed a small sigh.

"Whoever you are out there, don't shoot me," she begged.

He heard the men fix on her location and turn toward her.

"Ms. Reyes?" one of them asked.

"Yes."

"Where are you?"

"I want to make sure I'm not going to get hurt."

"Where is that information you took from Blake's office?"

"I'm not going to tell you unless I know my brother is safe."

As she spoke, he saw them moving in on her.

"Cut the chitchat. Where's Gallagher?"

"Dead."

"Like we should believe that?"

"Iverson shot him. He was bleeding badly. He went down. I kept going."

The man laughed, but Shane didn't.

"Too bad for him. And you. That leaves you in a pretty vulnerable position. Come out."

"If you won't hurt me."

"I will if you try to stay hidden."

He saw her stand up, although she stayed behind the duck blind, which offered only minimal protection.

Before the men could move in on her, Shane got off a shot.

That was a big clue that she had been lying through her teeth and Shane was behind them. In response, the two thugs switched their focus, whirling and discharging a hail of bullets.

He tried to fire again, but this time the gun that had been in the water failed.

With a curse, he ducked low and dodged behind a tree, hearing bullets follow him.

As Elena had told Shane earlier, she'd been a very successful softball pitcher in high school. She had thought of that when he'd left her in the duck blind. Knowing she needed a way to defend herself, she had picked up several baseball-sized rocks from the ground. Of course, she hadn't thrown a ball in years. And she'd only thrown overhand for fun. But her pitching arm was the only weapon she had. The question was, could she score on the first shot?

When the thugs turned and started shooting at Shane, she wound up and threw one of the missiles at the closest man, holding her breath until she saw she'd hit him square in the back of the head. He cried out in surprise and went down. Seeing he was out of commission, she threw another rock at the second attacker. This time, she was less successful and only hit him in the shoulder. He whirled back toward her, a look of fury suffusing his features.

"Bitch!"

As the man turned his attention to her, Shane leaped out of the bushes and pulled him down. The thug pivoted and tried to get his gun hand up. Shane banged his hand against the ground as the two men struggled, rolling through dry leaves.

Elena sprang forward, trying to get to Shane. But the man she had downed with the rock was functioning again. He shot out an arm and closed his hand around her ankle, yanking her roughly off her feet. As she toppled over, she managed to hold on to one of the rocks she'd collected. When he pushed his hand into her face, going for her eyes, she twisted around and brought her arm up, trying to crash the rock down on his head again.

But he was ready for her and reared away, anger flashing in his eyes. Knowing she had to take him out, she lunged forward and managed to slam him in the forehead with the rock. To her relief, he went still. She wiggled out of his grasp and, for good measure, hit him again, watching him go limp.

Pushing herself up, she ran toward Shane and the other man. They were still struggling. When the man rolled on top of Shane, she darted in, kicking at the attacker.

The distraction was enough for Shane to sock him in the face. And Elena slammed him on the head with the rock.

When the goon went still, Shane heaved him onto his back where he lay sprawled in the leaves.

"Thanks," Shane said.

"You, too."

"Have you ever seen these guys before?" he asked.

"No. Have you?"

"No. But I'd like to know who they're working for." He studied the men scattered on the ground like fallen logs, then looked back the way they'd come. "They drove here in a vehicle, obviously. We can use it to make a getaway."

He turned to the man he'd been fighting and reached into the guy's right front pocket.

"Jackpot," he said as he pulled out a set of keys. After hesitating for a moment, he went through more pockets. The man had a wallet with no identification. But there was a lot of cash. Shane put the money into his own pocket and wiped his fingerprints off the billfold. Then he took the gun from the man's hand.

"What happened to yours?" she asked. "You fired once, didn't you?"

"Yes. Then it jammed. Probably from the river water."

He got up, wavering on his feet, and she gave him a critical look. "You're sure you're okay?"

"Yes. And we need to get out of here before the cops show up."

Before she could ask another question, he said, "Nice pitching."

"Thanks."

"I thought softball pitching was underhand."

"It is. But I practiced the other way, too. To see if I could do it."

He stopped again to pick up his weapon. "We'd better not leave it for the cops to find. And when I get some gun oil, I can have it in working order again."

They continued down the access road, then stopped when they came to an SUV pulled into a clearing.

Shane opened the door and slipped behind the wheel. Then he inserted the key in the ignition. When the engine caught, he let out a breath.

Elena had already gotten into the passenger seat.

"Check the glove compartment," he said. "See if you can find out who owns this car."

She opened the glove box and looked inside.

"Anything interesting?"

"It's like the wallet. There's nothing to tie it to anyone. Not even a registration."

"Figures. And they probably stole the license plates. I guess if they got stopped by a cop, they'd shoot him."

She made a strangled sound. "Truly?"

"Just a theory. But I wouldn't discount it. They don't want anyone to know who they are or what they're doing."

"Where are we going?" she asked.

"Farther away. And maybe this time we'll be safe."

His face had turned gray, and she gave him a questioning look. "Are you hurt?"

"Not bad."

"You're sure?"

"Yeah. And our first priority is to get out of here," he said.

"In their car?"

"Only for a few miles. I've got faster transportation."

He drove to a small airport about twenty miles from the estate where they'd been hiding out.

After pulling up on a strip of grass where other vehicles were parked, he said. "Wait here."

"Okay."

"I'll be a few minutes," he added.

He went into the office and even though he'd warned her, he was gone long enough for her to start worrying. She was sure he wouldn't leave her here. But what was he doing?

When he finally reappeared, she felt some of her tension ebb.

He came back to the car and slipped into the driver's seat.

"Everything okay?"

"Yeah." He drove the car down the strip of grass and into a hangar where several planes were parked.

"Wipe off any surfaces you might have touched," he said.

She used her shirt to wipe the interior around the passenger seat while he did the same with the steering wheel and the driver's side. Once they'd left the building, he closed the door behind him.

"The owner's a friend of mine," he said. "He'll drive the car away from here and leave it in the woods."

He ushered her to a small single-engine plane that sat with a number of others in a field to the left.

"That's yours?" she asked.

"Rockfort's. We're all experienced pilots. I'm going to do a preflight check before we take off."

Shane focused on the checklist. He wanted to get out of the area, but he wasn't going to skip this important step, because if you took off without making sure everything was working properly, you could get yourself killed.

He started methodically, making sure the aircraft registration, certification, and other paperwork were in the cabin and up to date.

Next he turned on the master power switch and checked the fuel gauges, glad to see that the plane was gassed up. It helped steady him to focus on the plane and not his physical condition—or his relationship with Elena—or the surprise of finding out that Iverson was knee-deep in the S&D shit.

He pushed that out of his mind again as he listened to the sounds of equipment powering on. To his relief, everything sounded okay.

Finally he checked the flaps, landing gear lockdown levers, and other flight controllers for smooth, normal function.

When he was satisfied, he turned to Elena.

"All set."

"Do you have to…file a flight plan?"

"I did when I was in the office."

"Where are we going?"

"North Carolina. We have another facility down there." He snorted, then fought not to wince. "Let's hope it's better hidden than the one up here." He looked at her. "Buckle up."

She did as he asked, but she looked jittery as he taxied down the runway.

"You've flown before, haven't you?"

"Well, we flew here from Mexico, but I've never been in a plane this small," she said as he picked up speed and they sailed into the air.

"I'll try to make it fun," he answered, then gritted his teeth against the pain in his side. He probably shouldn't be flying at all, but getting out of here was his first priority.

When they were airborne and he'd gotten his bearings, he looked toward her. "Thanks for your help."

"I wasn't going to leave you in danger."

"I wasn't going to leave you, either."

He wanted to say a lot more, but he'd have to save it for later, because all he could deal with was flying the plane. He had to keep his emotions out of it until he got them to safety.

———~~~———

Elena had expected that once they were out of danger Shane might relax a little, but she didn't see any evidence of that. She wanted to touch him. Maybe put her hand on his arm, but distracting him now seemed like a bad idea.

Some of her own tension about the small plane dissipated as he flew south, staying along the coast, sometimes pointing out landmarks below them as they passed over.

Casting around for something to say, she murmured, "You said you filed a flight plan? Can't the men looking for us use it to find out where we went?"

He answered with a hollow laugh. "I guess they can try. They have to figure out we took a plane. And if they figure that out, the flight plan is false."

She absorbed that information. "You can do that?"

"The guy who owns the airport has helped us out before. He'll cover for me."

"Okay."

He didn't say anything more, and she kept stealing glances at him, thinking that he wasn't in good shape. But she figured that if he'd wanted to tell her about it, he would.

A couple of hours later, he landed at another small airport near Elizabeth City, North Carolina.

"While I was in the office, I arranged to have a car waiting," he said as he taxied down the runway, then pulled off onto a grassy strip similar to the airplane parking space where they'd taken off.

―――⚬⚭⚬―――

Elena followed Shane to a small office, similar to the one at the previous airport.

"Good flight?" the man behind the desk asked.

"Yeah." Shane reached into his pocket and got out some of the money he'd taken from the killer.

"Thanks. Your car's right outside the fence."

As Shane drove into the countryside, Elena watched his hands gripping the wheel.

"Do you want me to drive?" she asked.

"I'm fine."

"I don't think so."

"We don't have far to go," he answered, and she could tell that he was determined to do things his way.

They turned off onto a secondary road, and he slowed as he came to a long driveway. Again he turned, then stopped at a gate and punched in a code.

After driving inside, he waited for the gate to swing closed behind them, then proceeded to a house set well back from the road.

He took the driveway at a slow pace, then pulled up in front of another older house that looked like it had recently been renovated.

The key was under the edge of the front porch. Inside, the first floor was similar to the last safe house, with a comfortably furnished great room, a dining area, and a kitchen along one wall.

Shane crossed the room and sat down heavily on one of the couches. "I guess we made it," he said in a barely audible voice.

He looked wiped out, and she had the feeling that he'd kept himself going on willpower. Now that he was safe, his energy had suddenly drained away.

When he threw his head back, his jacket fell open, and she saw the red stain that had spread across the side of his shirt. She ran toward him.

Lincoln Kinkead looked up as one of his aides came into the room.

"You find out what happened to Iverson?" Kinkead asked.

"Yes, sir."

Without giving him any information, the aide stepped aside and a tough-looking man walked into the room.

Kinkead looked up at him, fairly sure that he knew who he was dealing with now. "And you are?"

"Detective Paul Raymond with the Maryland State Police."

Lincoln had expected that the police might show up at S&D, although he'd been thinking it would be local law enforcement — not the state cops. The introduction immediately put Kinkead on edge. "What's this about?"

Without answering the question, Raymond asked, "A man named Bert Iverson works for you?"

"He's my assistant chief of security."

"Did you send him out on an assignment?" Raymond asked.

Lincoln thought about that. He'd called Bert last night and he'd come in for a few hours. Then he'd disappeared. Like Shane had disappeared.

"He was here last night. Did something happen to him?" Lincoln didn't say that Iverson had been helping out with an emergency situation. He had learned that the less you volunteered to the cops, the better.

"He turned up dead at an estate on the Eastern Shore, outside St. Stephens."

Thrown off balance by the terse statement, Lincoln stared at the man. Of all the things the detective could have said, that was the last one he'd expected to hear.

"How? When?" he managed to ask.

"He was found a few hours ago when the owner went down there to spend some time at his vacation house."

Lincoln waited for more information.

"There was evidence that an intruder had been using some of the facilities at the estate without permission. Someone apparently spent the night on the owner's cabin cruiser docked there. And food was eaten at the guesthouse."

"And you think Iverson was responsible?"

"We don't think so. We searched the property.

There's evidence of a gun battle in the woods. Iverson was shot."

"By whom?"

"We don't know, but we'd like some information on your chief of security, Shane Gallagher, the man who's wanted for questioning about a shooting at his apartment."

Shane had gotten into trouble at his apartment—with Elena Reyes, who had been in the building after hours the evening before. Now there had been another gun battle today on an Eastern Shore estate. Both incidents had to be connected, but Lincoln couldn't put it together.

"Gallagher is missing," Lincoln said.

"And Reyes was with him at the apartment."

Lincoln sighed. "I called and asked him to come in, and he didn't show up."

"We'd appreciate it if you would contact us if you hear from him."

"Yes. Okay," Lincoln answered because he felt like he had no choice.

"What's going on at S&D?" the detective suddenly said.

"What do you mean?"

"Your chief of security is missing. His second-in-command is dead, and Elena Reyes, one of your IT people, is probably with Gallagher."

Lincoln nodded.

"Is there anything else you want to tell me?"

Lincoln swallowed. "Not at this time. I'm conducting an internal investigation."

"Of what?"

Wishing he hadn't given away that last part, Lincoln said, "Elena Reyes was in the building after hours."

The cop gave him a hard look. After several seconds, when Lincoln said nothing more, the man turned and left.

Lincoln waited for long moments, debating what to do. Finally he picked up the phone and called Rockfort Security.

"Max Lyon here."

"This is Lincoln Kinkead."

"Right."

"Have you heard from Shane Gallagher?"

"No."

"Are you lying to me?" he snapped.

"We've been at the office all night, hoping to hear from him and hoping you might call with information."

"He was supposed to come in. When I called to find out where he was, he said he was with Elena Reyes and that they'd escaped from thugs at his apartment. But you probably know that from the police report."

"Yeah."

"Apparently they went down to the Eastern Shore and got into some trouble again. My assistant head of security is down there—dead."

Lyon dragged in a quick breath. "Who killed him?"

"The state police are investigating that. Why would Shane go down there?"

"We have a safe house in St. Stephens."

"Did Shane call Iverson?"

"We don't have any information on that."

"Well, if you hear anything, let me know."

When Lyon was silent, Lincoln said, "I paid Rockfort good money to find out who was trying to steal proprietary information from me. Gallagher hasn't found out squat. And now it looks like he's gotten into bad trouble."

"Or he's trying to stay out of trouble," Lyon suggested.

Lincoln snorted. "If you hear from him, I expect a report."

"Will do," Lyon said, but Lincoln had the feeling the man was only saying what the client wanted to hear.

———

Max hung up the receiver, clicked off the speaker, and looked at Jack. "Kinkead's pissed off."

"He has a right to be."

"Which doesn't help Shane."

"What do you think is going on?"

"No way to be sure."

Max stood. "We're going down there."

"In the helo. That will be fastest."

They both checked their weapons, then headed for the safe house near Gaithersburg where the agency kept the helicopter.

Chapter 20

ELENA STARED AT THE BLOOD SPREADING ACROSS SHANE'S middle. "Shane. Oh Lord, Shane."

When she reached his side, she pulled the jacket farther back and inspected the bloodstain. It looked fresh, like something that had just happened. But that wasn't possible, was it?

Carefully she undid the shirt buttons and looked at his chest, then farther down. When he'd been in the airport office, he must have wound a sheet around his middle and tied it tightly in place. It was soaked with dried blood, but more fresh blood had come through onto the shirt.

"When were you were shot?" she breathed.

"By Iverson."

"And all this time you just…"

"Kept going—because I had to."

"Where is the wound?" she demanded.

"In the side."

She caught her breath. "The bullet…"

"Went through," he finished for her.

Her frantic gaze darted around the safe house as she tried to find a phone. "If you're shot, you could have internal damage."

"I don't."

"How do you know?"

"First, because I would have bled to death already. And second, because the bullet only traveled along my side."

"You can't be sure you're not badly hurt. You have to go to the hospital."

That got his attention. He grabbed her wrist and held her in place. "I went to a lot of trouble to make sure those bastards didn't know where I was. They've already tried to kill me three times. I'm not going to check into a hospital where they can find me."

She caught her breath at the blunt assessment. "Do you have to use your real name?"

"If I want them to treat me."

She kept her gaze on him. "Then what are we going to do?"

"This place is equipped for medical emergencies. And back at the airport in Maryland, I washed and disinfected the wound."

She winced.

"Maybe you can put on a real bandage. And I should take antibiotics."

"Okay," she whispered. Now that he knew he was safe, he had stopped trying to hold himself together. She could see that the effort to give her so much information had done him in. He closed his eyes again.

She wanted to lay her hand against his cheek, but she kept her arm at her side.

She could ask him where to find the first-aid supplies. Or she could go looking for them. She chose the latter, heading toward the kitchen area. In the other house, he'd kept pulling things out of kitchen drawers that you wouldn't expect to find there. Following that clue, she discovered the medical kit in one of the upper cabinets, with everything carefully labeled. A plastic box held an assortment of antibiotics, with instructions for various conditions.

One even said, "For gunshot wound." Apparently the Rockfort men were prepared for that, she thought as she took the bottle out of the container.

She also got sterile pads and gauze, along with a pan of warm water and some towels she found in the upstairs bathroom. She took a quick trip around the upper story, seeing several bedrooms. Hoping she'd be able to help Shane up there, she turned down one of the beds, then hurried back to the first floor.

When she brought all her supplies back to the sitting area, Shane's eyes blinked open, and he reached for the gun that he'd taken from the man on the ground. Her breath caught, and she froze.

"Shane?"

She watched his eyes come into focus. "I thought…"

"That I was one of the killers."

"Yeah. Sorry."

When he put the gun down, she relaxed. But she could see that he was on the edge of reality—ready to defend himself at a moment's notice. That made him dangerous if he truly did get her confused with the enemy. Moving slowly, she picked up the gun and put it out of his reach on the end of the table. When he didn't lunge for it, she relaxed a little.

"I've found the medical supplies, but first I've got to take off your jacket and shirt," she murmured.

He answered with a small sound of agreement.

She sat beside him on the sofa and eased the arm on his good side from the jacket and shirt at the same time, then the other arm, trying not to hurt him as she worked. Relieved that his skin didn't feel hot, she removed the makeshift dressing he'd put on and saw where the bullet had cut a path along his side. The long, thin wound was oozing blood, and when she gently washed it off, he sucked in a sharp breath.

"Sorry."

"Not your fault."

She kept working, cleaning his skin, then swabbing on antiseptic, which she could tell was worse than the water. But he didn't complain.

She finished by bringing him a glass of water and an antibiotic caplet, which he dutifully swallowed.

"Drink a little more," she said, thinking that when she'd seen shooting victims being taken care of on TV, they often had an IV line in their arm to replace lost fluids, which she wasn't equipped to do.

He drank more of the water, then laid his head back again. Afraid that he was going to sleep sitting up on the sofa, she asked, "Can you make it upstairs?"

"If I have to."

"You'll be more comfortable."

He grunted and heaved himself up, then wavered on his feet. She moved in and caught him around the waist, being careful not to touch his injuries. He tried to stand up straight, then gave up the effort and leaned on her as they made their slow way across the great room to the stairs, which they took very slowly, his weight almost too much for her as he used her to stay upright.

She was glad she'd chosen the closest room when he plopped down onto the bed.

"Thanks," he muttered as she swung his legs up and eased him back against the pillows.

She leaned over to unlace his shoes and take them

off, then set them on the floor. He was shirtless, but his jeans were dirty from the fight in the woods.

When she reached for the button at the waistband, his eyes blinked open.

"Better if I get these off you."

He answered with a small nod as she undid the button, then eased down the zipper. She'd made love with him the night before, but now she tried not to focus on the intimacy of undressing him. But that was difficult to do because, like her, he hadn't put back on his damp underwear. He was naked under the jeans, and she had a good view of his genitals as she eased the pants down his hips. Last night he'd been a magnificent lover. Today he was achingly vulnerable.

After she was finished, she pulled the covers up to his waist. When she looked back at his face, his eyes were closed and his breathing had changed. He was sleeping. Which must mean something about his state of mind, she hoped.

Before they'd had the encounter in the woods with Iverson and the two goons, she'd known that Shane didn't trust her. She hoped she had gotten his trust back. Or maybe now he was simply too worn out from the injury to stay awake.

She stood looking down at him, then couldn't stop herself from leaning over and laying her hand against his cheek. For medical reasons, she told herself. She was still concerned that he might develop a fever. But so far, his temperature seemed normal, *gracias a Dios*.

Her own outfit was a mess, and she opened the closet and some drawers, finding men's shirts and pants. Leaving Shane for a few minutes, she looked in the other rooms and found women's things in one of them. After discarding her clothes, she put on panties, a loose shirt, and sweatpants, then hurried back down the hall. When she saw that Shane was still sleeping, she made a quick trip downstairs to retrieve the gun, knowing that he'd want it close if he woke. But not right where he could reach it from the bed, she decided, thinking about the way he'd startled when she'd come back with the medical supplies.

After putting the gun on the dresser, she sat down in the chair across from him. But her eyes drifted closed, and she found herself jerking awake a couple of times.

Conceding that she needed rest almost as much as he did, she crossed the room and eased onto the bed beside him.

He didn't wake. But if he did and needed something, she was sure she'd know it.

—∽∿∾—

Sometime later, Elena's eyes blinked open. It took a moment to remember where she was and why. The man beside her was moving restlessly on the bed.

She raised up, looking down at him. His eyes were still closed, but when she touched his cheek, he made a low sound.

"Glenda?" he asked.

"No."

He ignored the answer, perhaps because he wasn't really awake. "What the hell are you doing here? You can't sleep with somebody else and then come back to my bed."

She caught her breath, wishing she hadn't heard.

"I'm not Glenda," she whispered, but she could tell that he wasn't aware of who was in bed with him.

"It's all right," she soothed. "I think it's time for your antibiotic. I'm going to get you a pill—and some water."

When she tried to ease off the bed, he closed his fingers around her upper arm.

"I trusted you," he said. "And you didn't give a damn about that, did you? Or maybe I was just too stupid to figure out what was going on."

She didn't want to hear what he was saying, but at the same time, she did, because it explained a lot about his closed-up emotions. It looked as though another woman had hurt him badly, and that had put his guard up.

Then he'd met Elena Reyes, and right from the start, she'd done things to make him suspicious. And she'd kept on doing them because of her brother.

She silently cursed Alesandro for getting her into this mess. And for getting Shane into it. If it was within her power, she vowed that she was going to get the two of them out again.

Shane's grip on her arm relaxed, and she eased her hand away. When she was free, she climbed off the bed, trying not to disturb him as she left the room. She used the bathroom, then went downstairs and looked at the food supplies in the kitchen. It was well stocked, considering that it probably wasn't used very often. There were several packages of milk that could keep in a cabinet until they were opened. Also coffee, cereal, and a number of canned and frozen foods ranging from soup to man-sized dinners.

She smiled when she found chicken soup. The universal medicine for convalescent patients.

She opened a can of vegetable soup for herself and

took a mug of it upstairs, along with the antibiotics. Then she sat in the chair across the room, waiting for Shane to wake up. She was relieved to see his color was better, and she couldn't help watching him as he slept, taking in details she hadn't been able to study when he'd been watching her. She loved his thick, dark lashes and the curve of his well-shaped lips.

He slept restlessly for several hours, but finally his eyes blinked open, and he looked around, focusing on her.

She crossed to him immediately. "How are you?"

"Better." He tried to push himself up and winced.

"You shouldn't get up."

"I have to pee. You probably don't want to look around for a urinal."

"I will, if you need it."

"I'd rather you help me up."

Because she knew that his dignity demanded it, she crossed to his side and helped him sit up, then held out an arm so that he could pull himself up. He slowly eased out of bed, and as the covers fell away, she realized he was naked except for the bandage around his middle. Following her gaze, he looked down.

"Sorry."

"It's okay."

She helped him slowly across the room and into the bathroom. He leaned against the wall, his face pale, and she had to bite her lip to keep from upbraiding him for getting out of bed.

"Close the door," he said in a low voice.

She stepped out of the room, closed the door, and waited, listening to the sounds from inside. When he'd flushed the toilet, she knocked. "Okay?"

He managed a hollow laugh. "I wouldn't exactly put it that way."

She stepped inside, and they reversed the process, the trip back to the bed even slower. She helped him under the covers, and he lay with his eyes closed. The walk across the room had obviously taken a lot out of him.

She thought he might have dozed off when he said, "I'd like some clothes."

Arguing was only going to use up more of his energy, so she opened the closet and inspected the contents. "How about a long-sleeved shirt?" That would cover down to his hips, and they could worry about putting pants on him later.

"Yeah."

She took down a flannel one and brought it back to the bed, where she helped him sit up and get his arms into the sleeves. When she was finished, she checked the bandage and was relieved to see there was no more blood oozing out.

Then she worked the buttons on the shirt and left him leaning against the pillows while she brought over antibiotics and a glass of water. When he'd taken the pill and drunk some water, she helped him ease down into the bed.

"Thanks," he murmured.

"You should sleep."

"Yeah." She heard the exhaustion in his voice. Then his eyes snapped open. "Where's the gun?"

"On the dresser."

"Put it on the nightstand."

"I'd rather not."

He gave her a sharp look. "And your reasoning is?"

"You were…upset about something…" she said, not wanting to go into details.

"What?"

"Someone named Glenda."

"I was talking about *her*?"

"A little in your sleep."

"That's great."

Changing back to the main topic, she said, "I think it's better if you can't wake up and grab the gun."

He considered that statement for several seconds, and she waited with her breath shallow. If he didn't trust her, he'd insist on having the weapon within reach.

Chapter 21

LONG SECONDS PASSED BEFORE SHANE MURMURED, "OKAY."

Elena let out the breath she'd been holding. At least that was something.

His eyes closed again, and he was asleep within minutes. She started for the chair across the room, then reconsidered. She needed to sleep, because she would be no good to him or anyone else if she was too tired to think straight. But she didn't want to leave him. The bed was queen-size. Plenty of room for the two of them. She pulled back the covers and eased onto the far side of the mattress. At first she kept her arms at her sides, but when he didn't wake, she stretched out the arm nearest him until they were lightly touching. She liked the contact, and she would have snuggled closer to him, but she wasn't going to focus on her own needs. Her top priority had to be taking care of him and making sure he got well.

She woke in the night and knew that he was awake.

"How are you?" she asked.

"Better."

His arm was still next to hers, and she felt him reach for her hand and link his fingers with hers. The gesture felt intimate, the most intimate thing they had done since they'd made love.

He squeezed her hand. "I'm sorry," he said in a low voice.

"About what?"

"About being so crappy to you."

"You had your reasons," she murmured.

"Don't make excuses for me. I know you were worried about your brother. That turned out to be entirely justified."

"But I should have told you what I was planning to do."

"You didn't because you knew I would stop you."

"Yes."

She heard him swallow. "You said I was talking about a woman. It was my wife. I went through a messy divorce about a year ago."

She felt her heart start to pound. "Oh," was all she managed to say, shocked that he'd told her about it. But maybe the darkness and the intimacy of lying next to her made him feel safer about talking.

"She cheated on me," he went on. "Starting when I was deployed. And I think that made me mistrustful of women in general. I was looking for reasons not to trust you."

"I gave you a lot."

He tightened his hold on her hand. "Stop trying to cast yourself in the worst possible light."

"I haven't stopped feeling guilty about looking through Arnold's desk and then taking that phone."

"You made a mistake. But you don't have to pay for it for the rest of your life."

"Which means what?"

"Forgive yourself for putting family loyalty above your own welfare. The focus has got to be on figuring out who those men are—then stopping them."

"How are we going to do it?"

"I'm working on it." He sighed. "But I need to be in better shape."

"You will be." She turned slightly and laid her head on his shoulder. She hadn't expected him to say the things he had. Now she was overwhelmed by the feeling of closeness.

"Got to go back to sleep," he whispered. "You, too."

She closed her eyes, feeling better than she had in days. Weeks. Maybe forever.

———

When she woke again, the side of the bed next to her was empty, and panic grabbed her by the throat.

She leaped out of bed, not sure where she was going. "Shane?"

He didn't answer, but she heard water running in the bathroom.

"Shane?" she said again as she hurried to the door.

"I'll be out in a minute."

She waited for the door to open, then stared at him. He was wearing fresh sweatpants, but he was naked to the waist, and he looked almost like himself.

"You're better," she said.

"Yeah."

Did he remember what he'd said to her last night— and what she'd said to him? And did it all mean the same thing in the light of day? She couldn't ask. Instead she said, "You should stay off the stairs. I'll bring you something to eat."

"Probably a good idea."

She hurried downstairs, opened a can of chicken

noodle soup, and poured some into a mug. She heated it in the microwave, then got herself some tomato soup from another can.

She put the mugs on a tray along with glasses of water, a box of crackers, and a couple of napkins. It was an odd breakfast, but it would do.

When she came back into the bedroom, he had plumped up the pillows and was sitting up.

"You should take your antibiotics," she said.

"I did."

"Okay."

She set the tray on the dresser and brought him the soup and the water, then sat across from him in the chair, sipping from her own mug.

"I know the other guys at Rockfort are worried about me," he said after taking a sip of soup. "But I don't want to get them involved."

"Why not?"

"Safer."

She nodded and took another swallow of her breakfast.

"Did your brother say anything about who the men were who wanted the information from S&D?"

"The only thing he said was that they would hurt him if he didn't deliver."

"How did they hook up with him?"

She closed her eyes for a moment. "I don't know. He probably didn't want me to know anything about it."

"Yeah."

"Was he always secretive?"

"Not when he was little." She stopped and thought about it. "He didn't have to work hard when he was little to get my parents' approval. Then stuff started happening. I mean, like he got a D in Algebra II. Or he didn't get on the football team. Things that he considered failures."

Shane nodded.

"He wanted them to be proud of him, and he wasn't living up to his own expectations. So he'd do things he knew were wrong, but he'd keep them from my parents."

"Like what?"

"He and some of his friends made themselves into expert shoplifters. They'd go into a store together, and one of them would get the clerk's attention while the other one stole some stuff. Then they'd sell what they took."

"And you know this—how?"

"I heard them talking about it. They didn't know I was on to them."

"And you never said anything?"

She shook her head. "I should have, but I knew it would kill my parents." She raised her head. "Did you have a perfect childhood?"

He laughed. "Of course not."

"What was wrong with it?" she asked, surprised that she was pressing him. But she didn't want the exchange of information to be one way.

He took a sip of soup before answering. "My dad came from a rough neighborhood in Pittsburgh. When he grew up, he worked at a steel plant. It was a hard life, and he wanted better for me. So he pushed me to do well in school, and if I slacked off, I was punished. At the same time, he wanted to make sure I was a tough guy— that I could take care of myself under any conditions."

"What about your mom?"

"She went along with his thinking."

"I guess that's like my mom," she murmured.

"I know you believe it has to do with your culture. But I think it's just as much a generational thing." His gaze turned inward. "Part of being a tough guy was not letting your emotions show. Maybe that's why my marriage got screwed up. I could only reveal so much of myself to my wife, and maybe she wanted more of me. But I couldn't give her any more."

She clasped her mug in her hand. So he did remember what he'd said the night before. And now he was saying more about himself—things that he'd kept private.

He was speaking again. "I could let myself go with my buddies better than I could with my wife—because the emotions that men show each other are 'tough' emotions, if that makes any sense."

"I think so. I guess like my brother and his buddies."

He sat up a little straighter. "And that's making me think that I'm not being fair to Max and Jack right now. I know they're worried about me, and I've been trying to protect them. But maybe it would be better if I clued them in on what's going on."

"That makes sense," she answered.

"Down in the kitchen, in the last lower cabinet on the right, there's a cell phone. It's plugged into an outlet inside the cabinet. Could you bring it to me?"

"Of course."

———

Shane watched Elena get up.

"Should I leave your mug?" she asked.

"Yeah, I'll finish the soup later."

As she left the room, he felt his tension mount. He

knew the guys were worried about him, and he knew he could only say so much. But he had to make the call.

Elena brought the phone and handed it to him.

"Do you want me to leave while you talk to them?" she asked.

He shook his head. He'd told her to go outside when he'd talked to Iverson, but not now. He was trying to change his relationship with her into something different, although he wasn't sure if it would work—for a lot of reasons. Like the way he'd started off suspecting her. And then his feelings of anger and betrayal when she'd called her brother.

He had told himself he trusted her now. He wanted it to be true. And also the reverse, because when he thought of her not trusting *him*, he felt his gut clench.

He switched his attention to the phone, which was a secure line that nobody should be able to tap into. The instrument at the other end of the line—at Rockfort Security—was similar.

Max picked up on the first ring.

"Shane?"

"Yeah."

"Are you okay?"

"Mostly."

He heard the relief in his partner's voice—and also the worry.

"What happened? Where are you?" Max asked.

"Down south. I don't want to be too specific," he answered, knowing that Max could probably figure it out.

When his partner said nothing, Shane said, "I know the cops are looking for me, and I want you to be able to deny that you know where I am. My SUV's at the

St. Stephens safe house, but you might as well leave it there."

"Yeah, we know. We were down there," Max said.

"Did you find anything?"

"Shell casings and exploded land mines."

"No clue about who was there besides us?"

"No."

"Did they search the house?" Shane asked.

"Yeah. It's pretty messed up, but we'll take care of it."

"The boat's somewhere on the other side of the river."

"Okay. We'll try to get it back. If not, it's insured." Max cleared his throat. "And you're not in danger at the moment?"

"Not at the moment." He laughed. "I'm not a hostage or anything. I'm just trying to lie low for a few days."

"Were you hurt?"

"Let's not get into that," Shane clipped out, knowing that his answer told his partners he'd been injured.

"What can we do?"

"Elena Reyes' brother was being pressured to make her turn over some proprietary information from S&D to a third party. If you can find out who wanted it, I'd be grateful."

"We're on it."

He hesitated for a moment, then said, "And if you could find out what was so valuable, that might also be helpful."

"You think Lincoln Kinkead's doing something illegal?" Max asked, picking up on the tone of Shane's voice.

Chapter 22

Shane glanced at Elena, knowing she was listening to his part of the conversation.

"I don't know. But it would help to find out."

He knew Max wanted to keep him on the line, but he wasn't going to let that happen.

"I'm getting off now," he said.

"When will we hear from you again?" his partner asked.

"I'm not sure. I just wanted you to know I'm okay." He clicked off.

He looked up to see Elena watching him.

"You think Lincoln Kinkead is doing something illegal?"

"I'm not sure, but I'm beginning to wonder about the way this whole thing was handled."

"I don't understand."

Shane sighed. "He hired someone from outside the company."

"Because maybe he didn't think Bert Iverson was good enough. Or he had a bad feeling about him—the way I did."

"Maybe," Shane conceded.

"Do you have any idea what Arnold Blake took?"

"No."

"Do you know about other products the company is developing?"

"Some. They're mostly for businesses. Some products

are similar to Microsoft's—only S&D's are easier for non-technical people to use. The way you use their word-processing software makes sense, for example."

"But this product's special—and secret."

She nodded, conceding the point, then said, "You want your partners to nose around and try to find out what it is."

"Yeah."

"We have to go back," she said suddenly.

"But not until I feel like I can defend myself," he snapped, then said, "Sorry. It's frustrating having to lie here."

"I understand."

"Yeah." He slid down in the bed so that he was more lying than sitting. "And I'd better get some rest if I want to heal."

Elena stood and gathered up her mug and the glasses of water she'd brought.

"Better not leave the house," he said.

"Okay," she answered.

"We have a big library of CDs and DVDs," he said. "It's probably better not to watch anything live—or streaming."

"Why not?"

"Because I'd like to keep this place sealed off." He gave her a direct look. "And you know it would be a bad idea to call your brother, right?"

"Yes." She exited the room. He watched her leave, wondering what she thought about the caution.

He didn't dwell on that. He had only so much energy, and he wanted to think about Lincoln Kinkead, about every interaction he'd had with the man. Had Kinkead set him up? Or what?

Downstairs, Elena focused on washing the mugs they'd used and putting the rest of the soup into the refrigerator for later.

She understood why Shane was being careful about outside contacts. And she understood why he wasn't exactly in a good mood.

She lay down on the couch and closed her eyes.

Somehow she was able to get a few hours of sleep. When she woke again, she went upstairs to check on Shane.

He had closed the blinds, darkening the room, but she could see he was lying in bed, staring toward the door.

"You're awake."

"Yeah."

"How do you feel?"

"Better," he answered, but she thought it might be an automatic response. She brought him more of his antibiotic and some water and waited while he took the medicine.

"Do you want some more soup?" she asked.

"In a while." He held up one side of the covers. "Come here."

She was surprised by the gesture, but she kicked off her shoes and slipped into bed beside him, on his good side.

He reached for her hand again and tangled his fingers in hers.

As they lay next to each other, he played with her hand, sliding his own fingers against hers and squeezing them, and she found herself responding to just that simple touch.

He turned his head toward her, stroking his lips against her cheek, then nibbling along the line of her jaw, before moving to her ear and stroking his tongue along the interior ridges, then sucking her lobe into his mouth.

No one had ever touched her like that, kissed her like that.

She felt tingles of sensation chase themselves over her nerve endings. She closed her eyes, letting herself ride the pleasure of it for a few moments before whispering, "What are you doing?"

"Enjoying myself."

"You shouldn't be doing this."

"Why not? Don't you like it?"

"I think you know I do, but you're still recovering. I mean, we shouldn't be doing anything…physical."

"Maybe this is helping me get better."

She felt him shifting carefully so he was half facing her. His lips moved to her neck, playing with her there the way he'd played with her jawline. With one hand, he found the bottom of her sweatshirt, reached under, and moved upward to stroke one of her breasts.

Her breasts felt full and achy, and her nipples were already hard. When he brushed back and forth against them, her breath caught.

"Don't," she said again.

"Why not?"

"Because you're making me…hot," she managed to say.

"Good."

As he spoke, he took her hardened nipple between his thumb and finger, squeezing and tugging gently on it, making her breath catch.

"Why are you doing this?" she asked.

"Because it feels good. And I haven't had much chance to feel good in the past few months."

The way he said it tore at her, and though she knew she should stop him, she didn't do it.

He moved so that he could slip one hand inside the waistband of her sweatpants, then lower, circling her navel and stroking her stomach, then her thighs, before slipping into the folds of her most intimate flesh.

"You're so nice and wet for me," he murmured.

She made a small sound, half embarrassment and half arousal. No one had ever focused on her pleasure like this. No one had ever teased her and tormented her this way. He didn't rush what he was doing, only glided his finger up and down, dipping into her vagina, then up to her clit, making it throb with need. And all the while, he kept his other hand on her breast, playing with her nipple.

He was watching her, and she felt more exposed than when she'd been naked making love with him. Unable to deal with that intimacy, she squeezed her eyes shut.

She heard her breath coming in gasps, felt her hips rising and falling to increase the friction as he sent her higher and higher toward orgasm.

Then she felt her body contract and gasped as climax grabbed her.

She came back to earth slowly and kept her eyes closed. She didn't want to look at him, but what was she going to do—get up and walk out of the room?

Reluctantly she turned her head toward him.

"Shane. You shouldn't have done that."

"I wanted to. Watching you was very satisfying to me."

That made her face heat, and she was glad that the room was dark. After a moment, she managed to say, "But you can't…I mean we can't."

"Yeah, unfortunate that if I start moving around too much, I could pull the wound open."

She rolled toward him, careful of his bad side as she slung her arm across his chest and laid her head on his shoulder. She could still feel the tension coursing through him.

He'd said what he'd just done was satisfying. She knew he probably meant "arousing."

Without looking at Shane, she moved her hand, sliding it down his body and pressing it over the hard shaft that stood up against the knit fabric of his sweatpants.

He made a low sound as she pressed against him, and she knew he liked her touch.

"Can I do the same thing for you that you did for me?" she whispered.

"Only if you want to."

"I do."

Of course, he'd known exactly how to give a woman pleasure, and she was a lot less experienced, but she had the feeling she could figure out what to do from his reactions.

She stayed pressed to him. And as he had done, she slipped her hand inside his sweatpants, reaching downward, finding his distended flesh. He felt so warm and alive, and so sexy. She had made love with him, but she hadn't touched his penis. Now she learned the shape of it, the size, the length, and the girth as she circled it with her hand.

She remembered the things he did to her. Playing with her nipples, stroking through her sex. She slid one hand to his chest, finding that his nipples were hard. When she stroked them the way he'd stroked her, his breath caught.

She was bolder with her other hand, squeezing his penis.

"Move your hand up and down," he said in a strangled voice.

She did, feeling the skin move as she worked her hand along his length.

His reactions told her what felt good, his rigid body, his heavy breathing, and then he whispered, "Harder. Faster."

She shifted over him, squeezed him more tightly, moving her hand more quickly, feeling the tension coiling through him. Then she felt his climax, felt it so intimately that she had to catch her breath.

It took a moment for his breathing to return to normal. "Thank you," he said in a gritty voice.

"Thank you for letting me get that close to you," she answered. She felt him reach to the bedside table and grab a wad of tissues from the box there. Under the covers he cleaned himself up, then dropped the tissues on the floor.

Cuddling against him, she felt overwhelmed by the intimacy of what they had done. Maybe it shouldn't be that way. Was this more intimate than really making love? Right now it seemed so.

She wanted to ask where they went from here, but she thought she might not like the answer. So she kept the question locked behind her lips.

Shane Gallagher and Elena Reyes had disappeared off the face of the earth, and two people were beating the bushes looking for them.

One was Lincoln Kinkead, who had no idea if his chief of security had defected to the enemy or was even alive.

The other was Jerome Weller. He wanted to kill Reyes' damn brother. But the little piece of shit was the only leverage he held over the woman. Of course she could have fled the country, for all he knew. But he didn't think so. He was fairly sure she was where he could get to her, if he could only figure out where that bastard Gallagher had taken her.

He started with where his men had first found them on the Eastern Shore and worked outward from there. He thought he'd had a major breakthrough when he found the airport from which Gallagher had flown away. Until the flight plan he'd filed turned out to be bogus. He'd disappeared into thin air, as it were. But the damn little plane only held so much fuel. There was a limit to where he could have gone. Would he try to get as far away as possible, or would he stay closer to home? And what were his plans after that?

Weller indulged in a string of curses. He had to find the guy, because if he didn't, he was in deep shit.

Alesandro Reyes could have said the same thing. He was still in the basement of the house where they'd taken him. The fat guy's house. But he'd heard his guards talking when they thought he was unconscious.

He'd learned the fat guy's name, and if he ever got out of here, he was going to tell the cops, and to hell with the consequences.

The *matones* had taken him off the torture table, which was a blessing. Then they'd thrown him into a dark, stinking room, with only a sliver of light coming in from under the door.

He thought his nose was probably broken and swollen to twice its size. And one of his fingers was broken, too.

He could have internal injuries, except that he thought the guys who had worked him over knew how to avoid killing someone. Their mission was to inflict pain, not kill.

The killing could always come later.

When he felt like he could move without throwing up, Alesandro pushed himself to his feet and began to explore his surroundings. The floor was cement. One wall of the room was brick, which told him that maybe the house had been constructed before the cinder-block era. Which was what the other three walls were made of.

The room seemed to be about eight feet by eight feet, and he thought it had been built in the corner of the basement. The door was metal and wouldn't budge when he tried to shake it or twist the knob. There was no bed, only a thin mattress on the floor and a dirty blanket that smelled like a dog had used it last. And for a toilet, there was a metal bucket in the corner.

Men came twice a day to empty the bucket—another blessing—and to give him a little food. Mostly junk like potato chips and cheese twists. After the nausea from the beatings subsided, he gobbled up the crappy food.

He could die in this room. He had come to know that. And he wasn't sure what would get him out.

He thought it had been days since he'd sent Elena into S&D to get that information, but he couldn't be absolutely sure of that—or anything else.

In the dark, cold, stinking cell where roaches skittered across the floor, he had plenty of time to think.

At first he'd been angry with Elena for leaving him in this situation. But the longer he stayed here, the more he came to realize it was his own damn fault.

He'd taken his status in his family for granted. And he hadn't worked very hard to improve his lot in life. Then he had gotten sucked into doing some little jobs for the mob. He'd thought stealing cars and carrying drugs would be a nice way to increase his income, since he hardly made enough for a decent lifestyle with his job as a rental-car clerk.

At first he'd liked the excitement and the *dinero*. Then they'd asked him to do bigger jobs—like carrying more dope and taking more chances. And last week they'd told him they'd get him arrested if he didn't make his sister get whatever it was from S&D. And then he'd found out that getting arrested wasn't the worst thing that could happen to him. And here he was in this miserable cell, wondering if he was going to make it home alive.

He hadn't prayed in years, but he prayed now.

"*Dios*, I know I did wrong. I got myself into bad trouble. It was little stuff at first. I didn't realize I was going to get into bad trouble. But if you help me now, I'll never do it again."

Was that the truth? He hoped so. He couldn't say the next part. But he knew what it was. If he couldn't get out of this alive, he hoped that he would die with no more pain. A simple shot to the head would do it, preferably from behind so he wouldn't have to see it coming.

Chapter 23

ELENA WATCHED SHANE CLOSELY, TRYING NOT TO MAKE IT obvious that she was evaluating his physical condition. To her relief, he continued to get better. By the next day, he was up and around, at least for short periods. He was eating more, and there was no infection in his wound.

And he had a new mission.

"Have you ever shot a gun?" he asked.

"My father taught me and my brother. He was always afraid of bad men coming after us."

"That's good. Because you might come up against a situation where throwing rocks isn't enough. So let's see what you know."

"But I thought you said I shouldn't go out. My father always took us out to the woods."

"On private property?"

"I don't know."

"There's a shooting range in the basement, among other special features."

He took her downstairs and showed her the safe room where she could lock herself in if there was trouble.

"But you're not expecting any," she clarified.

"No. But I wasn't expecting any in Maryland."

He showed her how to call for help from outside, then took her into a long, thin room set up as a pistol range.

"We've got twenty-five yards from firing position to target," he said.

"How did you do all that—under this house?"

"It took some special excavation and modifications to our specs. We've got an excellent ventilation system, so you won't be breathing in smoke or lead particles. But you will have to wear double ear protection."

"Which means?"

"Earplugs and over-the-head earmuffs, because the space is confined."

He showed her the paper targets, which were outlines of cartoon characters, then went to the gun rack along the wall and took down an automatic.

"I don't know what your father taught you. What kind of gun did you use?"

"An old revolver."

"Well, I think we can do better than that. There are a lot of considerations in choosing a gun for you. Some people think women should start with a twenty-two because it's lighter, with less recoil. But it's also the least accurate gun you could get for self-defense. I'm thinking it would be better for you to start with a nine-millimeter automatic."

She nodded, knowing what he taught her might save her life.

He picked up a Sig Sauer from the rack, holding it downward while he checked to see if it was loaded.

"What did he teach you about safety?"

"Not to point a loaded gun at anyone."

"Yeah. Actually, there are four basic rules to remember. You treat any gun as though it's loaded. Never point the gun at anything you don't intend to blow away. Keep your finger off the trigger until you are ready to fire, and be sure of your target and what's behind it."

"Behind it?"

"Yeah, like innocent bystanders—out in the woods."

He went on to talk about safety gear and where she might carry a concealed weapon, and then explained how the gun worked and how to load ammunition. His careful lesson was a lot more thorough than anything her father had imparted. It was like the difference between the Wild West and a police academy.

"It's a lot to remember," she murmured.

"Yeah." He dragged in a breath and let it out.

"What?"

"I'm getting tired," he answered. She was instantly worried about his health, until she realized he was probably using that as an excuse to slow down the lesson so she could absorb everything he was teaching.

They ate lunch—this time a couple of frozen meals. Then they went back to the range. Before he let her do any actual shooting, he made sure she was wearing a long-sleeved shirt with a collar and also a hat to minimize the chance of getting struck with a spent casing. He also instructed her on using a two-handed grip.

"After you fire the first clip, I'll show you how to reload. Obviously, it's not the same as with a revolver."

She was pleased when her first try impressed him.

"I suppose you were better than your brother," he said.

"How did you know?"

He laughed. "A lucky guess."

By the time they'd had several lessons, she was fairly confident about her ability to defend herself.

But as they ate dinner after her fourth lesson, she could sense his restlessness.

"What?"

"Those men found us twice before."

"But we came down here because it's far enough away to be safe," she argued.

"Yeah, I needed a place where I could heal. But I've been thinking about the time that's passed since we got here."

She waited for him to continue.

"They probably figured we flew out. And they know there's only so far we could get in that plane. And there are only so many small airports where I could have landed. If they're desperate to find us, they could start checking locations within the range of the plane."

"You think they'd do that?"

"I don't know. But I think to be safe, we'd better move on."

The way he made the statement sent a shiver over her skin. She felt like she'd been getting a reprieve from facing the problems that waited for her back in Maryland. Now he was telling her it was time to get back to reality. At least she felt better equipped now.

"We're flying back there?" she asked.

"Maybe. We're going to talk to Max and Jack to find out the situation first."

Again she nodded, and then she was surprised when Shane put the call on the speakerphone so she wouldn't be excluded from the conversation.

One of his partners picked up immediately.

"Shane?" The man sounded relieved to hear from them. "How are you?"

"I'm a lot better, Max. I have Elena on the speakerphone."

"Jack's on at this end, too. So we're all here," Max said.

"We're coming back up there to see if we can resolve the situation."

"Yeah, but you'll have to be cautious," Max said.

"What's the problem?"

"Someone's been nosing around here. I mean, around this office. Whoever the bad guys are, they know you're part of Rockfort Security. At least that's what we surmise. There's been a lot of unusual surveillance around the building. Also at the safe house in St. Stephens. And they broke into the airport offices."

Shane winced. "I figured they might. I filed a fake flight plan."

"Yeah."

"What do you suggest now?"

"Meeting at a location they won't suspect and making some plans."

Shane glanced at Elena, then back at the speaker.

"How about the Four Seasons Hotel in Washington, D.C.?"

Max laughed. "Yeah, if they're thinking you want to cut costs, that would be an excellent choice."

"Then let's do it. Get a two-bedroom suite. Use a set of alternate identities."

Elena kept her gaze on him. He was casually telling his partners that the two of them were sleeping together. But why should she care about that? she asked herself. Maybe it was a good thing. He had found an offhand way to tell his friends about the relationship.

He raised an eyebrow as he caught her reaction.

When she shrugged and looked away, he reached out and clasped her hand.

Max was speaking again, asking a question. "How are you traveling?"

"It's probably better not to tell you."

"Yeah, in case the guys hanging around here catch us and torture us."

Elena winced, even though she knew that Max was kidding. She hoped.

Max said he'd take care of the reservations—under their assumed names.

"Get us a late check-in, for tonight," Shane said, "in case we don't go straight there."

When they hung up, Elena looked at him.

"How are we traveling?"

"Surface transportation. It's about a six-hour drive. I'd use a delivery truck if I thought I was fit to drive that far. But I think our best bet is a limo—following the luxury theme."

"Okay."

He consulted his computer, got the number of a limo service, and made the arrangements.

"They'll be here in half an hour," he told Elena.

Her jaw dropped. "How could you arrange it that fast?"

"Money."

"This is costing a lot. I mean, it's like you've taken on a case but you're not getting paid for it."

"Lincoln Kinkead's going to pay me."

"Even though you…" She flapped her hand in a help-less gesture. "Even though you walked out on the job he hired you to do?"

"I didn't walk out. I'm still working for him, even if he doesn't know it. And you're forgetting that I'm the one who knows where that SIM card is hidden."

"At the first safe house," she breathed.

He nodded.

"You think it's still there?"

"I put it somewhere nobody's going to look. Partly because they don't even know what they're looking for."

She didn't ask where he'd put it because she didn't want him to speak the words aloud—just in case someone could hear them. Or maybe she was being paranoid.

The expression on her face made him shake his head.

"Don't worry about it now. And we don't have time for an argument. Pack some clothes you want to take."

"You mean something that will look like I belong at a five-star hotel?"

He laughed. "You'd be surprised what people wear at top-of-the-line hotels these days. The more money they have, the less they think they have to impress people, and the more casually they tend to dress."

"Okay."

Still, she hurried upstairs and looked through the women's clothing she'd found in the safe house, selecting nice slacks and jeans and several nice blouses, and packed them in a suitcase she found in the closet.

She was ready in twenty minutes. When she came down, Shane was coming up from the basement.

She gave him a questioning look.

"Something I had to do. Give me a couple of minutes to pack." He climbed the stairs while she waited in the great room. She'd felt okay here until he'd started making her nervous with his talk about her brother's pursuers finding them.

When he came back downstairs, he was carrying a small bag.

"I guess I took more clothes than you did," she blurted.

"Women always need more clothes than guys."

When a call came to his cell phone, she tensed, then waited while he answered. It was the limo driver down at the gate. Shane buzzed him into the compound, and they got into the luxury vehicle, with its wide leather seats, television, and wet bar.

She was looking back the way they'd come when she saw an SUV slow at the entrance to the property.

Shane was looking in the same direction.

"Who is that?" she asked.

"I don't know, but I think my instincts were correct. We may have gotten out of there just in time."

She shuddered. "You think they found where we were staying?"

"I think if they put enough resources into it, they could do it."

"Can they get in there?"

"The alarms are on, but they might ignore them."

"Another safe house compromised," she whispered.

"Rockfort will handle it." Shane moved to the facing jump seat and tapped on the window between the passenger compartment and the front seat. When the driver lowered the window, the two men had a hurried conference.

"What?" Elena asked when he settled back into his seat.

"We're changing cars in Richmond," he told her. "The driver's setting it up now."

She swallowed, thinking that she'd never been in a situation where she didn't know if she was going to be safe from one moment to the next. Then she changed that evaluation. It had been true when she'd been a little girl in San Marcos. Her parents had told her and her brother that everything would be fine once they got to North America. She'd believed them, and for her it had been true until the past few weeks—until her brother had messed everything up for the Reyes family.

She caught her breath.

Shane instantly picked up on her reaction. "What?"

"I was thinking that my brother had messed things up for our family. Then I started worrying that the bad *hombres* could have gone after my parents. I mean, they can't know anything, but that may not be any protection."

Shane still had his phone in his hand. As they sped north, he called Rockfort Security and explained the situation to his friends.

He looked up and said, "They're going to make sure your family is all right."

"*Gracias.*"

He nodded and went back to the conversation with the other Rockfort men. She could only hear his side of it, but she sensed his frustration. Apparently they hadn't figured out where her brother was and who was holding him. That was bad enough, but the thugs seemed to have put enormous effort into figuring out where she and Shane had gone.

As she listened to the conversation, a plan began to form in her mind.

Her brother had gotten her into bad trouble. She'd transferred that trouble to Shane and his partners, and she was thinking it was her responsibility to get them out of it.

Jerome Weller shoved his cell phone into his pocket. With his mouth set in a grim line, he got up and wandered onto the flagstone terrace outside his office. He stood in the shade of the awning for a few moments, then walked down a flagstone path to the fishpond that his gardening service had installed for him. The fish glided through the water, completely oblivious to any dangers.

He took out his phone and stared at the screen. When there was no indication of a call, he put it back and walked farther into the garden.

He was angry with himself for reacting to this situation. Over the past few days he'd lost weight. And every time he tried to eat a decent meal, it stuck in his throat. He took two antacid pills out of his other pocket, popped them into his mouth, and chewed. He hated the taste, but he found he was eating them like candy.

When the phone rang, he took it out of his pocket again and looked at the number on the screen. "Well?" he demanded.

The man on the other end of the line hesitated, the way he had after the failed attempt in St. Stephens, making Jerome's stomach clench.

"Spit it out."

"I think we just missed them."

Jerome responded with a string of curses, yet he couldn't fault the men he had sent to North Carolina. They'd figured out where Gallagher had landed. Then they'd started searching for secure properties. The whole process had taken a long time. Longer than Jerome would have liked, but there was nothing he could do about it. Not from here. And not from there, either.

He'd only been able to wait for word, and it hadn't turned out the way he'd hoped.

"They were at a safe house, and they left?"

"Yes."

"Did you search the property?"

"It's wired with explosives."

"That's just great." He thought for a moment. "I think we have to assume they're coming back here. Maybe by plane again."

"Maybe in a limo. We saw one on the road right outside the gate."

"Find it."

Chapter 24

As promised, Shane and Elena stopped outside of Richmond, at a gas station where another car was waiting for them.

While Elena was using the facilities, Shane spoke to the driver.

They were on the road again in the new car in a matter of minutes. When they were back on the highway, he opened a refrigerator at the side of the passenger compartment and pulled out a plastic bag from an upscale restaurant.

"Lunch. I ordered gourmet sandwiches."

He unfolded a table in the center of the seating area and set out the meal. "We've got shrimp salad, ham and cheese, roast beef, turkey. Sorry, they were too upscale to have tuna."

"That's okay."

She took the shrimp salad and managed to eat a few bites, but she was getting jittery as they approached the D.C. area. Too much had happened on so many levels. The stuff with her brother was enough to set her teeth on edge. But she was thinking about herself, as well.

She'd wondered if Shane still had a job with S&D. She should also be wondering about herself. Kinkead probably didn't want to set eyes on her again. And she couldn't imagine that he would give her a reference so that she could get another job. Maybe with her background, she could end up working at a local computer store.

Shane hadn't told her his exact plans, and she was surprised when they stopped at an upscale shopping center in the Virginia suburbs of D.C.

The limo pulled into a parking space at the far end of the lot near a major department store.

"What are we doing?" she asked.

"Changing cars again."

They got out, and the limo driver retrieved their luggage and set it beside a luxury SUV that was parked nearby.

"Anything else, sir?"

"No. That was great. Thanks." He gave the man a tip.

When the limo had pulled away, the driver of the SUV got out, along with another man. Both of them reminded her a lot of Shane. Tough, effective guys who looked like they knew how to handle themselves.

"Elena Reyes, these are my partners, Jack Brandt and Max Lyon," Shane said. "Max and Jack, this is Elena."

She kept her hands at her sides as they sized her up.

"Nice to meet you," both of them said.

The one named Max turned to Shane. "How are you feeling?"

"Not bad, considering I got shot in the side."

"Is that what happened?"

"Yeah." He laughed. "I'm feeling well enough to admit the truth. And Elena did an excellent job of patching me up."

As the attention turned to her, Jack said, "Let's not stand around here jawing."

"Right," Shane agreed.

Elena and Shane climbed into the back of the SUV, and the two other men took the front, with Max driving.

As they headed for D.C., Jack got out fake identification for them. She goggled as she looked at what appeared to be a legitimate Maryland driver's license with her picture on it. The statistics on her height, weight, and eye color were correct, but it said her name was Erica Garcia.

"How did you do that?" she asked.

"There's a very reliable company in the area that can get this stuff at short notice. You've also got a credit card, in case you need to buy anything."

"Okay." She looked over at Shane who was examining his own fake ID. He was now Stan Hamilton.

As the men talked, she gathered that they still hadn't found out who had her brother—and where. She wanted to jump into the conversation, but she kept her lips pressed together, thinking that it would be better if they were settled before she sprang her plan.

She'd lived in the area for years, but she'd never been to the Four Seasons Hotel, which was in Georgetown. The driveway of the red-brick building was inside a courtyard. Bellmen rushed to get their luggage and take the car away. And when they stepped into the elegant lobby with its black-and-white marble floor and soft beige-and-gold color scheme, she saw a carafe of lemon water waiting next to a plate of cookies.

The desk staff made her feel like a queen, and their suite was as luxurious as the lobby, with comfortable couches, thick carpeting, and a dining area. As promised, there were two bedrooms, which was the way Elena wanted it.

When the bellmen had departed, Jack gestured toward the sitting area. "We've got stuff to discuss."

He got out an electronic device and moved around the room, taking readings, and she knew he was checking for listening devices. He set another box on the coffee table.

"What's that?" she asked.

"Electronic sweeping and jamming—just in case. We need to be sure no one can listen to us."

She nodded and they all sat, she and Shane on the sofa and the other two men in chairs facing them.

When they were all comfortable, she got to the point. "If you can't figure out who has my brother, we're going to have to flush them out."

"How?" Max asked.

"I tell them I've got the information they want, and I'll trade it for Alesandro."

"No," Shane said immediately. "Too dangerous."

She pointed to the electronics equipment that Max and Jack had brought. "You can follow me every step of the way."

"And if it doesn't work, you're dead," Shane said.

She winced, knowing why he had put it that way. "I know you don't want me to do it," she said, "but I think it's the only way."

"Give us a little more time to find out where your brother is," he growled.

She didn't want to agree, but she understood that she had no choice. She couldn't do this alone. She needed the Rockfort men to pull off her plan.

And she was fairly sure they didn't want her hanging around, watching their efforts.

"I'm not going to hover," she said as she stood up and walked to the bedroom.

"I want to tell you something before you leave," Max said.

"Good or bad?" Shane asked.

"A piece of good news. You know that shoot-out in the garage of your apartment?"

"Hard to forget," he answered.

"It was all caught on tape. The police saw what happened. The man taking Elena hostage. The shooting. It was obviously a case of self-defense on your part."

"That's something," Shane muttered.

"More than something. It means you can operate around here without worrying about getting arrested."

Elena nodded. "That's a good place for me to leave you three to talk."

Shane watched Elena leave the room, frustrated and at the same time relieved that she was giving them some space.

As soon as the door closed behind her, Jack gave him a long look.

"I guess you've fallen for her."

"I wouldn't put it that way," Shane snapped, then ordered himself not to let his nerves show.

"How would you put it?"

"I care about her."

"Okay."

"What's that supposed to mean?" Shane asked, fighting to keep the edge out of his voice.

"I was simply agreeing with you. But if you care

about her, maybe we'd better figure out what happened to the brother."

Shane sighed. "I've been getting bits and pieces of news from you. How about a comprehensive rundown of what you managed to scrape up?"

"He was doing some part-time jobs for the mob. Car theft. Drug deliveries. Other delivery jobs."

"For whom, exactly?"

"The boss kept himself removed from the assignments. We don't know who he is."

"Dumb of Alesandro to get involved with the mob."

"From what I dug up, he never was all that smart," Jack said. "You can go back and look at his school records. A mostly C student, with an occasional B, if he was lucky. Not like Elena," he added. "She's pretty sharp."

"Right," Shane said. "And they used him to get to Elena."

Max nodded. "Unfortunately. They wanted a way to get into S&D, and they were willing to use the brother to get it."

"Bastards," Shane muttered. "And do we know how Alesandro got sucked into a life of crime?"

"Apparently through someone else who worked at the car agency."

"And you talked to the guy?"

"No. He's dead," Jack said in a flat voice.

"Jesus. How?"

"Hit and run accident."

"That's not the most reliable way to kill someone."

"In this case, it worked."

"And there's no lead on the driver."

"Of course not."

"Are we going to tell any of this to Lincoln Kinkead?" Jack asked.

"Not now. Maybe not at all," Shane answered.

"Why not?"

"Because none of that is going to change anything with him. He's not going to be happy unless we bring him that information that was stolen from S&D."

"And if we can't?" Max asked.

Shane turned to him and reflexively lowered his voice. "It's at the safe house on the Eastern Shore. We can't go back and get it until Mr. Big is taken out."

"Mr. Big?" Jack asked.

"The guy who's running the show. We do need a name for him."

"How about Mr. Big Ass?" Max asked.

Shane laughed. "I can think of a couple of better ones, but let's keep it clean since we'll need to talk about him in front of Elena. Mr. Big will do."

They discussed the other leads Jack and Max had tried to follow, but in the end Shane had to agree with his two friends. Everything led to a dead end.

"So what about Elena's suggestion?" Max asked.

Shane dragged in a breath and let it out. "If we can keep her safe."

"We'll do our damnedest," Max said. "Which means we need to go out and get some equipment."

Shane nodded.

His two partners exited the suite.

When the main door had closed, the door to the bedroom opened and Elena peered out.

"Did someone come in?" she asked, looking around the living room.

"Max and Jack went out to get the equipment we're going to need."

"Then you agree to my plan?"

"I don't like it, but I don't see an alternative."

"Okay."

He walked toward the doorway where she stood, and she backed up. He kept walking forward into the room, then closed the door behind him.

She gave him a questioning look.

"I don't like it," he said.

"I don't honestly like it either, but I'm not going to leave my brother in the hands of men who have been torturing him. I mean, they haven't heard from us in days. There's no telling what they've done to him."

"Don't think about that now."

"What should I think about?"

He took a step forward and pulled her close, wrapping her in his embrace. "Think about the two of us."

He felt a shiver go through her. "What are you saying, exactly?"

"That I want you in my life. I never thought I'd say that to any woman again, but it's true."

"*Gracias a Dios*," she whispered.

"And now…" He couldn't finish the sentence.

"And now you're going to do everything you can to protect me."

"It might not be enough."

"I'm the one making the decision that I have to go. Because if Alesandro dies and I could have done something about it, then I couldn't live with myself."

"I know. That's why I'm agreeing."

"Thank you," she whispered.

"But I want you to know exactly how I feel about you, so you won't take any crazy chances."

As he spoke, he slid his hands up and down her back, touching her with a need he hadn't felt before. She had aroused so many emotions in him that he hardly knew what to do with them.

Well, he knew, but he couldn't put them into words, only into physical terms.

"Shane."

He didn't ask what she was feeling. But when she raised her face to his, he thought he saw it in her eyes. Did he see desperation mixed with desire? Determination mixed with just a touch of uncertainty. Not about what they were doing now, he told himself. Or he hoped that wasn't true.

As she stared up at him, he brought his mouth down to hers.

It was like before when they'd kissed, when they'd held each other. He felt a jolt of heat, a desire that threatened to overwhelm rational thought. And perhaps for the moment that was all right.

Maybe he needed to wipe out the worry about her. At least for now. As his lips touched hers, he began to move them with a desperation that surprised him.

He lifted his head, looking toward the bed. She'd been lying down at some point because the spread was pulled down.

Good.

He started to scoop her up in his arms, then thought better of it. Not when he was still healing from a gunshot wound. Not when he had to be in the best shape possible when she went off on her insane mission.

He scrubbed that thought. No use thinking about the mission or what it might mean. He wanted to be with her now, and he wanted to show her what he felt for her.

He walked her backwards toward the bed, where she stopped when the edge of the mattress hit her legs. Her shoes were already off. He scuffed out of his and took her down to the horizontal surface, stretching out beside her and gathering her close. He saw her close her eyes as she clung to him, and he did the same for a moment, wanting her to be the only part of his reality that mattered.

It flitted through his mind that perhaps he could make her reconsider what she'd suggested. He pushed that away, knowing that if the situation were reversed, it would do more harm than good.

Instead he stroked his hand over her back, then pulled her blouse from the waistband of her slacks and slipped inside, flattening his palm against her warm skin, loving the feel of her.

When he shifted away, he saw her eyes fly open. He only smiled at her as he pulled his knit shirt over his head and tossed it onto the floor beside the bed.

Then he bent over her again and slowly began to undo the buttons at the front of her blouse.

She kept her gaze on him, watching his face as he opened the buttons one by one, revealing olive skin and a lacy bra. Something that she'd picked up at the safe house. And worn for him, he had to assume.

He could see her nipples sticking up against the cups of the bra, and he reached to touch one, circling it with his middle finger and watching the peak contract more.

She caught her breath, then caught it again as he

reached to unfasten the front clasp of the bra. Pushing the cups aside, he admired her breasts with their dark pink tips.

"So lovely," he whispered, then bent to swirl his tongue around one distended tip before sucking it into his mouth.

He continued to suck on her while he used his thumb and finger on the other side, tugging and twisting. She writhed on the bed, as small sounds came from her throat.

"Shane, *ah Dios*, Shane," she called out.

He lifted his head, smiling down at her as he slowly undid the button at the top of her slacks, then lowered the zipper, spreading the fly as he'd spread her shirt.

Again he kept his gaze on her as he slipped his hand inside, reaching into her panties and downward into her most intimate flesh, finding her hot and slick for him.

He stroked her neck, feeling her pulse accelerating and shivers racing over her skin, then bent to nibble and suck at her throat while he kept one hand on her breast and the other inside her panties.

He felt his lips curve into a smile before he brought his mouth back to hers for long thirsty kisses, drinking in the wonderful taste of her.

She arched her back as her hands came up to clasp his head.

He heard himself make a low sound as he feasted on her.

"Shane, please," she gasped.

"Please what?"

He heard her swallow.

Grinning to himself, he flicked his tongue over her nipple. "Please what?" he asked again, his gaze seeking hers.

"Last time we…"

"Yes?"

"You brought me to climax with your hand."

"And?"

"And if you keep up what you're doing, you'll do it again."

"Is that what you want?"

"I want to make love with you."

"That's what we did last time."

"I mean…you know what I mean."

He was through teasing her. And himself. He was dizzy with desire for her, desperate for the same thing she wanted.

He dragged her pants down her legs along with her panties. She fought with the fabric for a moment, then kicked them away and off the end of the bed.

Easing a little away, he managed to get his belt buckle undone, then his zipper.

When he was undressed, he pulled her into his arms, gasping at the feel of her naked skin against his.

"Shane, oh Shane!" she cried out.

He had never needed a woman more, yet he wasn't going to rush this. Not when he sensed the moment was so important.

He touched her and kissed her, tasted her, lifting his head to watch her face and judge her readiness as he continued to stroke his fingers through her slick folds.

"You promised," she gasped out.

He answered with a tight nod, knowing that both of them were near the breaking point.

He moved over her and parted her legs with his knee.

When her eyes met his, everything inside himself clenched, then clenched again as he sank into her.

He wanted to grab on to every sensation he could give and take. Every nuance of being with this woman. Lifting his head, he stared down at her, overcome with emotions he couldn't speak as he began to move inside her.

Her face was suffused with passion, and he liked that. And liked that she kept her gaze on him as she matched his rhythm, as though the two of them had been lovers for ages and each knew what the other craved.

He felt her fingers dig into his shoulders as she climbed toward orgasm with him. Summoning every ounce of self-control he possessed, he held himself back, waiting for her to reach the peak of her pleasure. When he felt her body start to contract around him, he let go, crying out as climax rocketed through him.

He collapsed on top of her, then hugged her to him as he rolled to his side.

"Elena," he murmured. "Oh Lord, Elena…don't… put yourself in danger."

"I have to."

"I know. But I had to ask."

"I'll be all right," she said.

He didn't know if she spoke the truth, but maybe he could give her something important to think about. "I love you," he said.

She reared back and her eyes widened.

"Oh Shane, are you just saying that to keep me from going out there?"

He kept his steady gaze on her. "No, I'm saying it because I mean it."

Chapter 25

SHANE WAITED WITH HIS HEART POUNDING TO HEAR HER response. Once he'd been sure he would never trust Elena or any other woman. She'd changed that. Now he'd worked up the guts to tell Elena how he felt about her, and she didn't seem to return his feelings.

Finally, she broke the silence. "I want to say the same thing."

He swallowed hard. "But you can't?"

"I want to," she said again. "I mean, it's what I feel."

He released the breath he'd been holding. "Thank God."

Her face reflected a host of conflicting emotions. "But I can't do it yet. First I have to get you out of the mess I got you into."

He bit back a sharp comment. But this was the wrong time to let his emotions take control—not when she didn't need any more stress. The irony of their relationship wasn't lost on him. He'd wanted her from the beginning, but he'd told himself he was simply trying to find out if she was the one stealing information from S&D. He'd practically stalked her, using surveillance as an excuse to stay close to her.

On the boat, she'd reached for him, giving him a gift that she'd given to no other man. At the time, he hadn't been sure how he'd felt about that. Today he was perfectly sure of his feelings, but he couldn't do anything about them until she returned from her self-imposed mission. And he was going to make damn sure she returned.

He leaned to tenderly stroke his lips against her cheek. "Then I guess I'll have to wait until you come back safe and sound," he said, hearing the roughness in his own voice.

A shadow crossed her face, and he pulled her into his arms.

"It's okay to be scared," he said.

"I know. But that doesn't change anything."

He wanted to argue with her. More than that, he wanted to tie her up and keep her in this bed. But he wouldn't do either one of those things. Instead he said, "The guys will be back in a while. We should get up and get dressed."

She gave him a flustered look. "Are you saying they left so we could…have some time alone together?"

"Yeah, that was part of it, but they really did need to pick up the equipment we're going to need."

The information spurred her to action. "I'm not going to look like I spent the past hour making love."

She started to get up, realized she was naked, and stopped short. Reaching over the side of the bed, she picked up her blouse and pulled it on before heading toward the bathroom.

He watched her go, enjoying the view because the blouse didn't hide much.

She closed the bathroom door, and when he heard the shower running, he got up. Without bothering to put anything on, he strode to the bathroom and stepped inside. The shower and toilet were in their own separate room. When he crossed the tile floor, opened the shower door, and stepped inside, she made a startled noise.

He grinned. "We both need to get ready."

"And you think this is going to save time?" she asked.

"Not really. But it's going to be more fun," he answered as he pulled her into his arms, reached for the bar of soap in the wall niche, and soaped his hands before starting to run them down her back and over her ass.

Forty very pleasant minutes later, they were both dried off, and she was using the hair dryer.

He stepped into the bedroom, pulled on clean clothes, and brought her bag to the bathroom.

By the time he'd left the bedroom, Jack and Max were back with some additional bags.

"I've thought about how we should work it," Max said.

"Me, too," Shane answered. "But let's wait for Elena before we start discussing strategies."

She came out of the bedroom trying to look nonchalant, and she was all business when she walked over to the bags they'd brought.

"What do you have for me?"

"A lot of good stuff," Max answered as he began taking out equipment. "I'll explain what we've got, and then we should talk about what you're going to say to the contact person."

She answered with a tight nod as he began showing her what he'd brought.

Shane paced nervously around as Max displayed his wares. His partner finally gave him a direct look. "Could you cut that out?"

"Sorry." He stopped, then cleared his throat. "I think there's something we need to do."

"Which is?" Jack asked.

"I was going to keep Lincoln Kinkead out of the loop, but I don't think I can. I want him to give me something that looks like the stolen material, in case Mr. Big wants to test it before he turns over Elena's brother."

"You think Kinkead will be glad to hear from you?" Max asked.

"I don't give a flying fig one way or the other. I just want him to cooperate." He turned to Elena. "I'm going to talk to him."

When she looked like she was going to object, he said, "Let's see what happens." He turned to Max. "Give me one of the burner phones you bought."

Max opened the plastic shopping bag and poured several phones onto the coffee table.

Shane picked up one and put it in his pocket. He was walking toward the door, when he turned and looked at his partners. "Car keys."

Jack handed over a set.

"Okay, thanks. Call down to the valet service and tell them I want the car."

Max reached for the phone.

"Be good while I'm gone," Shane tossed out.

Elena made a strangled sound. The two men simply watched him leave.

Once outside the room, he took the elevator to the lobby, then stepped into the courtyard to wait for the car.

Meanwhile, he called Kinkead's private office line.

The phone rang four times before the S&D executive picked up.

"Who is this?" he demanded. "I don't recognize this number."

"This is Shane Gallagher."

"You son of a bitch. Where are you?"

"I want to meet with you."

"I fired your ass while you were gone."

"And I've still been working on the case."

"And do you have the stolen information?"

"As a matter of fact, I do."

"Then bring it in."

"Not yet."

"What—are you blackmailing me or something?"

"The night the shit hit the fan, Elena Reyes came into the office to retrieve what Arnold Blake stole from you."

"Jesus."

"Yeah. We suspected Blake but we didn't know anything for sure."

Kinkead made a rough sound.

"Elena found the info and took it because the men who wanted it were holding her brother. They still are. We're going to exchange the program for him."

"Listen to me, Gallagher, you can't do that."

"I could, but I'm willing to do it another way. I want you to download some of that code onto a phone SIM card."

"Why?"

"That's where Blake hid it. He left the phone in his desk drawer. It was there all the time, but only Elena was smart enough to figure it out."

"Son of a bitch," Kinkead answered.

"Yeah. You could have found it and saved yourself a lot of trouble. Don't put everything on it, just enough to look real, because they may check it out before they turn over the brother. And if they think Elena's scamming them, they'll shoot her."

Kinkead winced.

"When you've got something plausible, meet me outside that restaurant where you took me after I accepted your job offer."

"You mean…"

"Don't say it," Shane cautioned, cutting him off.

"Then you're back in the area," Kinkead said.

"Yeah. How soon can you be there?"

"Forty minutes."

"It will take me a little longer. Wait in your car at the edge of the parking lot."

Shane hung up, wondering if the guy would show up—or if he was going to pull some kind of scam. Because as the S&D saga had unfolded, Shane had started thinking that Kinkead wasn't exactly playing straight with him—or anybody else.

But when Shane showed up at the parking lot outside the Mykonos Grill on Congressional Lane, he recognized Kinkead's Mercedes in the corner of the lot.

He checked out the area, then parked beside the other car.

"Thanks for coming," he said as he slipped into the passenger seat.

"I should have you arrested."

"For what?"

"Taking ten years off my life."

Shane ignored the comment.

"Why didn't you contact me?" Kinkead snapped.

"Because I was busy trying to save my life—and

Elena's. We were shot at in my apartment garage. We were shot at in the Rockfort Eastern Shore safe house. And then where we were hiding out after that."

"You got Bert Iverson killed."

Shane made a dismissive noise. "What the hell do you think he was doing down there?"

"Coming to bring you in."

"Did you tell him to do that?"

"No," Kinkead conceded.

"Well, he wasn't doing it for you. He was working for your opposition. He shot me."

Kinkead gaped at him.

Shane pulled up his knit shirt and showed him the healing wound.

"Jesus!" He gave Shane a direct look. "Who was Iverson working for?"

"I don't know yet. We hope we'll find out tonight. Give me the SIM card."

Kinkead got the little drive out of his pocket but held it in his hand. "And the real goods are safe?"

"Yes."

"And you won't tell me where the card is?"

"Nobody's going to find it," Shane said.

Kinkead sighed and handed over the SIM card.

"This will fool them?"

"Hopefully," Kinkead said.

———◇◇◇———

Lincoln Kinkead watched Shane Gallagher return to his car and drive away.

He'd given him a smidgen of the good stuff that had been stolen by Arnold Blake.

He made an angry sound. He'd come here thinking that he didn't owe Gallagher or Reyes anything and what happened to them was their fault, not his. Reyes had as good as stolen from the company. Gallagher had gone rogue. But now he was wondering if he was going to get one or both of them killed with what he'd put on the SIM drive. It was a very small part of Falcon's Flight. Maybe it would fool someone for five minutes. Maybe not.

Chapter 26

WHEN SHANE WALKED INTO THE HOTEL SUITE AN HOUR later, Elena rushed to him, and they embraced. She knew the other two men were watching them, but she didn't care what they thought. She only wanted to wrap her arms around Shane and feel his arms around her.

When Max cleared his throat, Shane eased away.

"You got something we can show Mr. Big?"

"Mr. Big?" Elena asked.

"That's what we call the boss man, since we don't know his name."

Shane pulled out the SIM card. "Kinkead says this will fool them."

"You believe him?"

"I hope so."

He looked toward the phones still lying in a pile on the coffee table. "We should make the call."

"After we eat," Jack answered. "We figured we wouldn't have much time for eating later, so we ordered something. It will be here soon."

The food came ten minutes later. Gourmet hamburgers, potato salad, and coleslaw for everyone, along with ice cream sundaes for dessert.

"If you can't handle the food, you can eat the ice cream for calories," Jack explained.

Elena forced herself to nibble some of her burger because she knew the men were watching her, and she didn't want to look like she was too nervous to swallow. But after a few bites she switched to the ice cream.

A knock at the door made her stiffen. Jack got to his feet quickly and crossed the room. After looking out the peephole, he opened the door, and a pretty woman with dark blond hair walked in.

Elena watched in surprise as the woman and Jack embraced. When they broke apart, he turned to the group.

"Elena, this is my wife, Morgan Rains."

"Your wife?" she said in surprise. "I didn't know you were married."

Jack grinned. "Very much so."

"I'm glad to meet you," Morgan said. "I thought you might want to have another female join you in this group of macho guys."

"Yes, thanks," Elena managed to say.

"Maybe we could go into the bedroom and talk," Morgan said.

Elena tipped her head to the side, wondering where this was leading, but she said, "Yes, all right."

She got up and took the other woman into the bedroom, glad that she'd made the bed before coming out.

Morgan closed the door behind them and gestured toward the armchairs by the window. "Why don't we sit down?"

Elena nodded and lowered herself into a chair, wondering where this was leading.

Morgan took the opposite chair. "Jack told me you're determined to go off on a dangerous mission."

"Are you here to talk me out of it?" Elena demanded.

"No. I'm here in case you need someone to talk to—besides the guys."

Elena knitted her hands in her lap. "I've made up my mind."

"At least you have a choice."

"What does that mean?"

"Let me give you the executive summary of what happened when I met Jack. He had infiltrated a homegrown militia planning to attack the U.S. Capitol. After they discovered he wasn't really one of them, they tortured him for information. He escaped and ended up naked and beaten in the woods near my house. I took him in and tried to patch him up. When they came after him, we had to escape together—and Shane and Max came to our rescue. Then when I was kidnapped and the militia leader told Jack I only had twenty-four hours to live, the three guys risked their lives to save me."

Elena sucked in a sharp breath. "Truly?"

"Yes. I told you all that because I wanted you to know that I understand how you're feeling now. And I also want to be here for you. I'm a psychologist." She stopped and laughed. "When I first met Jack, I thought I might have hooked up with a psychopath."

Elena blinked. "Why?"

"He did some pretty violent things to get us away from the militia."

"Okay," Elena answered, thinking of Shane's recent exploits—including flying a plane with a bullet wound in his side.

"Can I help you deal with what you're going through now?"

"It's the other way around," Elena blurted out, "from what you said about Jack. I did a lot of things that made Shane mistrust me."

"Is that why you're going off to meet a guy who could kill you—to prove your innocence?"

Elena blinked at her bluntness. Didn't therapists usually let the client bring stuff up? But maybe in this case, they didn't have time to draw it out.

"No," she answered. "It's the only way to rescue my brother. And I'm sorry I dragged Shane into it."

"I don't think he's sorry."

"He was."

"And now he's committed to you."

Elena kept her gaze fixed on Morgan. "How do you know?"

"I saw the way he looked at you."

"You can tell from that?"

"Yes."

Elena swallowed. "Which means I'm making him frantic."

Morgan shook her head. "These guys don't get frantic. They stay cool and do what has to be done. And if Shane is letting you meet up with the bad guys, he's going to be right behind you."

"I know. If he can."

"He will. It will help you to focus on that."

Elena nodded, knowing that the other woman was giving her a pep talk and praying that she spoke the truth.

"Is there anything I can do to help?" Morgan asked.

"You did," Elena answered.

"Then the sooner you get the hard part over with, the sooner you and Shane can plan the rest of your lives."

"The rest of our lives," Elena murmured. "I've hardly dared to think about that."

"Keep the thought with you."

They both got up and went back to the sitting room. "Let's make the call," Elena said in answer to Shane's anxious look.

"And hope he's been waiting to hear from us," Shane muttered under his breath.

—∿∿—

While Shane had been gone, Elena and the other two Rockfort men had talked about what she was going to say—and what she wasn't. And now was the moment of truth. The first test to see if she could pull this off.

The three men and Morgan all had Bluetooth earpieces so that they could hear the conversation—and give her pointers if she got into trouble.

Willing herself to steadiness, she punched in the number of her brother's cell. This time it rang three times before anyone answered. And it wasn't Alesandro on the other end of the line.

"This is Elena Reyes," she said.

"It's about time you called," a hard male voice said.

"I...I couldn't do it before."

"Why not?"

"I had to get away from Shane Gallagher."

"And you're saying you did that?"

"Yes."

"I don't believe it." The hard voice punched out the words. "You were with him for days."

She tried to picture the man on the other end of the line. He sounded like he wasn't young. Maybe he was in his sixties. She guessed that he was used to having people do what he told them, and he wasn't happy that she'd kept him dangling. Or that she had some say in the course of this call.

Answering his unspoken question, she said, "Not because I wanted to be with him. I had no choice. I had to pretend I was helping him, but I finally gave him the slip."

"How?"

She swallowed hard. "I waited until we left that hiding place in North Carolina. When his driver stopped for gas, I got out of the limo and ran."

"Ran where?"

She glanced at Shane, and he gave her an encouraging look before she went on with the story that they had worked out. "He was in the gas station restaurant, and I ran into a shopping mall. When he realized I was gone, he came after me, but I hid."

"You expect me to believe that?"

"It's the truth."

"What if you're really with him?"

"I'm not."

"Why did you run away from him?"

"Because he doesn't care anything about Alesandro." She gulped. "He just wants to get that information back. That's why I called. How is my brother?"

There was a long pause, and she wondered if the man was buying the story. "Where are you?" he finally asked.

"How is my brother?" she repeated.

"Alive."

The way he said it made her wince.

"Where are you?" he asked again.

"I'd be *muy estúpida* to tell you that."

"It looks like we don't trust each other."

"Truly. So I'm getting off the phone and calling you back in a minute."

"No! Wait."

She hung up, feeling a shiver go through her. The man had sounded panicked, which was a small victory for her.

Apparently the others agreed.

"I liked his reaction to that," Morgan said.

The three men nodded.

Shane came over and put his arm around Elena. "You did great."

"But we haven't gotten anywhere yet."

"You will," Morgan said. "I could hear the tension in his voice. He's fighting not to panic."

"Like me," Elena murmured.

"You have us," Morgan said. "I think he's got nobody."

Elena grasped at that. Her heart was pounding as she fought the urge to make the second call right away. Instead, she looked at the clock on the computer screen and forced herself to wait a minute and a half before picking up another cell phone and punching in her brother's number.

This time the man answered on the first ring. "Where were you?"

"Like I said, I don't trust you not to try and trace this call. I'm not going to talk to you for more than a few minutes on any one phone."

The man laughed. "And you thought of that all by yourself? What are you, a high-tech spy or something?"

"What, you think I'm some little twit? I'm a woman with a degree in computer science. I work in the IT department of a software company." She swallowed, readying herself for the real negotiation. "We'd better get down to business. We don't trust each other, but we each have something the other wants."

The man made another snorting sound. "Do you have the information from Arnold Blake's office?"

"Yes."

"You'd better bring it to me."

"I won't unless I know you're going to bring my brother."

His tone turned derisive. "You don't have much of a bargaining position."

"Neither do you."

Again there was a long silence. He finally said. "All right, what do you propose?"

"We drive to a location that we both agree on. You bring my brother and I'll bring the information you want. We'll make an exchange."

"And your friend Shane Gallagher will be there to kill me."

"No."

"And how will I know you're telling the truth?"

"I'll come alone."

"And he can put a tracking device on your car."

She sucked in a sharp breath.

"That's what you were planning, weren't you?"

"No," she answered, fighting the urge to scream, because that's exactly what she had known Shane would do.

Chapter 27

"CALL ME BACK IN FIFTEEN MINUTES," THE MAN ON THE phone said. Then the line went dead.

Elena looked at Shane in panic.

"Will he be there when I call back?" she asked.

"Of course," Morgan answered. "You have something he needs. Desperately, I'd say, from the way he's behaving."

Elena nodded, struggling for calm and glad a psychologist was judging the guy's reactions. "You were going to track my car, right?" she said to Shane.

"Yeah, but we were going to let him think that he'd fooled us by defeating the tracker."

"I'm not following."

"There will be a tracker and another one he won't find."

"All right," she answered, ordering herself not to freak out. Shane and his friends knew what they were doing.

She stood up, paced to the window, and stared out at the cars whizzing by on Rock Creek Parkway, then paced to the other end of the room.

Shane looked at his watch, keeping track of the time.

As the minutes ticked slowly by, Elena fought not to scream—or make the call early.

"He knows how to get to you," Shane muttered.

"Unfortunately."

Finally he gave the go-ahead.

With fingers that felt like they had lost their nerve

endings, she punched in the number again, and the man picked up on the second ring and got right to business. "Here's the deal. You come alone or your brother is dead."

"All right."

"You meet me at the following location."

She was ready with a pen and notepad. He gave her an address, which Max started checking out the moment she'd written it down.

"I want to talk to my brother now."

"You're not in a position to make demands."

"Neither are you," she shot back. "Not if you want that program."

"You know it's a program?" he asked with an edge in his voice.

"Yes, I looked at it," she lied.

He sighed and covered the phone, but she could hear him speaking to someone else.

Again the seconds ticked by, and finally she heard sounds from the other end of the line. Then her brother's shaky voice.

"Elena?"

"Alesandro. Are you all right?"

He gave a harsh laugh. "Not really."

"They hurt you," she whispered, expecting him to start berating her for disobeying his directions, but he didn't do it.

"I guess I deserve it," he said instead.

She couldn't believe his answer or the way his voice sounded. The last few times they'd talked, he'd been angry with her. Now his tone was completely different. He'd always acted so sure of himself and so sure that he deserved every good thing in the world. This time he was telling her that he knew he'd made a mistake.

"I'm going to trade the information for you," she said, feeling her chest tighten as she said the lie. Although she didn't have the SIM card, she had something that looked like it. The important point was that Shane and the other men from Rockfort Security would get to her before Mr. Big realized he'd been tricked.

"*Gracias*," Alesandro said, making her feel even worse. If this plan got messed up, he'd be dead. And maybe she would be, too.

She pushed those thoughts out of her mind and prepared to say something reassuring. Before she could get the words out, she heard her brother make a strangled sound.

"That's all for now," Mr. Big said.

"Please."

"We're wasting time."

"Who are you and why are you doing this?" she asked.

He laughed. "Just meet me at the place I told you. At nine p.m."

Before she could ask any questions, he had hung up.

Shane looked at his watch. "That doesn't give us much time."

"I guess that's what he wanted," Max said.

"Do you think he'll bring my brother?" Elena asked.

"Not to that location," Shane said.

"What do you mean?"

"He's going to make you go somewhere else when you get there."

"How?"

"There will probably be a cell phone waiting for you. Or written directions. I don't know exactly. But I know he's not stupid. He knows we can follow you."

"It's a warehouse in Gaithersburg," Jack said. "In a run-down industrial park."

He brought over the laptop and showed her a map of the area plus a Google Earth picture of the building. "See the street number at the upper right-hand corner of the buildings?"

"Yes."

They studied the map. "You'll take I-270 out of town."

He printed out the directions, which she studied.

"Any problems?" Jack asked.

"I think I can find it."

Shane looked at his watch. "We'd better get ready."

She gave Shane a direct look. "Would it have been better to have gotten that SIM card from the safe house? You know, in case…" Her voice trailed off.

"He won't know the difference until after you've got your brother," Shane said.

She nodded, hoping he was right.

They'd already started preparations, and now they had to snap to it.

Elena went into the bedroom and changed into the clothes she was going to wear. After a few minutes, there was a knock on the door.

"Shane?"

"Yes."

He came in with two pistols. "I want you to take these."

She didn't protest. They'd practiced with these particular weapons at the firing range in the basement of the southern safe house, and she was comfortable with both of them. One went into her purse and the other into a holster. He also gave her a SIM card.

"Tell him the program's on here. And tell him how you figured it out."

She answered with a little nod.

"You have to leave," he said.

"I know."

"I don't like sending you off alone."

"I know. But you can't exactly hide in the trunk of the car."

"Unfortunately." He pulled her into his arms, gathering her close, hanging on to her as though he never intended to let go. But of course, that was impossible. When he eased away, she saw that his eyes were shimmering.

"Be careful," he said.

"You, too."

He squeezed her hand, then stepped away. Her head was spinning with all the points they'd discussed. They both walked into the other room, where Max, Morgan, and Jack were waiting for them.

Jack made his voice all business. "I brought a car over for you to use. It's in the garage and they're bringing it up. I want you to drive down M Street, then up Wisconsin and turn left onto one of the lettered streets. Don't tell me which one. If the tracking equipment is working, we'll find you, come up behind you, and give you the all clear."

"Okay."

Morgan reached for her and gave her a quick hug. Then Jack and Max did the same.

"Good luck," all of them said.

When she started to leave the suite, Shane said, "Wait."

She gave him a questioning look.

"Let me see your purse."

She handed it over, and he made sure that everything that was supposed to be inside was there, but he also took out the hotel room key. "Let's not give away where we're staying," he said.

She answered with a nervous laugh.

Morgan stayed behind, and Elena and the three men all went down to the lobby, where they waited for the car she would be driving and also for the SUV. Other people were waiting for cars, and she looked at them, thinking that they were going to the Kennedy Center or restaurants or other fun locations in D.C. They all looked prosperous and confident, and she was sure they'd be shocked to know her mission.

Her car arrived. It was a Honda Civic. Basic and nondescript, but fast, Shane had told her, in case she needed to make a fast getaway from a bad situation.

And what? Leave her brother with the bad guys?

She drove through the evening Georgetown traffic, not bothering to look for Shane and the other Rockfort men. Either they'd be able to track her, or it wouldn't work.

———

Shane waited impatiently for the SUV to arrive. It was slow coming up from the garage, and he wanted to scream at the parking attendants to get a move on. But he knew that wasn't going to do him any good.

Finally the vehicle appeared, and they all climbed in with the equipment that Max had brought along.

When they had pulled out of the hotel courtyard, he opened the suitcase in his lap and turned on the tracker.

Shane's stomach knotted as he waited for the verdict.

"Got her," Max said, and they took off toward Wisconsin Avenue and the location Elena had chosen.

When Elena saw the SUV pull up behind her, she breathed out a little sigh. So far, so good.

Shane waved to her, and she waved back, like they were going off to a ball game or something and were meeting at that location.

Her chest was so tight she could hardly breathe as she took off up N Street, then worked her way toward Bethesda, Rockville, and finally Gaithersburg.

As she took the ramp to I-270, she looked behind her but saw no sign of Shane. Which was good, she supposed. If anyone was checking on her, they'd think she wasn't being followed.

The flaw in the plan was that she couldn't talk to Shane and the Rockfort men. They could follow her, and they would be able to hear if she spoke to anyone. But it was one-way communication because any microphones on her or the car would show up. She had to trust that they were behind her.

She made it to the vicinity of the warehouse early and pulled up on a side street, sitting in the darkness and waiting for the appointed meeting time. It looked like a rough neighborhood with trash lying around on the ground and warehouse facilities in need of repair. She made sure the car doors were locked as she scanned the area, but no other cars passed. Which meant what? Probably that Mr. Big already had his plans in place.

At nine thirty on the dot, she drove to the correct

building, which had a ground-level garage door that stood open. Another car, a blue Hyundai, was parked inside, and she pulled up next to it, looking around at the open space. There were oil slicks on the floor, as well as a dark circle painted in the middle of the space. Aside from that, the interior seemed entirely empty except for the other vehicle.

But someone must have been waiting for her to arrive because as soon as she cut her engine, she heard a phone ringing. It sounded like it was inside the other car. Getting out, she hurried to the driver's door, pulled it open, and found the ringing phone lying on the driver's seat.

When she picked it up and answered it, the man Shane called "Mr. Big" was on the other end of the line.

"I see you made it to your first destination," he said.

"My first?" she asked, acting as though she thought he was going to show up with her brother.

"You don't think I'm stupid enough to let the Rockfort men follow you, do you?"

She sucked in a sharp breath. He was letting her know that he knew Max and Jack were following her, as well as Shane.

"I don't think you're stupid," she murmured.

"Good. See that camera mounted on the wall to your right?"

She turned and looked. "Yes."

"I'm watching everything you do."

"Okay."

"And now we're going to make sure they can't follow you. You'll be taking the car I left for you. The keys are in the ignition."

She swallowed. Shane had warned her about something like that.

"And I'm going to make sure that you don't have a tracker or a gun on you," he added.

"How?"

"You will take off all your clothing and stand in front of the camera so I can make sure you're not wearing a wire and you're not armed."

Chapter 28

SHANE HAD NO TROUBLE FOLLOWING THE TRACKER ON Elena's car. When she'd arrived early, he'd driven past the entrance to the industrial park and kept following the secondary road for ten minutes in case someone was watching to see if he was behind her.

He pulled off onto a side street and turned around, waiting with his lights off to find out what would happen.

Elena's car started again, and she drove toward the warehouse.

Max looked at his equipment. "She's driven inside."

Shane heard a cell phone ring, then Elena getting out of the car and opening another vehicle door.

Then she was speaking on the phone. To Mr. Big, he presumed.

"He figured we'd track her," Max said.

They listened as the man said, "You will take off all your clothing and stand in front of the camera so I can make sure you're not wearing a wire and you're not armed."

"Jesus," Shane swore. "Did I hear that right?"

"I think so. He's making her get undressed."

Shane clenched his hands on the wheel. "I want to go in there and get her out of this."

Max put a hand on his arm. "You can't."

"I know," Shane shouted. "But I want to. I mean, that bastard is making her strip."

"And hopefully she's alone there," Jack said from the backseat.

All Shane could do was clutch the wheel and wait.

———

Elena looked up at the camera. "You want me to take my clothes off?"

"That's the only way I can be sure you're not wearing a wire."

She gulped.

"Think of it like a visit to the doctor's office. You get undressed for the doctor, don't you?"

She wanted to curse at the man, but she knew that would do her no good.

"Step into the middle of the garage where there's a circle painted on the floor. Stand in front of your car and start stripping," Mr. Big ordered.

She stepped to the spot he'd indicated.

"Or think of it like strip poker," the voice from the phone said. "Did you ever play strip poker?"

"No," she bit out.

"Pity. Probably you were too much of a straight arrow. That's what got you in trouble now, you know. If you'd just brought that information to Alesandro, none of this mess would have happened."

Of course, he was right, but she felt like she was standing in an open field, being buffeted by a howling wind.

She'd thought she was prepared for whatever this guy was going to throw at her, but she hadn't been prepared for *this*. And she'd brought it on herself, like he'd said.

With her teeth clenched and her eyes cast down, she started unbuttoning her blouse. When it was undone, she laid it on the hood of the car. Next, she unzipped her slacks, folded them, and laid them with the blouse.

"Take off the rest of it," Mr. Big ordered.

She fought to keep her hands steady as she unhooked her bra and took it off, then her panties, so that she was standing naked in front of the camera.

"Look at me."

"What?"

"Look up at the camera."

Silently she did as he asked.

"You are under my control now."

She wanted to scream at him, but she kept the protest locked behind her clenched teeth.

"Very nice," he purred. "Turn around so I can see the back of you."

She did, then faced the camera again. "Can I get dressed now?"

"Say please."

"Please."

"Actually, no. Take off your socks and shoes."

She gulped. With no other choice, she bent to comply.

There was a long moment of silence. She stood with her heart pounding, wondering how good a view he was getting.

"You have a gun strapped to your ankle," her tormenter said. "And a tracking device on your other ankle. Is that right?"

"Yes," she managed.

"Take them off."

She fought to keep silent as she took off the holster with the gun and untaped the tracker.

"That's better," he said. "Stand up and turn around again, so I can make sure you don't have any more tricks up your…" He laughed.

As ordered, she turned in a slow circle, coming back to her starting position.

"One more thing. Lift up that beautiful shiny, black hair of yours and turn so I can see both ears. I want to know for sure you're not wearing a Bluetooth."

Grimly, she lifted her arms, lifting her breasts as she displayed her ears.

"Nice," he murmured. "You can get dressed in the clothes I put in the backseat of your new car."

She walked stiffly to the car and pulled out a T-shirt, slacks, and bedroom slippers. There was no underwear. But at least she'd be covered.

Quickly she dressed in the T-shirt and pants, feeling marginally better. Then she scuffed her feet into the slippers.

"Very good. I'll tell you where to go after you get into the car and leave the garage. Be sure to take the phone with you."

"Wait a minute," she called out.

"For what?"

"The information you want is in my purse. I have to get it from my car."

"Not the whole purse. Take out the memory stick or whatever it is and hold it up."

"How do I know you won't…come in and take it?"

"Because I'm assuming your boyfriend's close enough to rescue you. At least for now."

Instead of arguing, she walked slowly back to the car, planning her moves as she went. Leaning inside, she pulled her purse toward her, hoping that her body hid what she was doing. She had one chance to get this right, and only one.

She reached inside, taking out the twenty-two revolver and shoving it into the waistband of her slacks. Then she took out the SIM card, the one that had the fake information, and held it up.

"Here it is."

"What the hell is that?"

"A SIM card. From the phone Blake left in his office drawer."

She heard the man on the other end of the line curse. Probably he'd sent Bert to search the office, and Bert had left the phone where it was. "Bring it to the new car."

Again she complied, then slipped behind the wheel and adjusted the seat so she could reach the pedals before starting the engine and driving slowly out of the garage.

He'd separated her from the tracker on the other car and from the one strapped to her leg, but maybe...

She didn't finish the thought. Mr. Big was speaking to her again.

"We're going to take back roads to Columbia. That way I can tell if anyone's following you."

"Columbia?"

"Yes, to another industrial park."

"And my brother will be there."

"If you do what you're supposed to. Get going. I'll give you directions as you drive. And, of course, I'll know where you are at all times."

Feeling sick, she did as he directed. As she drove down the road, thunder rumbled and a fork of lightning split the sky in front of her like a warning sign.

In the next moment, rain began to pound down on the car.

—⁓—

"Shit!" In the other car, Shane shouted out his frustration. "We've lost the sound. We can't hear what he's saying to her."

"We can still track her," Max said.

"We hope."

Max fiddled with some dials on his equipment, and Shane could tell from his actions that he wasn't having any success.

"What's wrong?" Shane growled.

"The storm is interfering with the tracker we had her swallow. I don't know…" He didn't have to finish the sentence.

"Shit." Shane repeated his earlier assessment. "I thought that thing might not work."

"It's the storm. Give me a few minutes, and I'll get her back."

—⁓—

Shane drummed his fingers against the steering wheel, praying that Max could work it out, because if he didn't, Shane wasn't sure he could keep his sanity.

He would lose his mind if anything happened to her.

He'd been going through the motions of living until he'd met her. And even when he'd told himself he didn't trust her, he knew he was forming an attachment to her.

He didn't want to go back to the life where it was a struggle to heave himself out of bed and get through every day.

He wanted to shout in frustration. He wanted to pray aloud. He wanted to start driving and hope that he was going in the right direction and that when they found her, they'd be close enough to save her. But he did none of those things because he was in the car with his two friends, and he wasn't going to let them see that he was skating on the edge of his emotions.

Yeah, who was he fooling? He was sure they knew what he was suffering, but at least he could hang on to his illusions.

"What have you got?" he said to Max, trying to keep his voice even.

"Nothing yet."

He didn't bother cursing again. It wasn't going to do any good.

He watched rain sheet down the windshield and prayed that the storm would pass.

Finally, there was an electronic beeping from the machine in Max's lap.

"I got her," he said.

"Where is she?"

"On back roads. I guess to make it easy to see if anyone's following."

"Where's she going?"

Max was silent for several moments. "If I had to guess, I'd say Ellicott City or Columbia. But the rendezvous point could be a vacant farm out in the country, for all we know."

"That's just great."

"We can circle around, then head for the Columbia-Ellicott City area and see if the signal gets stronger."

"And if it doesn't?"

"We can head into the backcountry."

—᠊ᨆ᠊—

Elena hunched forward, struggling to see where she was going with water pouring down on her windshield. Her headlights cut through the steady rain, making the road in front of her murky as the storm unleashed its worst. She didn't know this part of Maryland, and she didn't like driving these narrow roads in a downpour, but she had no choice.

Max had told her that the tracker on her car was only part of their plan to follow her. The tracker on her leg had been a decoy that the men expected Mr. Big to find and make her throw away. That had happened as predicted. But before she'd left the hotel, she'd swallowed a capsule with another tracker inside. They still should be able to follow her—if the thing was working correctly. She'd been able to tell from Max's face that he wasn't one hundred percent certain that it was going to work. But he had acted confident, and she had to be, too.

She drove on through the downpour. It had been an eternity since she'd heard from Mr. Big. Had she lost the connection in the storm? If she had, then what?

Her tension mounted. With no other option, she kept driving, praying that she would hear from the man who was holding her brother. Finally, the phone next to her crackled.

"A road is coming in on the right. Take it."

She dragged in a breath and let it out before answering, "Okay."

"Don't have an accident in the rain," Mr. Big said, his voice cheerful, and she knew he was confident that he had total control of this situation. Hopefully, he was dead wrong.

"I won't," she answered, thinking that he probably was hoping she'd crash, and then he wouldn't have to trade anything for the SIM card.

—⁓—

Shane drove as fast as he could through the pelting rain and darkness, feeling sick as he calculated his chances of getting Elena out of this alive.

"Take it easy," Max murmured as the car skidded on the wet pavement and Shane fought to keep control. "If we crash, you're not going to be any good to her."

"I know that," Shane snapped and slowed down a few miles per hour.

"We're getting closer to her," Max said.

"Thank God."

"We're going faster than she is. We should be able to catch up."

"Well, not entirely," Shane cautioned. "We don't want anyone to think we picked up her trail."

In the backseat, Jack was consulting computer maps while Max manned the tracker up front.

"I think she's headed for another industrial park," Jack said.

"Okay, good. That's better than an isolated farmhouse where we'd have to get out and sneak through the fields."

Max made a sound of agreement, then caught his breath.

"What?"

"She's stopped abruptly. Either she's there or she had an accident."

"How fast can we get to her?"

"If you don't crash, in ten minutes."

Shane gripped the wheel, knowing that ten minutes could mean the difference between life and death.

—⁓—

Elena pressed on the brake, the car fishtailing on the slick road surface. Ahead of her she could see water flowing across the pavement.

"There's a flood," she said aloud.

"What are you talking about?" the man on the other end of the line snapped.

"Water is flowing across the road."

"Go through it."

"It looks like it's too deep."

She was greeted with a string of curses, then "Just a minute."

She waited with her heart pounding.

"Back up," he snarled. "Go to the last intersection. Take Owen Mills Road."

"Okay."

She looked behind her and saw that nobody else was dumb enough to be out in this storm.

Turning the wheel, she tried to make a U-turn, but the road wasn't wide enough for her to do it and stay on the blacktop. Her right front tire crunched onto the wet gravel shoulder. There must be a thin layer hiding mud below because the tire sank in, and she had to back up, the wheel grinding as she fought to gain the pavement again.

Chapter 29

SHANE HAD PULLED TO THE SIDE OF THE ROAD AS HE WAITED for Max to tell him which way to go.

"Wait a minute, she's moving again."

"Still heading in the same direction?"

"She's backtracking, but I think the ultimate destination is going to be the same. She must have hit a spot where she couldn't get through."

"You guess," Shane snapped, then said, "I'm sorry. I'm on edge."

"We know. Slow down again until we find out what direction she's going."

Shane slowed, fighting anger and frustration and his need to save Elena. At this point, he didn't give a damn what happened to the brother, but if she didn't come out of this okay, he was going to smash Lincoln Kinkead.

Was this Kinkead's fault? Maybe, maybe not. But the man had been up to something he wasn't talking about. Maybe Elena could explain what that was—if he asked her the right questions.

But for the moment, he had to keep his focus on making sure she came back to him, safe and sound.

Elena backtracked along the rain-slick pavement, then made the next turn, as directed. She could see more houses in the area now, although she still didn't know exactly where she was going.

"Take the next right," Mr. Big directed. She slowed and turned, seeing that she was coming into another industrial park, although this one was a lot more upscale than the previous location.

"Drive down to location 651 and stop," the man directed.

Oh Lord, this was it. She was going to exchange the fake information for her brother.

She drove down an access road lined on either side with buildings that held warehouse facilities. At the far end, some of the buildings were illuminated with exterior lights. But for three-fourths of the length, the lane was dark and silent.

She had to squint to see the numbers, which were high up on the buildings and thankfully painted white. When she saw 651, she pulled to a stop, the car parallel to the buildings instead of perpendicular. Looking around, she saw no other vehicles. But that didn't prove anything. Mr. Big had probably been here for hours, waiting for her to arrive. Making preparations. She shuddered as she wondered what he was planning.

But maybe she didn't have long to wait.

A light clicked on inside building 651, and she looked up at the back of the small warehouse. It had a loading dock with a garage door that opened onto a platform about four feet above ground level, a pedestrian door, a landing, and a set of stairs leading to ground level.

"Get out of the car," Mr. Big ordered. He was still speaking to her from the phone.

—∿∿—

"She's stopped again," Max said. "I think this could be the place."

Shane sped up, trying to drive as fast as he could and stay on the slick pavement.

At least the rain had slowed to a drizzle.

"Turn here." He did, leaning forward and peering through the windshield, hoping to see something.

"Slow down," Max warned.

"Why?"

"We're almost there. We don't want the Big Guy to figure out that Elena's not alone."

Shane slowed and switched off the lights. He waited a moment for his eyes to adjust before proceeding along the two-lane highway. Luckily, at this time of night and in this weather, nobody else was on the road.

"There's a turn ahead," Max said. "Into an industrial park."

"But the unit where she is won't be visible from the access road."

"Good. That means we can get close before we have to get out of the car."

Shane's tension mounted as he glided into the complex and looked around at the darkened buildings. Nobody seemed to be here, but that was the point. It was the way Mr. Big wanted it, and he'd had a long time to plan this confrontation. Too bad Shane couldn't say the same for himself and Elena. Still, he'd given her some strategies, and he hoped to hell she kept her head and used them. The danger was that when she saw her brother, she'd forget that she was already standing in a lion's den.

—⁓—

Elena had pulled up so that the driver's door was facing away from the building. She cut the lights on the
borrowed car and picked up the cell phone. Clutching it
in her hand, she exited the vehicle, keeping it between
her and the warehouse. Would the thin metal sides stop
bullets? Probably not, but it helped that she was on the
wrong side of the car to get ambushed. At least not yet.

"Bring my brother out," she said into the phone.

"You first."

"Not until I see Alesandro," she said, wondering how
Mr. Big was working this. Was he here at the warehouse,
or was he giving someone inside directions? She thought
it was more likely the former than the latter since he was
so anxious to get his hands on the S&D program.

She looked back the way she'd come. Did Shane and
the Rockfort men even know where she was? Maybe
not, so maybe she was on her own.

A flash of light at the warehouse drew her attention. The door at the top of the stairs opened, and three
men came out. Two of them looked tough and capable.
The middle one was Alesandro, and the two other guys
were holding him up. They each grasped one of his
arms with a large hand. In the other, they both held
automatic weapons.

She took in the trio at a swift glance. The two on the
outside both had buzz cuts and were wearing neat slacks
and dark-colored button-down shirts. Her brother's dark
hair was matted, his face was covered with bruises and
dried blood, and his clothing was rumpled, with a tear
in one arm of his shirt. As she stared at him, the world

seemed to sway around her. He looked like he'd been to hell—and hadn't been able to claw his way back.

The voice on the phone brought her to her senses. "Come and get the miserable slug," Mr. Big growled.

Keeping her voice hard as steel, she answered, "I'm not coming any closer. I want him to walk down the stairs by himself and come toward me."

Again there was no response.

She waited a beat before saying, "You don't get the information until I get my brother."

"Now that you're here, we could just shoot him."

She felt her throat clog. "And you won't get what you dragged me here to deliver. I can still get back in the car and drive away."

"You won't."

"I will if you shoot him. Send him to me."

"How do I know you won't do it when he gets to you?"

She dragged in a breath and let it out, knowing she was about to take a big risk. "I'll give you the car keys."

Mr. Big's voice brightened. "Great suggestion. Toss the keys toward the steps."

"When my brother is halfway here."

There must have been a conference among the men that Elena couldn't hear. One of the tough guys let go of Alesandro, and he wavered on rubbery legs, then grabbed the railing to keep himself from falling. When he was almost steady on his feet, he started down slowly, his hand gripping the rail, and she thought he looked like he'd aged fifty years since the last time she'd seen him in her apartment.

As he descended the steps, he raised his face to Elena. She watched his mouth as his lips formed the word "run."

Dios, he was telling her to leave him. But she couldn't do that, because she knew he wouldn't get out of this alive.

She focused on her brother's shaky progress toward her, which was probably what the men had intended. But something warned her to look up, and she saw one of the men raise his arm.

When it registered that he was pointing a gun at her, she ducked behind the vehicle as a bullet slammed into the wall in back of where she'd been standing.

The weapon she'd taken from her purse was already in her hand before she had made a conscious decision, and to her relief, she noted that her brother had dropped to the ground.

Reaching above the top of the hood, she returned fire.

Obviously the man who had shot at her thought she'd be an easy target. And he certainly didn't think she'd be armed. Not after that remote-control strip search at the last warehouse. But she'd hidden her movements from the camera when she'd gotten the SIM card from the purse.

Now she had a clear shot at the two men who had come out of the warehouse with her brother. She pulled the trigger and one of them dropped. The other one was already firing at her. He ducked back up the steps, shooting as he went and weaving a zigzag pattern across the open space, heading for the door from which he'd exited the warehouse with Alesandro.

She heard her brother cry out, but she couldn't go to him, not when the thug was still laying down a spray of bullets, intent on getting back into the building before she could drop him.

It was then that she heard the roar of an engine.

From out of the darkness, a vehicle with its lights out came barreling down the access road toward the scene of the confrontation.

But who was it?

Shane or reinforcements from Mr. Big?

Elena gasped as she saw it speeding toward her brother, who was lying where he'd fallen in the middle of the blacktop—halfway between her and the bad guys.

"Alesandro, watch out!" she screamed.

Chapter 30

THE VEHICLE SKIDDED TO A STOP, ITS WHEELS INCHES FROM Alesandro's head and shoulders.

Shane jumped out the driver's door. Max flew from the passenger side.

Jack came from the back.

"They're inside the building," Elena shouted.

"Are you all right?" Shane called urgently.

"Yes."

He turned toward the warehouse as the loading-dock door opened, followed by a blast of gunfire.

Elena screamed. She couldn't see Shane, and she dashed around the borrowed car, using the SUV for cover.

As she peeked around the fender, she saw the Rockfort men crouching below the level of the loading dock, using the concrete barrier as a shield.

Shane had a backpack with him. He set it down and reached inside, pulling out something and tossing it through the open door into the warehouse interior.

It exploded inside with a terrible noise, a burst of smoke, and a concussion that shook the surrounding area.

He tossed in a second, then pulled a gas mask over his face. The other Rockfort men followed suit before dashing up the steps and pulling the door open.

Gunfire rattled through the smoke. The Rockfort men went in shooting, and Elena could see nothing. But she heard the sounds of battle.

Shane led the way up the stairs. Instead of pulling the pedestrian door open, he eased around to the garage opening. Beyond was a large room with cinder-block walls and industrial shelving clustered in several locations. At the back were spaces partitioned off into what might be offices. One of their opponents lay on the floor about halfway between the front and back of the open area. Jack moved toward him and rolled him over.

"Dead."

As he spoke a burst of gunfire came from the back of the building.

While Jack retreated to the staging area, Shane and Max were already leaping toward the nearest shelves. They pulled them away from the wall and toppled them on their sides. Using the barrier as a shield, all three Rockfort men began to advance on the back of the building, pushing the shelves in front of them.

"It sounds like only one guy firing," Shane said.

"Hopefully, the rest are dead," Jack answered.

They kept moving toward the lone gunman, who must be holed up in one of the offices.

"Wait," the gunman shouted.

"For what?"

"I'll cut a deal with you."

"Now? After you've spent so much time going after S&D?"

"Because Kinkead has something worth billions."

"What?"

"A program that can predict which stocks are going to make fantastic short-term gains. Nothing like it exists.

He's going to market it to investors, and it will make them some money, but he's keeping the best parts for himself."

"Where did he get it?"

"From the father of a smart-as-shit kid."

"Oh, yeah."

"Your girlfriend's got a copy of it. And we can share it."

—◦◦◦—

Elena knew she should stay where she was. She knew, but her brother was still lying in the middle of the road.

She ran to him, caught him under the shoulders, and dragged him back so that the bulk of the SUV was between him and the gunfight.

She'd gotten Alesandro to safety, but she gasped as she saw the smear she'd left on the wet pavement. He'd been lying in a pool of blood, and a red trail had followed him to the shelter of the SUV.

"Alesandro," she gasped.

His eyes flickered open. "Elena…you came for me."

She frantically pulled at his shirt. She had tended Shane's wounds. She could do the same for Alesandro. "Where are you hit?"

He reached for her hand to stop her. "Don't. It doesn't matter."

"But…"

"They beat me up pretty bad. Stuff inside me is broken. This is a mercy."

"No!"

"Listen to me. I don't have much time. I heard them talking…" He stopped and took a breath. "They called him Mr. Weller."

"Just stay quiet," she soothed as she leaned over her brother.

"Elena, you're a good girl. I was always going to disappoint our parents." He stopped and coughed, then started talking again. "Tell them I'll wait for them in heaven."

"Alesandro."

He didn't answer, and when she leaned over him and felt for a pulse in his neck, there was none.

Tears welled in her eyes as she reached to close his eyelids. She had thought she could rescue him, but she'd been wrong. He had suffered so much, and now he was dead.

"Nice of you to offer, but I don't think so," Shane growled.

"Wait. Why not?"

There were a lot of things Shane could have said, but he kept it simple. "Because you're a motherfucking scumbag."

He pushed the metal shelving forward, advancing on the man who began to shoot again, the sound of the automatic weapon echoing in the towering space.

Shane reached the wall of the first office, picked up the shelving, and smashed it through the window as an arc of gunfire followed the unexpected intrusion.

Taking advantage of the distraction, Shane darted around the corner and saw a tubby guy wielding an assault rifle. He shot the man in the chest. Cautiously he advanced on him, but the bastard wasn't playing possum. He was dead, and as Shane stared down at him, irony washed over him. They'd called this guy Mr. Big. And he was bulky enough to live up to the name.

"Check the back of the building," he called to his friends as he dashed back the way he'd come.

—~~~—

Elena looked up, seeing a figure running toward her. In the light spilling from the warehouse, she couldn't see who it was, and she raised her gun.

"Elena, it's me."

"Shane!" She stood, dashing toward him. He leaped off the edge of the loading dock, landed on the pavement, and sprinted toward her.

They fell into each other's arms, clinging and rocking.

"Mr. Big?" she gasped out.

"He's not going to be after us any longer."

"*Gracias a Dios*." Then she raised her face. "He's dead?"

"Yeah. He might be alive if he hadn't tried to kill me." Shane looked past to see the crumpled figure lying nearby. "That's your brother?"

"*Sí*."

"I'm sorry," he whispered.

"Thank you."

He stroked his hands comfortingly over her back.

"He said they had hurt him badly when they tortured him. He said he wasn't going to make it." As she said the last part, she struggled to hold back a sob.

"I'm sorry," Shane said again. "You came all this way to rescue him."

"Nobody could rescue him," she answered, finally understanding the truth. "He lost his sense of direction, and there was no way…" She let the sentence trail off.

"I know." Shane continued to stroke her, holding her close, and she could have stayed there forever.

In the next moment, he broke the spell. "We can't stay here," he murmured.

"I know."

As she acknowledged the urgency in his voice, he eased away.

She raised her head, taking in the scene of carnage.

"But the police..." she began.

"We've still got things to do, and we won't get to do them if we're all balled up with the cops."

The two other Rockfort men had joined them outside the warehouse.

"Where's your gun?" Shane asked.

She pulled the weapon out of the waistband of her slacks and held it downward, the way he'd taught her.

Shane took it, wiped it off, and knelt, pressing it into Alesandro's hand, wrapping his fingers around the butt, and slipping his finger into the trigger guard.

"You're making it look like he and Weller's men had a gun battle?" she asked.

"Weller?"

"He said that's the guy's name."

"Okay, that's good. The cops will know other people were here. Only the bullet in the guy you shot will match this gun. But they won't trace the rest of them to us."

"How will they know who Alesandro is?"

"Maybe through his fingerprints. Or maybe they'll need an anonymous call."

Max was inside the borrowed car, wiping off the steering wheel and the other surfaces.

"He was directing you by phone?" Shane asked.

She nodded and pointed to the hood of the car where she'd left the phone.

Shane retrieved it, wiped it off again, and put it in Alesandro's other hand.

"And the keys?"

She pointed to where they lay on the pavement.

Again, he wiped them off before putting them back into the ignition.

Then they all climbed into the SUV and drove away.

Shane and Elena sat in the backseat, his arm firmly around her.

"You did good," he said.

"I couldn't have held them off by myself."

"You held them off long enough for us to get here."

"I've got the tape from the camera," Jack said from the front seat.

She winced. "With me naked."

"Nobody's going to look at it," he answered.

She leaned into Shane and closed her eyes, but they snapped open moments later.

"Where are we going?"

"The Eastern Shore, to retrieve the SIM card."

"And return it to Kinkead?"

"After we find out what's on it."

"Something important to S&D."

"From what…Weller said, I think it's more than that."

"What?"

"We have to get the information off it."

—⁓—

Emotional exhaustion finally overcame Elena. She knew that everything wasn't settled, but she was too worn out to care. She drifted off to sleep. Her eyes didn't open until she felt the car slow at the gate of the safe house.

She winced, remembering the last time they'd been there.

Shane stroked her shoulder. "Weller sent the men who came here before. He's not giving any more orders."

She answered with a tight nod.

"You stay here," he said to the other two Rockfort men as they pulled up in front of the door. He slipped his arm away from Elena and climbed out of the car, heading for the front porch. The front door was unlocked, and as he pushed it open, he stopped short.

"What?" Max called.

"The place is a mess."

"Mr. Big, I mean Weller, must have been looking for the S&D stuff."

Shane's jaw firmed. "If I had to guess, I'd say Kinkead was here, too."

Jack and Max nodded.

"But we know Weller didn't find it," Shane said as he disappeared inside. "Otherwise there would have been no point in having you meet him. And I'll know in a few minutes if Kinkead managed to get it."

Elena waited with heart pounding. It felt as if Shane had been gone for years, but it was probably only a few minutes before he reappeared with the SIM card in his hand.

"Where was it?" Max asked.

"I slipped it into a crack between one of the legs and the top of the workbench."

His partner grinned. "Clever."

"Let's find out what's on it," he said.

Jack looked toward the former safe house. "But not here. We don't know who is going to show up next."

"Right," Shane agreed.

They all got back in the car. As they drove back toward D.C., Elena loaded the card into a slot in the computer that Jack had brought along. But when she directed the machine to the card, all they got was gibberish.

Chapter 31

BESIDE ELENA, SHANE MADE AN ANGRY SOUND. "WE WENT through a hell of a lot of grief to make sure this card was safe, and now…"

She put a hand on his arm. "It's encrypted."

His voice was hard. "Which means we can't get into it unless we have the key?"

She nodded.

"That's just great."

"I think I may know how to get it."

He gave her a questioning look.

"Remember I told you that Arnold sent me SIMon Sez puzzles. That was how I thought of the SIM card in the phone."

"Yeah."

"Well, what if he also sent me the encryption key in one of his emails?"

"How do we get the emails?" Max asked from the front seat.

"They're in my mail system. I can access them from here."

"My guess is that Kinkead locked you out of your office mail."

"Probably true. But I wanted to think about the puzzles, so I sent them to my home address."

"Lucky for us," Shane muttered.

As they drove through the darkness, Elena kept her

eyes on the computer screen, downloading messages and collecting them into a folder.

When the car slowed, she looked up and saw that they were back at the Four Seasons Hotel in D.C.

"Might as well enjoy the luxury for a little while longer," Max said.

The men unloaded their equipment, and they all returned to the suite they'd left six hours earlier. Or was it a lifetime ago?

Morgan was waiting for them. When they came in the door, she jumped up and embraced Jack. "Is everything okay?"

"Yes."

She turned to Elena, taking in her appearance and the clothing she was wearing. "You made it."

"Yes."

"I knew you would."

Elena gulped. "I wasn't so sure."

Shane gave Elena a considering look. "Why don't you take a shower and change?"

She glanced down and grimaced as she realized she was still wearing the outfit Weller had supplied.

"While you're gone, I'll copy the messages from Blake onto the other laptops so we can get started."

"Good idea."

The shower helped revive her, and she was glad to put on slacks and a shirt she'd brought from the southern safe house. When she came back to the sitting room, she saw the men had ordered breakfast.

"Better?" Shane asked.

"A lot." She looked around. "Where is everybody else?"

"While you were in the shower, we decided to split

up. We did some research and figured out that Weller was a mob boss named Jerome Weller. We got the address of his estate. Jack and Max have gone over there, and Morgan had a meeting with a client."

Her hands clamped on the mug of coffee with cream and sugar that he'd handed her.

"What will Jack and Max find?"

"Something helpful, I hope. Come eat."

She saw a cart at the side of the room and found bacon and eggs and various pastries. As she sat down with a plate of food, she decided that her appetite had finally come back.

She ate with the computer on the coffee table in front of her, looking at the puzzles Arnold had sent her. Many of them were grids with letters in them, where you had to spell words going up, down, or diagonally across the grid. All of them had a theme, like names of movies or books, authors, sports terms, or even zoo animals.

Shane was looking at the same material.

"Something interesting," he said.

She looked at him.

"Even when the theme is movies or something unrelated, other words show up."

"Like what?"

"Well, he's put his name into the puzzles, for example. And one particular word keeps appearing. Corruption."

Elena went through the puzzles. Now that Shane mentioned it, she saw the word in various forms. Usually backwards or backwards and diagonally.

Going back to the SIM card, she typed in "corruption."

She thought at first that she'd blown up the whole

program when pictures of fireworks erupted on the screen, accompanied by loud blasts.

Then the graphics disappeared, and the screen said, "Congratulations, Elena."

Her heart stopped, then started up again in double time as she gave Shane a quick glance. "It's for me."

When she saw that his expression had hardened, her mouth went dry. With this message, she was back where she'd started with Shane—in the middle of a conspiracy. "I know what this must look like."

"I know what it *looks like*. And I know what it's not." He slung his arm around her and pulled her close. "Elena, I trust you. I know you weren't working with Blake."

Her mouth was so dry she could barely speak, but she managed to ask, "How do you know?"

"Because I know what kind of person you are."

Leaning over, he gave her a quick kiss. "Let's see the rest of the message."

Praying that Blake hadn't said something that would implicate her in his theft, she scrolled down and saw:

"When I was streamlining the S&D files, I accidentally got into a proprietary S&D program called Falcon's Flight. The purpose is to analyze trends in the stock market and identify which stocks were going to have short-term gains of 15 to 20 percent. I didn't know why Lincoln Kinkead was keeping it secret, so I started investigating further. I did some research and found out that the program was developed by Kinkead's nephew, Josh Rosenbloom, his sister's son."

Elena glanced at Shane, then moved the cursor down so they could both read more.

"I've investigated this from a lot of angles. Kinkead

took Josh's original work and had a programmer in Romania improve it. It appears that Kinkead plans to market part of the improved program and share the profits with the Rosenblooms, but it also appears that he is planning to keep the most effective part of the program secret and use it for his own gains, thus depriving Josh's family of enormous income.

"While I was trying to decide what to do about this, I was approached by a man who wanted me to steal a copy of the improved program. He's offered me a lot of money to do this, and I am playing along with him while I decide how to handle the problem. I don't know the man's real name, and I don't know how he found out about the program. And I am reluctant to go to the police because I want to persuade Kinkead to do the right thing by the Rosenbloom family.

"In case something happens to me, Elena, I'm counting on you to see this through. I've included a copy of the entire program on this SIM card."

Elena could barely breathe when she finished reading.

"Arnold wasn't stealing it," she managed to say. "He was trying to make sure that Josh Rosenbloom and his family got their fair share of the profits."

Shane socked his fist against his hand. "And I fell for what Kinkead told me."

"It was true as far as it went. Weller somehow found out about the program and was trying to steal it," Elena answered.

"At the same time Kinkead was planning to screw his own nephew," Shane said. "Blake wanted to stop him, but he put you in terrible danger."

"It wasn't just him. My brother helped."

He reached for her, pulling her close.

She laid her head against his shoulder as she whispered, "We need to finish what Blake started. But how do we do it?"

Shane squeezed her hand. "I think we can figure it out together."

———

Max pulled up at the entrance to Jerome Weller's estate and pressed the button on the intercom.

After several seconds, a man's voice asked, "Who is it?"

"FBI, here to inform you that Jerome Weller is dead," Max answered. "Killed in a gun battle at a warehouse in Columbia."

They heard the guy on the other end of the line catch his breath.

"We're only interested in gathering relevant information," Max said. "We're not going to arrest anybody on the estate if you cooperate. In fact, we'll give you twenty minutes to clear out."

"How do we know that's not a trick, and we won't be arrested if we try to leave?" the voice asked.

"You'll have to take our word for it. But our best advice is to get yourselves out of this mess."

"Okay," the voice answered.

Max backed up and pulled across the road.

Five minutes later, the gate opened and a black SUV barreled out.

They waited another ten minutes before proceeding through the open gate.

"Are they really that stupid?" Jack asked.

"Let's hope so. And hope that the house isn't going to blow up when we start looking for evidence."

Jack laughed. "Right. And the first thing we'd better do is make sure nobody can pinpoint when we were here."

———

Shane and Elena talked about how to handle Kinkead. Then Shane got out one of the burner phones and called the head of S&D, using the speaker capacity of the phone so Elena could listen.

"Who is this?" the S&D owner snapped.

"Shane Gallagher."

"Where the hell have you been?"

"We've been busy."

"Where are you?"

"Somewhere safe."

"You said you knew where that SIM card was."

"We have it."

"Thank God."

"I'm going to send you the first part of the information on it," Shane answered. "Then we'll talk."

"What about the rest of it?"

"You have the rest of it. I'm sending Arnold Blake's conclusion." He looked at Elena. She pressed Send on the email she'd already prepared.

In a few minutes, there was an explosion of cursing from the other end of the line.

"What is this crap?" Lincoln Kinkead demanded.

"It's Arnold Blake's last will and testament. Your little shell game with Falcon's Flight got him killed."

"No," Kinkead breathed.

"Should we go to the police with this information?" Shane asked.

"No!"

"Then this is what we're going to do. I'm sending you a contract which you will sign. In it, you will give seventy-five percent of the profits from Falcon's Flight to the Rosenbloom family."

"Seventy-five percent. That's outrageous."

"Jesus, Kinkead, the kid developed it, not you. I'm letting you keep twenty-five percent, since you've got the marketing ability they don't."

"What else?" Kinkead demanded.

"I did the job you hired me for. I'm leaving your employ, but I want full pay for the next year."

"Fuck, no!"

"You're getting off easy on that one. Again, I'm assuming you don't want any of this made public."

"That's right," Kinkead growled.

"I'll take monthly payments instead of demanding you pay me in a lump sum."

Again, Kinkead didn't like it, but he agreed.

Shane glanced at Elena, and she nodded.

"And Elena Reyes is leaving the company," he said.

"Good."

"She'll get a year's pay and an excellent reference letter."

"Now, wait a minute."

"Again, I think we're in a position to dictate terms."

"All right," Kinkead snapped. "Do you have any more demands?"

"If the cops have any questions about what I've been doing for the past few days, you need to say I was on an assignment for you. And if you have any second thoughts, we still have a copy of Blake's account of your double-dealings. If anything happens to us, that will go to the authorities. Understood?"

"Yes," Kinkead bit out.

"That's all for now," Shane said as he clicked off.

Elena breathed a sigh, then looked at Shane.

"I have to tell my parents about Alesandro."

"Yeah. I'm sorry. I know that's going to be tough."

"I don't know exactly what to say to them."

"That he had gotten himself in with a bad crowd, there was a fight, and they killed him."

"And how do I know about any of that?"

"Let me check in with Max and Jack."

He called the other two Rockfort agents.

"You got anything?" he asked when Max answered the phone.

"Yeah. A lot of good stuff. We're on our way back. Sit tight."

Elena looked at Shane, "What does that mean?"

"That he doesn't want to talk about it on the phone."

Chapter 32

Max and Jack were back a half hour later.

"What have you got?" Shane asked as they came in carrying a desktop computer and a laptop.

"Weller's records."

Elena's eyes widened. "Is that legal?"

"Well, you hired us to help your brother, didn't you?" Max said.

"Did I?"

"Yeah. We'll postdate an agreement. We were trying to extricate him from a dangerous situation and ran across a lot of other information. Unfortunately, when we tried to rescue Alesandro, he was killed."

She stared at the Rockfort men. "You can do all that?"

"Yes," Max answered. "And if we all agree on what happened and keep our stories straight, we'll be fine."

"I don't like being dishonest," she whispered.

"In this case, you can think of it as protecting your ass," Max said. "Plus, what would be gained by dragging your brother into a media exposé? Weller's dead. And they can't prosecute him for anything he's done."

She thought about that for a few moments, then nodded.

"But I have to tell my parents what happened. And I need to get there before the police do."

"And I'm going with you," Shane said.

She stared at him. "Why?"

"Because I know how hard it's going to be for you, and there's no way I'd let you go there alone."

He called for the car, and then they went down to the lobby. When the SUV arrived, they got in and he drove away. After turning up Wisconsin Avenue, he took a side street, where he pulled into a parking space.

Elena looked at him questioningly. "What are you doing?"

"I know you need to go to your parents', but there's something I want to talk to you about first."

The way he said it made her chest tighten, but she only answered with a little nod.

The look on his face turned the breath in her lungs shallow.

"What is it?"

"After everything that's happened, would you consider marrying me?"

The words stunned her. "Did I hear that right? You want to marry me?"

"Yes. But if I've been too big a jerk, I'll understand…"

She stopped him before he could go any further. "You haven't been a jerk."

"I kept finding reasons to mistrust you."

"And I kept giving you reasons why you should. I should have gone to you in the first place."

Before he could answer that, she reached for him. He reached at the same time, and they came into each other's arms, holding on tightly.

"Elena, I love you. I had a hard time admitting that to myself. And it was hard to say it."

"Oh, Shane, I knew I was falling in love with you, and I felt like I was messing it up."

"Not anymore."

She raised her head, and their lips met in a long, emotional kiss.

"I'd take you back to the hotel," he said in a thick voice. "But that will have to wait."

"Yes." She turned toward him. "You know where my parents live?"

"I looked it up. But you can give me directions."

She leaned toward him and put her hand over his for a moment as he started the car again and drove toward Germantown.

They pulled up in front of the modest ranch house and both got out.

"Watch for my mother pulling the curtains aside and checking us out," Elena murmured as they started up the walk.

When the curtains shifted, she cut Shane a glance.

They both walked inside and stood awkwardly by the front door.

Her father eyed her and Shane. "Who is this man, and why are you here? You look like you're on your way to a funeral."

"*Sí*," Elena whispered. "In a way we are. I came to give you some bad news. I'm sorry, but there's no easy way to say it. Alesandro is dead."

Her mother gasped. "No."

"I'm sorry."

Her father looked like he didn't believe her. "How? Why? How do you know?" he demanded.

Shane spoke. "Elena and I almost got killed tonight trying to save her brother's life. He was being stalked by a man who had given him some illegal jobs."

"No," her mother protested again. "He wouldn't do that."

"I'm afraid he did," Shane answered.

Elena went to her mother and held out her arms. "I'm so sorry."

Momma backed away. "Don't."

Shane strode to Elena's side. "She came to tell you because she wanted to help you through it. But I see you don't need her."

Anger flashed in her father's eyes. "And who are you to meddle in our family business?" His gaze drilled into Shane. "Wait a minute. I know who you are. You're the man from the TV news. You were at that hostage thing with Elena."

"Yes. I'm Shane Gallagher. And I'm your daughter's fiancé."

Both parents gaped at him.

Papa folded his arms across his chest. "Her fiancé? Since when? How long have you known her?"

"A few months."

Her father snorted. "Not very long. We don't even know you. She didn't ask our permission to marry."

"She doesn't have to," Shane said. "I wanted you to know about us, but I think you probably want to be alone now."

He slung his arm around Elena, and she leaned into him.

"If you need me, call me," she said.

Neither of her parents answered, and Shane ushered her out of the house.

She turned to him with tears in her eyes. "I'm sorry."

"For what?"

"For the way they acted."

"They had a bad shock."

"Don't make excuses for them."

"Okay. But I'm not going to let them hurt you anymore."

"They didn't…"

"I can see how they are with you."

"I could never please them." She kept her gaze on him. "I went out on my own as soon as I could. And I dreamed of finding a man who would be on my side. A man I could trust. Then I met you…and I hoped."

"I met you, and I knew you were the right woman for me. It took me a couple of months to admit it to myself. Before that, I kept coming up with excuses to be with you."

They climbed back into his car, and he pulled her to him, holding her for a long moment before easing away.

"Are you all right?" he asked.

"Better than all right."

"I think you said that once before."

She grinned at him. "I remember. I didn't know how true it was going to be."

He started the engine and drove away. Into a future Elena had hoped for but had secretly thought she would never find.

About the Author

New York Times and *USA Today* bestselling author Rebecca York's writing has been compared to that of Dick Francis, Sherrilyn Kenyon, and Maggie Shayne. Her award-winning books have been translated into twenty-two languages and optioned for film. A recipient of the RWA Centennial Award, she lives in Maryland near Washington, D.C., which is often the setting of her romantic suspense novels.